Henry McBride Series on Modernism and Modernity

The artistic movement known as modernism, which includes the historical avant-garde, produced the most radical and comprehensive change in Western culture since Romanticism. Its effects reverberated through all the arts, permanently altering their formal repertories and their relations with society at large, and its products still surround us in our workplaces and homes. Although modernism produced a pervasive cultural upheaval, it can never be assessed as an artistic movement alone: its contours took shape against the background of social, political, and intellectual change, and it was always bound up with larger questions of modernity and modernization and with the intellectual challenge of sifting their meanings. Henry McBride (1867–1962) became perhaps the leading American critic of his time to write perceptively and engagingly on modern art. The Henry McBride Series in Modernism and Modernity, which focuses on modernism and the arts in their many contexts, is respectfully dedicated to his memory.

Italo Svevo

A NEW TRANSLATION BY BETH ARCHER BROMBERT

WITH AN INTRODUCTION BY VICTOR BROMBERT

 *Emilio's Carnival*

(SENILITÀ)

YALE UNIVERSITY PRESS

NEW HAVEN AND LONDON

 YALE NOTA BENE

This book has been published with assistance from the fund for the Henry McBride Series in Modernism and Modernity established by Maximilian Miltzlaff.

For information about this and other Yale University Press publications, please contact:

U.S. office sales.press@yale.edu
Europe office sales@yaleup.co.uk

Designed by Nancy Ovedovitz and set in Janson Oldstyle type by Keystone Typesetting, Inc. Printed in the United States of America by R. R. Donnelley & Sons, Harrisonburg, Virginia.

Library of Congress Cataloging-in-Publication Data

Svevo, Italo, 1861–1928.
[Senilità. English]
Emilio's carnival, or, Senilità / Italo Svevo ; a new translation by Beth Archer Brombert ; with an introduction by Victor Brombert.
    p.   cm. — (Henry McBride series in modernism and modernity)
ISBN 0-300-09047-1 (cloth) — ISBN 0-300-09049-8 (paper)
1. Title: Emilio's carnival. II. Title: Senilità. III. Brombert, Beth Archer. IV. Title. V. Series.
PQ4841.C482 S8413 2001
853'.8 — dc21   2001000914

A catalogue record for this book is available from the British Library.

The paper in this book meets the guidelines for permanence and durability of the Committee on Production Guidelines for Book Longevity of the Council on Library Resources.

10 9 8 7 6 5 4 3 2 1

Introduction | VICTOR BROMBERT

Ettore Schmitz (1861–1928), a successful Trieste businessman whose books published under the pen name of Italo
Svevo had passed largely unnoticed in Italy, made his entrance into world literature in 1925, by way of Paris. James
Joyce, who had known Schmitz/Svevo in Trieste years earlier and admired what he had read, brought his writings to
the attention of Parisian literary friends. Thanks to Joyce's
efforts, and to those of Valery Larbaud and Benjamin Cré-
mieux, all of them connoisseurs of Italian letters, *La coscienza
di Zeno* (1923) was hailed as a major literary event. Almost an
entire issue of the review *Le Navire d'Argent* was devoted to
Svevo, giving some extracts in translation. Italo Svevo was
launched. He was sixty-four years old.

La coscienza di Zeno ("coscienza" meaning consciousness
as well as conscience) now holds a secure place among the
important novels of the twentieth century. It is by far Svevo's
best-known work. But many Svevo admirers — including
Joyce and Larbaud, but also the great Italian poet Eugenio
Montale — expressed a preference for the earlier *Senilità*
(1898). They considered it his masterpiece, his most perfect
novel. Joyce, when he first read it upon meeting Svevo,
learned the final paragraphs by heart. He still remembered
them years later.

Senilità is indeed a remarkable achievement, especially
for its time and place. Its powerful social and sexual themes
are treated with an economy of means and a subtle psy-
chology that free this novel from the limiting methods of

naturalism. Svevo examines the amorous entanglements of a self-centered, ineffectual middle-class intellectual with a carnal and flagrantly amoral young woman from the lower classes. The novel is a study in frustration, jealousy, moral smugness and bad faith, suggesting currents of cruelty and violence beneath self-indulgent aestheticism.

The technical sophistication of this novel, though it does not aim at revolutionizing the rhetoric of fiction, tightly weaves parallel and contrapuntal stories by means of deft stylistic indirections and an imaginative use of love/hate transfers that exploit the possible complications of a "quadrangular" situation involving Emilio the protagonist, his sister Amalia, his rival-friend Balli, and the alluring Angiolina. This system of transfers has undertones that make it clear why Svevo was later bound to become interested in Freud.

Joyce's unexpected praise when he read the totally forgotten novel was like a balm for Svevo. To hear Joyce compare it to works by the best French masters surely encouraged Svevo to think of writing again. For he had given up all literary ambitions, wounded by unsuccess. There was another reason why he had given up publishing anything and remained silent for more than twenty years. He had married and entered into his in-laws' prosperous family business firm, producing anticorrosive paint used by a number of European navies. Which is precisely why he came to know the much younger Joyce, who was teaching English at the Berlitz school in Trieste, and also giving private lessons. Having to supervise the family factory in England, Svevo wanted to improve his conversational English. That is how he and his wife Livia (whose flowing reddish-blond hair was to inspire the figure of Joyce's Anna Livia Plurabelle) read Joyce's notyet-published story "The Dead," which served as the text for one of their English lessons. As for Svevo himself, it is by now well known that he served as an important model for Leopold Bloom in Joyce's *Ulysses*.

Admirers of *Senilità*—Valery Larbaud among the first—have over the years expressed some doubts about the appropriateness of the title. Joyce recommended that it be changed when there was talk of an English translation. Svevo, however, was steadfastly committed to his title. He felt that it was crucial, that to change it was to mutilate the novel. This stubborn allegiance is especially interesting as Svevo himself originally had another title in mind: *Il carnevale di Emilio* (Emilio's carnival).

This title makes perfect sense, not only because the important sixth chapter deals with carnival time just before Lent (a period of escapism, masquerades, and cheap illusions), but because it is in this carnival chapter that Angiolina is seen conspicuously betraying her lover, who follows her and her companion in vain through a labyrinth of streets, hatching dreams of vengeance—an obsessive, hallucinatory nocturnal search for phantoms during which he mistakes identities, loses the couple's trace, and, almost hysterical, turns his powerless rage against himself, biting his own hand. And it is in this same carnival chapter that Emilio's sister Amalia, in contrast to the uninhibited sexuality of the lower-class girl, betrays her repressed sexual yearnings as she is overheard dreaming aloud of her honeymoon with Emilio's friend, who in fact sees in her nothing but a drab, graceless person, destined to remain a spinster.

An even stronger case can be made for Svevo's original title. Carnival time is a period, though fleeting, of permissiveness and transgression of norms. The broader connotations are indeed inscribed in the etymology of the word "carnevale," *carne* meaning flesh and *levare* suggesting removal or denial — a denial of the flesh, a farewell to carnality. This is precisely the situation of the protagonist Emilio Brentani when he finally gives up Angiolina, closing the entire episode of physical passion for which he was poorly suited in the first place.

Which brings us to the title Svevo finally preferred, *Senilità* — a word which in the context of his writings in no way implies mental impairment caused by old age. The *senilità* in question refers neither to the pathology of aging nor to precocious decrepitude. Rather it suggests a special sensibility (some people are indeed born old); or better still, a special kind of inertia, the inertia of the dreamer, a modern version of acedia, or ironic ennui — devoid, however, of the metaphysical dimension Baudelaire gave to that term. *Senilità*, in Svevo's perspective, accompanies the tragic sense of existence; it represents a permanent premonition of life as disaster, a deep skepticism concerning one's own potential, a ceaseless meditation on vulnerability and death, a wisdom that can be put to no use, an awareness of the unavoidable loss of that which one never possessed, a suffering sharpened while consciousness views itself both as object and subject.

The silence that greeted *Senilità* in Italy when the novel first appeared could be attributed to the marginality of Trieste. That city had a significant Italian-speaking community but was at the time part of the Austro-Hungarian empire. In Trieste itself, where Schmitz/Svevo was known in intellectual circles, the book was read primarily as a roman à clef, everyone claiming to recognize the living models that had inspired the characters. Disappointed and embittered by the absence of any serious critical response (his first novel, *Una vita*, which appeared in 1892, had been equally unsuccessful), Svevo promised himself to give up all dreams of literary fame. His lifelong ambivalent attitude toward literature goes back to those early years. He confided to his diary that "outside of writing there is no salvation," but almost in the same breath he denounced all literary efforts as "ridiculous and harmful."[1]

The hard fact is that Italy in 1898 was not ready for Italo Svevo. The style and tone of *Senilità* were as far removed as possible from the aestheticism and sumptuous grandiloquence of Gabriele d'Annunzio, who was then in fashion. There was, moreover, the automatic prejudice against a Triestino writer. How could an Italian stylist be born in Trieste? "Svevo does not write good Italian," affirmed people who had hardly taken the trouble to read a single page of Svevo, even after he had acquired an international reputation. This kind of response remained an unexamined cliché echoed by many Italians, and well into our own period. Yet Eugenio Montale, an expert of the resources of the Italian tongue, had praised the almost Goldoni-like quality of Svevo's idiom, which had, as he put it, a music all its own.[2] To be sure, intonation and peculiarities of the Triestino dialect can be detected in Svevo's work. To Tuscan ears, Svevo doubtless writes with a foreign accent.

Trieste and "triestino" are indeed keywords when it comes to Svevo's cultural background. And Trieste at the end of the nineteenth century was less Italian than broadly European, though it was also attached to its specific mode of being, to its fragmented identity. Polyglot and cosmopolitan, incorporating a mixture of ethnic groups — German, Italian, Jewish, Slovene, but also Levantine and Greek — this prosperous "free" port, or *porto franco*, had since the eighteenth century days of Marie-Thérèse enjoyed special privileges and franchise. Although it was not central in a geographic sense, Trieste came to represent the very spirit of *Mitteleuropa*. Its solid bourgeoisie, driven by a business ethos, held to the emancipated notions of the European enlightenment. In Svevo's own words, it was a "crogiolo assimilatore," a crucible of people and ideas.[3] Trieste itself became a literary subject for Svevo, whose writings remain associated with the city's physical and mental setting, much as Balzac is linked with Paris, Joyce with Dublin, and Kafka with Prague.

But in this home city of his, astride the Austro-Hungarian and Mediterranean mentalities, Svevo/Schmitz was in a sense a multiple outsider. A subject of Austria, educated in a German school, he was writing in Italian; a Jew, he was living in a predominantly Christian society; the son of a small-time merchant, surrounded by mercantile concerns, he was consumed by artistic longings. He felt alienated, and Zeno, the name of his memorable fictional character, surely refers in part to *xenos*, the Greek word for foreigner. The language Svevo chose to write in was not really his own. Zeno makes a revealing statement: "With every word we speak in the Tuscan tongue we lie."[4] This statement has far-reaching implications about the nature of any verbal communication, as well as about the gap between ordinary speech and literary language. But at a quite literal level, it is a reminder that Tuscan or Italian was not really Svevo's language. His wife Livia, writing about her husband, made the point that the Triestino dialect was used even by educated people in Trieste. It was their natural speech.[5]

Even Ettore Schmitz's choice of pen name self-consciously points to his complicated foreignness. On the surface, the pseudonym Italo Svevo — Italo the Swabian (or Italo the German) — suggests his divided background, combining Germanic schooling, Triestino irredentist hopes of becoming part of Italy, and the personal desire to establish a literary reputation in a foreign tongue. Moreover, the

Italian-sounding Svevo, referring to the German-speaking region of Swabia, may well be a sly embedded reminder of his Jewishness on the pattern of many names of Italian Jews (like Morpurgo or Moravia — in fact his mother's name) derived from the names of specific towns or regions.

The Trieste that Svevo describes in *Senilità* — with its sea-front and surrounding hills, but also its popular caffès, taverns, forlorn alleys, outlying districts and shipyards — provides the poetic unity of the book, as well as its symbolic background. The beauty of the natural setting is perceived in sharp contrast to the monotony of constricted existences, the pathetic disillusionments, and the shabby realities that do not reflect the reputed prosperity of this money-driven city. Svevo brings out the distance separating two types of penury: that of a fallen, penny-pinching middle class striving nevertheless to maintain decorum in modest apartments; and the less veiled economic distress of a lower class, afflicted with the idleness and alcoholism of its men, and its women driven to promiscuous relations if not to downright prostitution.

Svevo is especially attentive to physical details and to gestures. The brief appearances of Angiolina's obsequious mother, ever eager not to indispose a prospective protector or client of her daughter's, are truly memorable. Svevo proceeds with brevity, by light touches, revealing the tenuous and constantly shifting web of emotional involvements. The novel is in that sense a novel of psychological choreography. But Svevo's real strength lies in the subtle delineations of individual characters and the wily resources of a narrative voice at the same time compassionate, clinically lucid and relentless in denouncing the abject mendacities of the protagonist. The novel is in fact a series of variations on the theme of lies. But there are lies and lies. Brazen and sluttish

Angiolina lies shamelessly from beginning to end. Yet her lies, which most often are unskillful, come naturally to her. They are not really perverse. The same cannot be said for Emilio, who is duplicitous to the core.

Svevo is a master of indirections, and more precisely of the indirect discourse which allows him to move in and out of the mind of his protagonist, sometimes in the same sentence. He thus reveals Emilio's bad faith and his crises of jealousy, both from inside and outside, subjectively and objectively. Better still, his method allows him to formulate thoughts, feelings, impulses of which his character is only dimly aware, or which he would be unwilling to admit. Flaubert had shown the way in *Madame Bovary*, and Svevo had not forgotten the lesson. The modernity of his narrative voice is furthermore dependent on its not being truly omniscient. It is a slightly unstable, deliberately weakened voice well adapted to conveying the instabilities of the novel's leading figure: the rapid switches in mood, the sudden changes in intention, the oscillations and fluctuations of his psychic states, the vibrations of his susceptibilities, the fragmentation of instants as registered by his consciousness. Unobtrusively, Svevo's devices bring the reader into contact with states of mind that blend latent anguish, obsessions, flat reality, and stubborn denial.

When reality is grim, Svevo does not hesitate to handle it realistically. The slow breakdown of Amalia's already weakened organism, the symptoms of her delirium, her mental and physical suffering, the pathos of her facial expressions, the sounds of her congested breathing and of her racking coughs, her final agony, are all described with clinical precision. But Svevo's realism is not devoid of poetry and meaning. It does not appear for its own sake; it fulfills thematic functions. Amalia's final malady exacerbates the specific combination of guilt and self-pity from which her brother Emilio suffers. It establishes a significant resemblance between brother and sister, in that they are both victims of their dreams and inflamed imagination. In a broader perspective, the realistic stress on Amalia's death-struggle brings into sharp focus the theme of a fatal psychological pathology that lies at the heart of this novel.

Not all the characters, to be sure, are afflicted by illness. Angiolina, who seems to move indefatigably from tryst to tryst, in fact brags about her good health. She is a splendidly endowed creature, whose feline strength and beauty exert animal-like magnetism. She is the one character in the novel we never see from within; she matters only because of her effect on others. Her tall, slender, provocative figure as she walks through the streets of Trieste, obviously pleased that everyone looks at her, brings to mind immediate thoughts of a bedroom. Her strong, flexible body, her luminous skin, her golden locks playfully touched by the sun have an intoxicating effect on Emilio from the moment he first sees her. It does not matter that he quickly comes to suspect that she has been promiscuous with much of Trieste. Determined to have an adventure for once in his drab life, yet unwilling to get seriously involved, he chooses to idealize Angiolina, preferring to give her the more exalted name of Ange, though there is not a trace of the angelic in the easily available creature.

Emilio is aware, of course, that Angiolina's childlike coloration, her pure profile and innocent look, her contagious physical laughter, stand in vivid contrast to her sordid background. She lives in what resembles an army barracks together with a mother who has some of the mannerisms of a procuress, a demented father who seems to be nothing but a lazy lout, and a younger sister who promises to become a fine understudy in the tricks of the trade. As for the love sessions with Angiolina, they take place not in a temple of love (as Emilio would like to imagine), but in a shabby room rented out by an unsavory old woman with whom Angiolina appears to have a long-standing professional relation.

Angiolina's wiles and betrayals are so obvious that even a willfully blind Emilio cannot long remain in doubt. At times he is aware that she comes to him still flushed and warm from the bed of another lover. She is a habitual liar. Yet the real lie in the novel is the Ange created by Emilio's imagination, the woman he wants her to be. Angiolina herself lies more simply—with a mixture of spontaneity, cunning, disarming freshness, and natural duplicity. She is, so to speak, innocently perverse.[6] She is not even a good liar. She may be supremely selfish and indifferent to the suffering she causes, but there seems to be in her not a shred of cruelty. She is even capable of being moved. Her type of candid perversity is best summed up by Emilio when he recognizes that there is no use trying to reform her: "She was already completely corrupted in her mother's belly."

Objectively speaking, Angiolina is literal-minded, vulgar, unintelligent. Her dismal background may account for certain traits. She has known poverty and is afraid of it. A child of the working class, she is filled with contempt for common people, siding with the rich against the poor. Svevo was evidently intrigued by the psychological and social phenomenon of class disloyalty. He may have recalled the case of Rosanette Bron, the high-class prostitute in Flaubert's *Sentimental Education* who was equally inclined to look down with fear and scorn on the working class from which she had sprung.

Eugenio Montale felt that there were two distinct Angiolinas, the Angiolina whom Emilio makes love to and comes to hate, and the Ange he idealizes, who is entirely a creation of his fantasy.[7] In fact, there is a whole range of Angiolinas who are creations of Emilio's feverish imagination. And the one who survives at the end of the novel, after he has fully tasted the cup of abjection and lost her for good, is surely his most complete invention. This absurdly poetic figure of Angiolina, already seen from a posthumous point of view, made a strong impression on James Joyce who would not forget this greatest "lie" of all: the metamorphosis of an unimaginative, carnal woman into a disembodied personification of thoughtfulness and compassion, a totally incongruous yet deeply moving reincarnation of the *donna angelica* of early Renaissance poetry — a symbol of lofty sadness and insight into the mystery of things.

The "real" Angiolina, of course, is of little importance. *Senilità* is not about her but about her besotted lover, Emilio. A prematurely tired aesthete living with an anemic sister, Emilio is a would-be writer who is aware of having missed out on the excitements of life and who, upon meeting Angiolina, wants to live the novel he cannot write. But he is no more gifted for living an adventure than for writing about it. Bookish, inert, passive, indecisive, this daydreamer knows occasional flashes of energy only when galvanized by fear, anger, or morbid jealousy. And reasons for jealousy Angiolina richly provides.

Emilio's portrait is developed in all its complexity. Socially clumsy, easily wounded (even by his one close friend), easily fatigued, Emilio dreams of action but is lacking in willpower and afraid to act. His frenzied imagination makes him exceedingly vulnerable. He lives in permanent expectation of something decisive, yet shuns responsibility and seeks refuge in his anxieties. He thus lives in unproductive agitation, a victim of his endlessly ruminating mind. Suffering from his passivity as a lover, Emilio does not really want to possess the woman he is attracted to. He fears and envies the rivals he imagines — men who are virile, true males. Yet he needs the very rivals he so fears. Endowed with an unremarkable libido, convinced that other men satisfy Angiolina better in bed, dimly afraid of sex the way one can be afraid of existence itself, he needs the image of the rival in order to experience desire. For here is the problem: Emilio cannot have a direct, unmediated contact with life. Cerebral even in moments of lovemaking, he self-consciously observes himself and his partner, watching every caress, scrutinizing every gesture, every facial expression, every word that might betray an as yet undiscovered lie.

But surely, the greatest liar in this relationship, as in all others, is Emilio himself, deeply immersed in self-deception and bad faith, invoking morality when it suits his purposes, and ultimately always a victim of his own subterfuges, concealments, and evasions to the point of no longer knowing what it is he really wants. Even in that confusion, however, Emilio remains painfully lucid. A spectator of the self, he is addicted to self-analysis, relentlessly directing his irony against himself, reaching ineffectual diagnoses that only augment his loathing for his own weaknesses and wretched behavior. Even his jealously lacks tragic vigor. The parodic reference to Othello in the fifth chapter underlines Emilio's unheroic suffering.

For Emilio loves his suffering and prefers not to engage in decisive acts. He cuddles his pain, finding satisfaction even in self-abasement. As for his anger and ultimate violence against Angiolina at the end of the novel, they too remain laughable. When he looks for a stone to throw at the woman he now calls a whore, he finds only small pebbles with which to pelt her.

Svevo is at his best registering the ceaseless mobility of Emilio's mind as it oscillates between remorse and guilt, between self-accusation and self-indulgence, caught in recurrent cycles of agitation and calm, with the inevitable relapses into anguish. Emilio's mental games are part of a system of justifications, alibis, and shifts of responsibility that make him insensitive to the suffering of others — in particular, to the suffering of his sister Amalia, who is wasting away, toward whom he feels a sense of duty when it provides him with a good conscience, and for whom he feels compassion only when it feeds his self-pity.

This ungainly sister, colorless and withdrawn, is of crucial importance to the thematic structure of the book. Living in silent sadness, busy keeping house for her brother, she seems condemned to spinsterhood. Repressed and starved for affection, Amalia too has secret dreams. She falls in love with her brother's friend the sculptor Balli, a jocular and domineering male who barely notices her. Amalia's speechless distress, as she constructs a dreamworld of her own, is contrasted with her brother's verbose misery. Sharing modest quarters, Amalia and Emilio are separated by their private dreams and anguish, illustrating the unbreachable distance between one consciousness and another.

Yet there are telling resemblances between Amalia and Emilio — even their names sound alike. Amalia also fabricates a self-destructive fiction and experiences the nightmare of jealousy. She too is submissive with the loved one, except that this loved one does not even notice it. Viewed in the broader context of the novel, her delusions appear like a grotesque parody of Emilio's obsessive jealousy. But the parody is tragic. In her despair and solitude, Amalia seeks oblivion in addictive use of ether, which undermines her already fragile organism. On her deathbed, she continues to have hallucinatory visions of her wedding day and of her betrayal. Her personal tragedy, moreover, illustrates a general law implicit in *Senilità*. Pain does not bring human beings closer together. In love especially, it separates them. Not even friendship can provide solace.

Which leads us to the fourth partner in this quadripartite human relationship, namely, the sculptor Stefano Balli, who is Emilio's close and devoted friend. Emilio stands in need of Balli's strength and sane advice. The two men could not be more unlike. Balli is a free spirit, a pleasure seeker, a domineering but quite likable individual. Used to being admired, successful with women, he is intolerant of the weak and the ugly, though capable of compassion. He has little patience for suffering and sickness. He and Angiolina are the only "healthy" specimens in the novel.

Yet even this close and devoted friend causes suffering for Emilio, who comes to view him as a rival. Emilio envies the sculptor's self-assurance and carefree manner, his easy success with women. Hurt by Balli's notion that life is a fierce competition and that only the fittest survive, Emilio is irritated when his sister listens with rapt attention as his friend tells of his adventures as a bohemian artist. And he becomes jealous to the point of hatred when Angiolina (who already gives him enough reasons to be jealous) appears awed by Balli and flattered to serve him as a model for a statue.

Balli and Emilio have only one feature in common: a propensity to view life (and even death) in an artistic perspective. When Balli watches Amalia in her final hours, as she lies on her deathbed with the yellow light of the candle reflected on her face, he looks at her for the first time admiringly. But what he sees is not a person; it is a work of art: Amalia's shining bare face seems to him the plastic image of a shriek of pain.

This aesthetic transformation of reality suggests that Balli, much like Amalia in her delirium, has a broader thematic function in the book's structure. He is not only the friend, the adviser, the rival; he shares with Emilio the temperament and condition of the artist. But both of them, he as sculptor and Emilio as writer, are failed artists, though to different degrees. Emilio is sterile, and has given up writing. Balli is productive, but what he creates is unsuccessful. He knows, moreover, that his work is not good. His amatory conquests are a poor substitute for the success he yearns for in his profession.

The frustration he and Emilio experience may well reflect Svevo's own disappointments and doubts concerning his artistic endeavors. The relation between life and literature was never an easy one for Svevo. Nor was it merely a matter of a difficult choice between living and writing. The matter was complicated because he continued to live astride writing and living, attempting to "literaturize" life in order to transcend the emptiness of existence.[8] What distinguishes Svevo from both Balli and Emilio is that he was able successfully to translate ineptness and defeat into the victory of artistic form.

In no other work has Svevo been more attentive to formal elements than in *Senilità*. The cityscape of Trieste, the surrounding countryside, the sea's presence and shifts of mood, the frequent changes of weather, the variations of light and seasons, the human habitat, the rain and moonlight provide an elegantly controlled accompaniment to the passions at play. The natural background and unstable climatic conditions are effective in projecting temporal discontinuities and the swift movements of mental processes. The drizzle and the mist, the shades of color, the aggressive Trieste wind (the "bora"), idyllic spring days giving way to stormy hours intensify the dramatic twists of the narrative. Amalia's death is illuminated by a yellow sunset and weird colors announcing an impending storm, by reflections as from a fire. And the violent final meeting with Angiolina takes place to the accompaniment of the sea's wild roar. At times, contrapuntal effects lead to painful ironic contrasts, as when Emilio becomes aware of the "strident contradictions" between the balmy weather and his own torment.

But these narrative devices are themselves forms of aesthetic mediation. The cityscape is easily translated into painterly effects. Much like Balli, Svevo the author transmutes the street scene into a work of art. The fifth chapter offers an interesting example:

> The air was balmy, but the sky, covered by a dense white mist, like a white cape, was really wintry. The long bare branches still unpruned, and the ground, whitish in that diffused and overcast light, made Sant'Andrea look like a snowy landscape. With no way of rendering the softness of the air, a painter trying to reproduce the scene would have set down this erroneous impression.

Erroneous impression, illusion, make-believe, deceit: we join up again with a major theme of the book. The interplay of lies will also be at the heart of Svevo's *La coscienza di Zeno:* talking as lying, lying as a compulsion, the entanglements of lies with truths, the truth of the lie, lying as invention.

These variations on mendacity are linked in both novels to basic human flaws. When Svevo was still an adolescent, so his brother Elio reports, he one day proudly announced that he had discovered his great subject. It was to be called "difetto moderno" (modern flaw).[9] But the underlying sense of ineptness, pessimism, and pathology curiously imply throughout Svevo's work a compelling attraction to illness, a refusal to be cured, and even the notion that illness is essential to the creative mind.

In *Senilità*, there are furthermore strong hints of "bovarysm." Like Emma Bovary, Emilio lives in daily expectation of something great to happen. He too would like to be other than he is. He experiences the corrupting force of dreams, learning at the same time the obverse truth, namely, that possession destroys the dream. Unlike Emma Bovary, however, he continues to dream, so to speak, in a posthumous manner. The ultimate lie, bitterly ironic, is the work of his memory when it transmutes Angiolina into a spiritual allegory of meditation and deep sorrow. The poetic irony of this preposterous transfiguration is heightened by the further irony of a postromantic parodic version of the highly romantic theme of the redeemed and redeeming fallen woman.

It is in this ironic sense that Svevo's work in general exemplifies literary modernity. His narrative instabilities, his conviction that communication itself is flawed, that language is an unreliable and scabrous tool, bring him close to other contemporary writers who thematize their distrust of the very words they must necessarily depend on. Svevo's writings illustrate T. S. Eliot's notion of language as shifty and treacherous.

> Words strain,
> Crack and sometimes break, under the burden,
> Under the tension, slip, slide, perish,
> Decay with imprecision . . .[10]

This problematization of language is not unrelated to Svevo's interest in psychoanalysis, which reached Italy precisely by way of Trieste. The haunting resonance of uttered words, the obsessive time of repetition and recurrence, the indelible memory of an original trauma inflicting what Zeno calls his "big wound," a complex system of transfers and psychological simultaneities are well-known features of psychoanalytic theory. But illness and psychoanalysis interested Svevo for literary, not therapeutic, reasons. "That Freud of ours was a great man, but more so for novelists than for patients," he declared in a letter to Valerio Jahier.[11] His interest in psychoanalysis was more often than not a questioning of psychoanalysis. In his introduction to the English translation of *La coscienza di Zeno*, Renato Poggioli shrewdly stated that Svevo had "psychoanalyzed psychoanalysis itself."[12] Certainly Svevo was a practitioner of what has been called undecidability. A supremely ironic writer, he ironizes irony. Had he known the term and the concept, he would probably have set out to deconstruct deconstruction.

When it comes to narrative duplicities, Svevo is in tune with the subtlest modern examples through his practice of indirections and obliquities, disingenuous narrative flatness, instabilities of point of view, dissonances between self and world, and the unreliability of a narrative voice that is both subject and object. Commentators of European modernity have rightfully sensed that Svevo, more keenly perhaps than any other writer, has glimpsed the demise of the hero as well as of the subject, and that the authority of the text itself was steadily sapped by him.

In that specific sense, one could say that Svevo is more modern than Marcel Proust, who seemingly writes about evanescence and change but is in fact seeking to recapture and fixate the essence of reality and give it an unalterable structure. There is no essence in Svevo's work, which remains mobile and committed to flux.

1. In a diary entry of December 1902, Svevo refers to literature as "quella ridicola e dannosa cosa." *Opera Omnia*, Milan: Dall' Oglio, 1966–1969, 3: 818.

2. See Eugenio Montale's preface to Livia Veneziani Svevo, *Vita di mio marito*, Milan: Dall' Oglio, 1976, p. 6.

3. "Profilo autobiografico," *Opera Omnia*, 3: 799.

4. "Con ogni nostra parola toscana noi mentiamo!" *La coscienza di Zeno*, Milan: Dall' Oglio, 1984, p. 445.

5. Livia Veneziani Svevo, *Vita*, pp. 17, 99.

6. The Italian reads: "ingenuamente perversa." *Senilità*, Milan: Dall' Oglio, 1962, p. 58.

7. Eugenio Montale, preface to *La coscienza di Zeno*, Milan: Dall' Oglio, 1976, p. 13.

8. For an interesting development of Svevo's notion of *vita literaturizzata* see the passage quoted in Livia Veneziani Svevo, *Vita*, p. 150.

9. See Elio Schmitz, *Diario*, Milan: Dall' Oglio, 1973, p. 244.

10. *Four Quartets*, "Burnt Norton," section V, *The Complete Poems and Plays*, New York: Harcourt, Brace, 1950, p. 121.

11. Letter of 10 December 1927, *Epistolario*, in *Opera Omnia*, Milan: Dall' Oglio, 1: 857.

12. Renato Poggioli, "A Note on Svevo," introduction to *Confessions of Zeno*, New York: New Directions, 1930, p. 5.

Emilio's Carnival (SENILITÀ)

one

With his first words to her, he wanted to inform her straight away that he had no intention of getting involved in a serious relationship. What he said was roughly this: "I love you very much and for your sake I want us to agree to proceed with great caution." His declaration was so prudent it could hardly have been made out of love; with a little more candor it would have sounded like this: "I like you a lot, but you could never be more than a plaything in my life. I have other obligations. I have my career, my family."

His family? Only one sister, neither physically nor morally burdensome, pale and petite, a few years younger than he, but older by nature or perhaps by fate. Of the two, he was the egoist, the younger one. She lived for him like a selfless mother, but that did not prevent him from talking about her as though her destiny were a separate one bound to his own. Bowed by so many responsibilities, he thus went through life with great caution, circumventing every kind of risk at the price of enjoyment and happiness. At thirty-five he was discovering in his soul unsated longings for pleasure and love and the bitterness of having experienced neither, and in his head a fear of himself and of the weakness of his character; really more a suspicion than a proven fact.

Emilio Brentani's career was further complicated because it comprised at the same time two occupations and two objectives that were quite distinct. From an insignificant job in an insurance company he earned just enough for his small household. His other career was literary, which, aside from a minor reputation more gratifying to vanity than to ambition, yielded him nothing and demanded even less of him. For many years, after having published a novel highly praised by the local press, he had done nothing, more out of inertia than distrust in his talent. Printed on inferior paper, the novel yellowed in the bookseller's stockroom. At the time of its publication Emilio had been considered a great hope for the future, but since then he had come to be regarded as an exemplar of literary respectability, inscribed in the city's meager artistic ledger. The first judgment was not revised; it evolved.

Because he was keenly aware of the worthlessness of his own work, he did not glory in the past, although he did believe, in life as in art, that he was still in a preparatory stage, that the deepest recesses of his being harbored an ingenious mechanism of great power, not yet functioning but still under construction. He continually lived in impatient anticipation of something his brain was sure to produce: artistry of some kind that would come to him from some source, wealth, success — as though the age of youthful creativity had not already passed him by.

Angiolina — a blonde with big blue eyes, tall and strong but slender and lithe, her face aglow with vitality, her complexion a golden amber suffused with the rosiness of robust health — walked beside him, her head tilted to one side as though bent by all the gold that enveloped her, her eyes fixed on the ground, which she tapped at every step with her elegant parasol as though she were trying to make a reply to the words she was hearing gush up from it. When she thought she had understood, she said, stealing a glance at him, "How strange. No one has ever talked to me that way." She had not understood and was flattered to see him assume the unexpected role of protecting her from danger. The affection he was offering her appeared to be brotherly tenderness.

With those introductory remarks, he felt secure and spoke in a manner better suited to the circumstances. He showered her blond curls with lyrical declarations that his long frustrated desires had polished and refined, but in his own ears they sounded new and young again, as though born just then in the azure of Angiolina's eyes. He had the sensation, not experienced in years, of composing, of extracting ideas and words from deep within himself. A sense of relief endowed that moment of his unfulfilled life with a strange unforgettable quality of repose, of peace. A woman had entered it! Radiant with youth and beauty, she would brighten it, making him forget his sorry past of yearning and solitude, promising him future joys which she would surely not withhold.

He had approached her with the notion of a casual and brief adventure, like those he had so often heard described but which had always eluded him or were not worth remembering. This one had certainly started out as casual and brief. Her parasol had fallen at just the right moment to provide him with a pretext to approach her and instead — as though by design! — it caught in the lace at her waist and could only be detached after much indelicate pulling. But once he caught sight of that astonishingly pure profile, that splendid vitality — to rhetoricians, depravity and vitality always appear to be irreconcilable — he restrained his impulse, fearful of miscalculating, and in the end became so entranced in his admiration of a mysterious face whose contours were both lovely and well defined that he found satisfaction and happiness merely in that.

She had told him little about herself. At the time, completely taken as he was with his own emotions, he did not even hear that little. She was doubtless poor, very poor, but for the moment—she had announced this with a touch of haughtiness—she did not have to work for a living. That made the adventure all the more appealing, since the proximity of hunger is an antidote to pleasure. Emilio's inquiries were therefore not exhaustive but he was convinced that his logical conclusions, even if based on such slim evidence, were enough to reassure him. If the young woman, as one would be led to believe by the candor of her glance, were respectable, he would surely not be exposing himself to the risk of corrupting her. If, on the other hand, her profile and her look were false, then so much the better. In either case there was room for enjoyment, and danger in neither.

Angiolina had understood little of his opening remarks, but she visibly had no need of additional commentary to understand the rest; even his most convoluted language carried an unambiguous ring. Her naturally bright tints returned to her lovely face, and her hand, perfectly shaped though somewhat large, was not withdrawn from Emilio's very chaste kiss.

They stopped for a long while on the Passeggio di Sant'Andrea and looked out at the deep-blue calm of the sea under a star-filled moonless sky. A wagon went by on the avenue below, and in the profound silence around them, they continued to hear the noise of the wheels on the uneven ground long after it passed. They found it amusing to follow the sound as it grew fainter and fainter until it faded into the total silence and were delighted that it vanished at the same moment for both of them. "Our ears are very much in tune with each other," Emilio smiled.

He had said all there was to say and felt no further need to speak. He interrupted a long silence to say: "Who knows if our meeting will bring us luck!" He meant it. He felt the need to question his happiness out loud.

"Who knows?" she repeated, trying to express in her own voice the emotion she heard in his.

Emilio smiled again but this time he thought he should conceal it. Given his stipulations, what kind of luck could possibly befall Angiolina from having met him?

Then they parted. She did not want him to accompany her back to town, and so he, reluctant to leave her so soon, followed her from a distance. What a lovely figure! She walked with the easy stride of a healthy body, her step secure on the slick muddied street. How much power and grace were united in those movements as sure as a feline's.

As luck would have it, the very next day he learned much more about Angiolina than she had told him.

He ran into her at noon, on the Corso. His unexpected good fortune made him greet her playfully with a grand gesture of sweeping his hat almost to the ground. She replied with a discreet nod, enhanced by a magnificent shimmering glance.

A certain Sorniani, small, skinny, and sallow, rumored to be a great skirtchaser, and unquestionably vain and gossipy to the detriment of other people's reputations as well as his own, took hold of Emilio's arm and asked him how he happened to know that girl. They had been boyhood friends but had not exchanged a word in years. It took a beautiful woman passing between them for Sorniani to feel the need to approach Emilio.

"I met her at a friend's house," he replied.

"And what is she up to now?" Sorniani asked, implying that he was familiar with Angiolina's past but was considerably put out not to know her present.

"I wouldn't know," he answered, adding with feigned indifference, "She looked to me like a decent girl."

"Not so fast!" Sorniani said with assurance, as though to infer the contrary. Only after a brief pause did he correct himself. "I don't know anything about her now, but when I did know her everybody thought she was respectable even though she was once in a somewhat equivocal situation." Without any further urging from Emilio, Sorniani related that the poor thing had come close to a sizable fortune but, out of her doing or someone else's, it turned into a disaster of no small proportions. In her early youth she had captivated a certain Merighi, a very handsome man — a quality Sorniani was willing to recognize even though the man was not to his liking — and a prosperous businessman. He had approached her with the most honorable proposals. He had taken her from her family, for which he had little respect, and brought her into his own mother's house. "His own mother!" Sorniani exclaimed. "As though that fool" — he was determined to make the man out to be foolish and the girl disreputable — "couldn't have taken his pleasure with the girl somewhere else and not under his mother's eyes. Then, after a few months, Angiolina went back to her own home, which she should never have left, and Merighi and his mother left town, giving the impression that they had been ruined by misbegotten speculations. According to others, the story went somewhat differently. It is said that when Merighi's mother caught Angiolina in one of her disgraceful intrigues, she threw the girl out of the house." Unsolicited, he continued to elaborate other variations on the same theme.

Since it was all too obvious that Sorniani enjoyed wallowing in this titillating subject, Brentani retained only what he considered completely trustworthy, that is, facts that were doubtless common knowledge. He had known Merighi by sight and remembered a tall athletic figure, just the man for Angiolina. He recalled having heard him described, or rather criticized, as unrealistic in business, a man far too daring who thought his dynamism could conquer the world. In short, from people he saw daily at work Emilio learned that Merighi's daring had cost him dearly: he ended up having to liquidate his business under disastrous conditions. Sorniani was therefore wasting his breath because Emilio thought he now knew exactly what had happened. Because Merighi, impoverished, his confidence shaken, no longer had the courage to start a family, Angiolina, who was to have become a rich and respectable upper-class woman, was now becoming a plaything for Emilio. He was overwhelmed by deep compassion for her.

Sorniani had seen with his own eyes Merighi's demonstrations of love. On a number of Sundays he had seen Merighi waiting patiently at the entrance to the church of Saint Anthony the Great for Angiolina, on her knees before the altar, to finish her prayers. And the whole time his gaze was fixed on that blond head gleaming in the shadows. "A double adoration," Emilio thought with emotion. It was easy for him to intuit the tenderness that kept Merighi rooted to the threshold of the church.

"An idiot," Sorniani said in conclusion.

Through Sorniani's account, his own adventure gained importance in Emilio's eyes. His anticipation of Thursday, when he was to see her again, became feverish and his impatience made him garrulous.

His most intimate friend, a sculptor by the name of Balli, was immediately informed of the meeting the day after it took place. "Why shouldn't I also have some fun, when I can do it at so little cost?"

Balli heard him out in amazement. He had been Brentani's friend for more than ten years, but this was the first time he had ever seen him excited about a woman. He was instantly alarmed by the danger that threatened Brentani.

"Danger, me? At my age, with my experience?" he protested. Brentani often talked about his experience. What he thought could be called experience had been extracted from books and consisted of regarding his peers with great distrust and great contempt.

Balli, on the other hand, had put his forty years to better use, so that his experience better qualified him to judge his friend's. Though less cultivated than Brentani, he had always exercised over him a kind of paternal authority, which Emilio not only accepted but desired. For despite a joyless but in no way threatening existence and a life in which nothing was unexpected, Emilio needed approval to feel secure. Stefano Balli was tall and strong, with boyish blue eyes in one of those tanned faces that never grow old. The only trace of his age was the silver streaking his chestnut hair. His beard was neatly trimmed, his features regular and a bit hard. His observant eyes could nonetheless grow soft when animated by curiosity or compassion, but turned steely in conflict or in even lesser disagreements.

Success had not smiled on him, either. From time to time a jury had praised individual elements while rejecting his projects, so that not one of his works found a place on any of the many squares in Italy. Nonetheless, he had never felt the despair of failure. He was satisfied with the admiration of one or two artists, convinced that his originality was what prevented him from enjoying celebrity and the acclaim of a wide public. He continued to live according to his own ideal of spontaneity, a certain willful roughness, a simplicity, or, as he said, a perspicuity that would reveal his artistic self, purified of all borrowed ideas or forms. He did not consider that the outcome of his work might demean him, but no amount of rationalization would have saved him from discouragement if his extraordinary personal success had not given him the satisfactions he concealed and even denied, but which contributed in no small way to maintaining the proud carriage of his fine slender figure. His interest in women was much more for him than the mere satisfaction of his vanity, although he was too ambitious to love; it amounted to success, or something like it, since the women who loved the artist also loved his art, however little suited it was to feminine taste. And so, unshakably convinced of his genius and feeling loved and admired, he maintained his air of superiority with no pretension whatever. In art, his judgments were harsh and tactless, and in society he was less than considerate. Men did not care much for him, and he sought out only those he knew were impressed with him.

Some ten years earlier, he had come across Emilio Brentani, very young at the time, an egotist like him but not as lucky, to whom he had taken a liking. At first he appreciated him simply because he felt admired; much later, habit made his friend more valuable, almost indispensable. Their relationship was shaped by Balli. It became more intimate than Emilio's prudence would have wished, in the way that all of the sculptor's few relationships were intimate. Their intellectual exchanges remained limited to the plastic arts, and in that they were in perfect agreement, for on that subject there was only one idea, Balli's: the retrieval of the simplicity or spontaneity which the so-called classicists had taken from those arts. It was an effortless agreement. Balli did all the teaching; his pupil made no attempt to learn. They never discussed Emilio's complex literary theories, since Balli despised whatever he did not already know. Balli's influence went so far as to affect Emilio's manner of walking, talking, gesturing. Masculine in the truest sense of the word, Balli gave, he did not take, and when he and Brentani walked side by side, he felt that he was being accompanied by one of the many women he held in thrall.

"True enough," he said after hearing all the details of the adventure from Emilio, "there should be no danger. The nature of the adventure was already determined by the parasol that fell so opportunely from her hand and by the rendezvous immediately accorded."

"Indeed," Emilio concurred, without however admitting the scant importance he had given to those two details, so that when pointed out by Balli, they struck him as completely new factors.

"So you think Sorniani may be right?" He had certainly not taken those factors into account when he passed judgment on Sorniani's story.

"You will introduce her to me," Balli said cautiously, "and then we will decide."

Not even with his sister was Brentani able to restrain himself. Signorina Amalia had never been pretty. Scrawny, dried out, colorless—Balli said she was born gray—the only trace of her youth was her hands—white, graceful, meticulously groomed—to which she dedicated all her attentions.

It was the first time he had ever talked to her about a woman, and Amalia listened attentively and amazed, her expression suddenly altered by words which to his ears were proper and chaste but which fell from his lips heavy with love and desire. He had told her hardly anything, yet she was already frightened and murmured the same warning as Balli: "Be careful that you don't do something foolish."

Then she wanted him to tell her everything, and Emilio thought he could confide his admiration and the happiness he had felt that first evening while withholding his intentions and his hopes. He was unaware that what he did tell her was even more disturbing. She continued listening to him, serving his meal silently and quickly so that he would not have to interrupt himself to ask her for something. It was with a similar look of avidity that she had read the hundreds of novels stuffed into the old cupboard, now serving as a bookcase, but the fascination that held her now — to her surprise, she already understood — was entirely different. She was not a passive auditor, nor was it the destiny of some unknown person that held her spellbound: her own destiny was being resuscitated. Love had entered the house and now cohabited with her, anxiously, oppressively. With one breath it had blown away the stagnant environment in which she had spent her life, while unaware of it. Looking into herself, she was surprised that given her sensibility she had not wanted to experience the joy and pain of love.

Brother and sister embarked together on the same adventure.

two

Although it was dark, he recognized her instantly at the crossroads of Campo Marzio. By then, all he needed to recognize her was her shadow gliding without rhythm because of its even stride, the stride of a body carried with assurance and self-esteem. He ran toward her, and seeing the remarkable color of that face, an uncommon color, intense, smooth, unmottled, he felt rising in his chest a hymn of joy. She had come, and when she leaned on his arm, it seemed to him she was abandoning herself to him unreservedly.

He led her toward the sea, far from the avenue still peopled with a few passersby. Once at the shore they felt truly alone. He would have kissed her at once but did not dare, even though she, silent until then, was smiling at him encouragingly. Just the thought that if he dared he could have placed his lips on her eyes or her mouth moved him so deeply that his breath caught in his throat.

"Oh, why were you so late? I was afraid you were not coming." That is what he said, but his resentment was already forgotten. Like certain animals in rut he felt the need to yowl, so much so that later he thought he had revealed his displeasure with the playful words: "I can hardly believe I have you here beside me." The remark lay bare the full extent of his happiness. "And I had thought no evening could be lovelier than the one last week." Oh, now his happiness was so much greater that he could relish his conquest as though already achieved.

The kiss came too soon, for after that first impulse to wrap his arms around her, he would have been satisfied just to gaze at her and dream. But she understood even less about Emilio's emotions than he did himself. He had ventured a timid caress across her hair — so golden. But her complexion was golden too, he noted further, in fact, all of her was golden. He thought that with these words he had said everything there was to say; Angiolina was not of the same mind. She remained pensive for a moment and then spoke of an aching tooth. "Here," she said, showing him her exquisite mouth, her pink gums, her strong white teeth, a jewel box of precious stones placed and set by a matchless craftsman: good health. He did not laugh but kissed the mouth that had been offered.

Her insatiable vanity did not upset him so long as he was benefiting from it; he was not even aware of it. He, like all who shy away from life, who considered himself stronger than the highest power and more indifferent than the most consummate pessimist, now looked around to see what had witnessed this extraordinary event.

It was not half bad. The moon had not yet risen, but over there, on the sea, was an iridescent sheen as though the sun had just passed over, leaving everything aglow in its wake. On either side, however, the blue of the promontories was shaded by the deep black of night. Everything was enormous, boundless, and in all that vastness the only movement was the color of the sea. In that instant, in the immensity of that setting, he had the feeling that he alone acted and loved.

He talked to her about what he had learned from Sorniani and then questioned her about her past. She became very serious and in dramatic tones began telling him about her relationship with Merighi. Abandoned? That was not the right word for it, since she was the one who had spoken the decisive word that freed Merighi from his commitment. The truth was that his family had gotten on her nerves in every way, letting her understand that they considered her a burden. Merighi's mother (oh, that old grouch, that nasty bilious crone) let her have it straight out: "You are our ruination, because without you who knows what great dowry he might find." And so, of her own free will, she left that house, returned to her mother — she said that tender word with such tenderness — and from grief fell sick soon after. Her illness was a solace, since high fever obliterates troubled thoughts.

Then she wanted to know from whom he had heard this story.

"From Sorniani."

She did not recognize the name at first, then exclaimed laughing, "That ugly yellow what's-his-name who is always with Leardi."

She knew Leardi too, a young man who was just beginning to sow his wild oats but was going about it with an ardor that immediately placed him in the front rank of the city's playboys. Merighi had introduced him a number of years before, when all three of them were practically children: they used to play together. "I'm very fond of him," she said in conclusion, with a candor that made the sincerity of her other remarks believable. And even Brentani, beginning to worry about that formidable young Leardi who was running after her, on hearing her last words felt reassured. "Poor girl! Honest but not very clever."

Would it not have been better to make her less honest and more calculating? Once he asked himself the question, he had the brilliant idea of taking upon himself the education of the girl. In exchange for the gift of her love, he could give her only one thing: an understanding of life and the art of enjoying it. And his was also an extremely precious gift, for with her beauty and grace, under the direction of a competent person like himself, she could be a winner in the struggle for life. With his help, she would be able to acquire, all by herself, the fortune he was unable to give her. He wanted to communicate to her right away some of the ideas that were going through his mind. He stopped kissing her and flattering her, and to instruct her in vice, took on the austere demeanor of a teacher of virtue.

Turning his irony on himself, which he often enjoyed doing, he began pitying her for having fallen into the hands of a man like him, lacking money and something else as well — energy and courage. Because if he were courageous — making for the first time a declaration of love more serious than any he had made to her before, his voice choking from the intensity of his emotions — he would have taken his lovely blonde in his arms, pressed her to his chest, and carried her off for life. But instead, he did not feel up to that. Penury for two was a horrible thing; it meant slavery, of the worst kind. He dreaded it for himself as well as for her.

At that, she interrupted him. "I would not be afraid."

He interpreted this as her wish to grab him by the collar and fling him into the very condition he so dreaded.

"If I lived with a man I loved, I could endure poverty."

"But not I," he said after a short pause, pretending to have hesitated for a moment. "I know myself. In penury I would be incapable of loving." After another brief pause, he added in a deep, somber voice, "Impossible!" while she continued to look at him attentively, her chin resting on the handle of her parasol.

Having settled the matter, he remarked — and this was the beginning of the education he wanted to give her — that it would be better for her if she took up with one of the other young men who had admired her that day she was with him, like Carlini, a rich man, or Bardi, who was squandering the last of his youth and great fortune, or Nelli, a businessman who made a lot of money. Each of them, in one way or another, was worth more than he.

Her reaction at that moment was right on the mark: she was offended! It was all too obvious that his bitterness was deliberate, exaggerated — Emilio himself had to admit it — but she did not hold this fabrication against him. Twisting her whole body, she turned as though to detach herself from him and get away, but the force of her movement did not reach her arms, by which he held her fast. They remained almost limp as he stroked and kissed them, until he finally released his grasp.

He apologized. He had not explained himself well, and courageously repeated in different words what he had already said. She did not acknowledge this new offense but for a while maintained her reproachful tone: "I do not want you to think that I would have permitted any one of those gentlemen to approach me. I would not have allowed them to speak to me." At their first meeting they had vaguely remembered having seen each other on the avenue a year before; so that he, Angiolina said, was not just some unknown.

"All I wanted to say," Emilio declared solemnly, "was that I do not deserve you."

Only then did he succeed in communicating to her the lessons that were to be so useful to her. He found her too disinterested and felt sorry for her. A girl in her situation had to watch out for her own welfare. What did honesty mean in this world? Self-interest! Honest women were those who knew how to find a buyer at the highest price, who did not yield to love until the bottom line turned out right. Saying these things he felt like a superior immoral man who saw and wanted things as they really are. The powerful thinking machine he considered himself to be rose out of his inertia. A wave of pride swelled his chest.

Listening attentively and wide-eyed, she remained glued to his lips. She seemed to think that a rich woman and an honest woman were the one and the same. "So that's how all those women with grand airs got that way?" Then, seeing his surprise, she denied having meant what she had said, but had he been as observant as he thought he was, he would have recognized that she no longer understood the argument that had amazed her a moment before.

He repeated and annotated the ideas he had already expressed: an honest woman knows her worth, and that is her secret. One must be honest or at least give that impression. It was already bad that a Sorniani could speak cavalierly about her, and even worse that she should declare her fondness for Leardi — and here he vented his jealousy — that most compromising skirtchaser of all. It was better to be wicked than to be seen as wicked.

All at once she forgot the general ideas that he had elucidated and began defending herself vigorously against those attacks. Sorniani could not have bad-mouthed her, and as for Leardi, he was a just a kid and in no way compromising.

That evening his instruction ended there, because he decided that such potent medicine should be administered in small doses. Moreover, in his eyes he had already made an enormous sacrifice by interrupting their embraces for a few minutes.

His literary sensibility was offended by Angiolina's name. He called her Lina, then, still dissatisfied with that endearing abbreviation, he bestowed the French name Angèle on her and occasionally refined it further by shortening it to Ange. He taught her to say in French that she loved him. When she learned the meaning of the words she refused to say them, but at their next meeting she spoke them without being asked: *Zhe tem bokú*.

He was not at all surprised to have come so far so soon. That corresponded precisely to his wish. She had obviously found him so reasonable that she felt she could trust him, and in fact, for quite some time she had no cause to refuse him anything.

They always met out in the open. They embraced in all the suburban streets of Trieste. After their first appointments they left Sant'Andrea, which was too crowded, and for some time after chose the road to Opicina, flanked by dense horse chestnut trees, a broad unfrequented thoroughfare that climbed almost imperceptibly. They would stop at a piece of low wall that became the goal of their promenades merely because they had sat there the first time. They exchanged languorous kisses while the city, still, silent, like the sea, stretched out below their feet. From up there it looked like little more than a vast expanse of some indeterminate mysterious color. And in the silence and the stillness, city, sea, and hills seemed all of a piece, the same material molded and colored by some weird artist, divided into sectors by the dotted yellow lines of the streetlamps.

Moonlight did nothing to alter the color. Objects whose contours became clearer were not so much illumined as veiled by light. A still whiteness lay over everything, but underneath, the color slumbered torpidly, darkly. Even now with the sea's endless motion visible, its surface rippling with silver, the dormant color remained muted. The green of the hills and the variegated colors of the houses remained dull, while the light above — deflected, separate, an aura saturating the air — was incorruptibly white, since nothing blended into it.

The moonlight became one with the face of the young

woman close to his own, replacing the tones of baby pink without eliminating the suffused gold that Emilio thought he could taste with his lips. An austere expression came over her whole face, and as he kissed her Emilio felt more corrupt than ever before. He was kissing chaste white light.

Later they chose the woods of Hunter's Hill in their growing need for privacy. They would sit beside a tree and eat, drink, kiss. Flowers quickly disappeared from their relationship, supplanted by sweets, which she later refused so as not to ruin her teeth. Then came cheeses, sausages, bottles of wine and liqueurs, very costly delicacies for Emilio's limited means.

But he was more than willing to sacrifice to Angiolina all of the meager savings he had made over the long years of his regimented life. Once the little nest egg was empty, he would reduce his expenses. He was more preoccupied by other considerations: who had taught Angiolina how to kiss? He no longer remembered their first kisses. At the time, he was too busy with the kiss he was giving; all he felt in the kiss he was receiving was the sweetness needed to complement his own, but it seemed to him that if her mouth had been all that active, he would have been somewhat surprised. Was it he, then, who taught her the art in which he himself was a novice?

She confessed! It was Merighi who used to kiss her a lot. She laughed as she told him about it. Emilio certainly looked silly to her to have imagined that Merighi would not have taken advantage of his position of fiancé to have at least kissed her to his heart's content.

Brentani was not made at all jealous by the memory of Merighi, who had many more rights than he. On the contrary, he was pained that she spoke so lightly about him. Should she not have wept each time she mentioned his name? When he expressed his own regrets at not seeing her more unhappy, she, in confirmation, arranged her lovely face in an expression of sadness, and to defend herself against what she took as a reproach, reminded him that she had fallen sick over Merighi's abandonment: "Oh! If I had died then, I would not have been at all sorry." Moments later, she was laughing uproariously in his arms which had opened to console her.

She had no regrets whatever, and he was as surprised by that as he was by his own pained compassion. How he loved her! Or was it merely gratitude toward that adorable creature for behaving as though she had been created for him alone, undemanding, obliging lover that he was?

When he returned home late in the evening and his pale sister put down her sewing to keep him company at supper, he, still tingling with excitement, not only was incapable of talking about anything else, he could not even pretend to take an interest in the little domestic banalities that made up Amalia's life and which she usually shared with him. In the end, sitting beside him, she took up her sewing again, and they remained in the room together, each lost in private thoughts.

One evening, after looking at him for a long time without his notice, she asked, trying hard to smile, "Were you with her until now?"

"Which *her?*" he asked bursting into laughter. Then he confessed, out of a need to talk. Oh, what an unforgettable evening. He had loved in the moonlight, in the warm air, looking out on an endless smiling landscape created just for them, for their love. But he did not know how to express himself. What notion of that evening could he give his sister without talking about Angiolina's kisses?

But while he kept repeating, "What light, what air!" she

intuited the kisses on his lips that filled his thoughts. She despised that women whom she did not know but who had robbed her of her companion, her solace. Now that she was seeing him love just like all the others, she was losing the only other example she knew of voluntary resignation to her own pitiful state. So pitiful! She began to cry, at first with silent tears that she tried to hide, then, when he became aware of her tears, with an outburst of sobs that she was unable to repress.

She tried to explain her tears: she had not been well all day, she had not slept the night before, she had not eaten, she felt very weak. Naturally, he believed her. "Tomorrow if you don't feel better, we'll call the doctor."

Added now to Amalia's pain was rage that he could be so easily taken in by the cause of her tears; that was a proof of his utter indifference. Abandoning all restraint, she told him that her pain could stay just as it was; given the life she led, it wasn't worth the trouble to cure it. For whom was she living and for what? Seeing that he still made no effort to understand and continued to look at her ecstatically, she poured out the whole of her heartache: "Not even you need me any more." Obviously, he did not understand, for instead of becoming compassionate, he became angry. He had spent his youth in solitude and sadness; it was only fair that from time to time he should allow himself some distraction. Angiolina held no importance in his life; she was an adventure that would last a few months and no more. "It is mean of you to make reproaches." He was moved only when he saw that she was still weeping, in silent brokenhearted immobility. To console her he promised that he would keep her company more often; they would read and study together as they had in the past. But she would have to be more cheerful because he did not like sad people. His thoughts flew to *Ange!* How she could laugh, with her prolonged contagious laughter. He could not keep from smiling at the thought of how out of place those peals of laughter would have sounded in his cheerless house.

three

One evening, he was to meet her at eight o'clock sharp, but half an hour before that, Balli sent word to tell him that he would wait for him at the Caffè Chiozza, at that very hour, because he had some important information to communicate. He had previously declined similar invitations, knowing their only purpose was to keep him away from Angiolina for a while, but this time, by accepting, he had a pretext for going to the young woman's house to inform her of the postponement. He would thus be able to examine within the context of her existence, her surroundings, her family, the person who had become so important to him. In his blindness, he continued to see himself as endowed with clear vision.

Angiolina's house was located just beyond via Fabio Severo. Broad and tall, in the middle of fields, it looked like a barracks. The caretaker's lodge was closed, but Emilio, somewhat hesitant, to tell the truth, not knowing how he would be received, nonetheless climbed up to the third floor. "This hardly looks prosperous," he murmured aloud to register his observations. The staircase was obviously made with little care: the stones were badly squared, the railing cheap iron, the walls whitewashed. Nothing was dirty, but the whole place smacked of poverty.

A little girl, perhaps ten years old, came to the door in a dress too big and too long and sheer as a spider's web, blonde like Angiolina but her eyes lifeless, her complexion sallow, anemic. She seemed not at all surprised to see an unfamiliar face. All she did was raise her hand to close the edges of her jacket across her chest — the buttons were missing.

"Good evening! May I help you?" Such ceremonious courtesy in a little person of her age seemed inappropriate.

"Is Signorina Angiolina at home?"

"Angiolina!" yelled a woman who in the meantime had come forward from the back of the hallway. "A gentleman is asking for you."

That was doubtless the dear mother to whom Angiolina devotedly returned when Merighi left her. The old woman was dressed like a servant, in bright though somewhat faded colors, her apron a bright blue, as was her scarf, which she wore around her head like the women of Friuli. For the rest, her face still held traces of former beauty, in fact, her profile resembled Angiolina's. But the bony expressionless face and small black eyes filled with anxiety had something of the wary animal trying to escape a beating. "Angiolina!" she yelled once more. "She'll be right here," she informed him with extreme courtesy. Then, without ever looking him in the face, she said insistently: "Please make yourself comfortable in the meantime." Her nasal voice was incapable of sounding pleasant. She hesitated like a stutterer at the beginning of a sentence, then the entire sentence tumbled out of her mouth without a break, all in one breath, without a trace of human warmth.

Walking quickly from the other end of the hallway, Angiolina appeared, already dressed to go out. Seeing him, she started to laugh but greeted him cordially: "Oh, Signor Brentani. What a nice surprise." She breezily made the introduction: "My mother, my sister."

So that was the cherished mother. Nevertheless, Emilio, pleased to have been so well received, extended his hand while the old woman, unaccustomed to such marks of distinction, hesitated before extending her own. She had not understood his intentions, and her nervous wolverine eyes stared at him for a moment with instantaneous and unconcealed distrust. The little girl, imitating her mother, also gave him her hand while her other one remained clenched on her chest. Now that she had attained that honor, she calmly said, "Thank you."

"Come in here," Angiolina said, running to a door at the back of the hallway and opening it. Brentani was ecstatic to find himself alone with Angiolina, for the old woman and the child remained outside the door after one more pleasantry. Once the door was closed, he forgot all about being an observer and pulled her to him.

"No," she implored, "my father is sick and asleep in the next room."

"I can kiss without making noise," he declared and pressed his lips to her mouth while she continued to protest. The result was a long interrupted kiss on warm breath.

Impatient with his attentions, she liberated herself and opened the door. "Now sit down and behave, because they can see us from the kitchen."

She was laughing again, and long after, he remembered her like that, pleased to have played that trick on him, like a mischievous child repulsing someone who loves her. The hair at her temples was ruffled by his arm, which he had placed around her blond head, as he always did. His eyes caressed the traces of his own caress.

Only a little later did he see the room surrounding them. The draperies were not too fresh, but the furniture, in view of the staircase, the hallway, and the way her mother and sister were dressed, looked surprisingly sumptuous, all made of walnut, the bed covered with a generously fringed spread, in a corner an enormous vase with tall artificial flowers, and on the wall above it, numerous photographs carefully grouped. In a word, luxury.

He looked at the photographs. An elderly man had himself photographed in the pose of an important figure, hand resting on a stack of papers. Emilio smiled. "My godfather," Angiolina explained. A young man, nicely dressed but looking like a worker in his Sunday best, with a bright face and a bold expression. "My sister's godfather," Angiolina said, "and this," showing him the portrait of another young man, gentler and more refined than the first, "is the godfather of my youngest brother."

"Are there any others?" Emilio asked, but the joke died on his lips because among the photographs, he came upon two men he knew: Leardi and Sorniani! Sorniani, yellow even on the photograph, with a grim look on his face, still seemed to be talking disparagingly about Angiolina. The best picture was the one of Leardi: the camera in this case had done a good job of reproducing all the gradations of light and shade, and the handsome Leardi seemed to be portrayed in color. He stood there jauntily, not leaning against any table, his gloved hands free, as though entering a room where he was perhaps awaited by an unaccompanied woman. He looked out at Emilio in a kind of proprietary way, natural enough in an attractive boyish face like his. Overcome with rancor and envy, Emilio tore his glance away.

Angiolina did not understand at first why Emilio's brow had darkened so suddenly. His jealousy revealed itself for the first time, and with force. "I am hardly pleased to find so many other men in this bedroom." Then, seeing she considered herself so guiltless that his reproach astonished her, he softened his words: "This is what I was talking about the other evening. It is not becoming to see you surrounded by such people, and it can do you harm. The mere fact that you know them is compromising."

An expression of great hilarity spread over her face. She claimed to be delighted to see him so jealous. "Jealous of such people!" Then, becoming serious, she said reproachfully, "What kind of respect can you have for me?" But just as he was about to relax, she made a fatal error. "See, you I will give not one but two photographs of me." And she dashed over to the cupboard to get them. So, all the others had Angiolina's picture. She told him about it, but with such innocence that he did not dare berate her. Then, there was worse.

Forcing himself to smile, he looked at the two photographs she had handed him, curtsying playfully. The first, in profile, had been made by one of the city's finest photographers. The other was a beautiful snapshot, but more because of the elegant lace-trimmed dress — which she had worn the first time he spoke to her — than the face, contorted from squinting in the sunlight.

"Who took this one?" Emilio asked. "Leardi, perhaps?" He remembered having seen Leardi in the street with a camera under his arm.

"No, not at all jealous!" she teased. "It was taken by a reputable man, a married man: the painter Datti."

Married, yes, but reputable? "Not jealous," Brentani said in a low voice, "just sad, very sad." And then among the photographs he saw one of Datti, a big chap with a red beard, warmly regarded by all the painters in the city. Seeing him, Emilio felt a sharp stab at the memory of one of his remarks: "The women I deal with are unworthy of constituting an offense to my wife."

He had no further need to look for evidence: it was falling all over him, squashing him, and her awkwardness only confirmed it, made it stand out all the more. Humiliated and offended, she muttered: "Merighi introduced me to all these people." She was lying, because it was inconceivable that Merighi, a hardworking businessman, could have known those young blades and those artists or, even if he did know them, would have gone out of his way to introduce them all to his bride-to-be.

He looked at her for a long time with an interrogating expression on his face, as though seeing her for the first time, and she caught the seriousness of that look. Staring at the floor, she waited, her face drained of color. Then Brentani suddenly reminded himself how little right he had to be jealous. He had none, nor any right whatever to humiliate her or make her suffer! Ever! Gently, to show her that he still loved her — he sensed that he had already exhibited a very different kind of sentiment — he tried to kiss her.

At first she appeared to be placated but moved away and would not let him kiss her again. He was surprised that she should refuse a kiss of such importance and ended up being even angrier than he had been before.

"I already have so many sins on my conscience," she said very gravely, "that it will be hard enough for me to obtain absolution today, and because of you I will go to my confessor in an unsuitable state of mind."

Hope sprang anew in Emilio. Oh, the beauty of religion.

He had banished it from his home and from Amalia's heart — it had been his greatest achievement — but rediscovering it with Angiolina, he welcomed it with ineffable joy. In the light of the religion of honorable women, the men on the wall seemed less aggressive. Taking his leave, he respectfully kissed Angiolina's hand. She accepted this homage as a tribute to her virtue. All the evidence gathered was incinerated in the flame of a sacred candle.

Thus the only result of his visit was that he knew the way to her house. He got into the habit of bringing pastries for her morning coffee. That too was a momentous occasion. He held in his arms that magnificent body, just out of bed, and felt its warmth though the thin dressing gown, giving him the feeling of being in direct contact with her nudity. The enchantment of religion had quickly vanished because Angiolina's religion was not of the kind that protects or defends those who are defenseless. Even so, Emilio was no longer tormented by the terrible suspicions of his first visit. In that room he did not take the time to look around.

Angiolina tried to simulate the religiosity that had served her so well on that one occasion, but she was unsuccessful and soon travestied it shamelessly. When she tired of his kisses, she pushed him away saying: *Ite missa est*, soiling a mystical notion that Emilio had often expressed with profound sincerity when saying goodbye to her. She would ask for a *Deo gratias* when she wanted a small favor, shouted *mea maxima culpa* when he became too demanding, *libera nos Domine* when she did not want him to talk about something.

Even so, Emilio enjoyed complete satisfaction from his incomplete possession of this women and tried to go farther only out of embarrassment, for fear of being ridiculed by all those men looking down at him from the wall. She vigorously resisted: her brothers would kill her. She even burst into tears on one occasion when he became particularly aggressive. He did not really love her if he wanted to make her unhappy. Thus reassured and delighted, he desisted from his aggressions. Since she had never belonged to anyone else, he could be confident that he would not be ridiculed.

She did, however, make him a solemn promise that she would be his when she could give herself to him without the risk of trouble for him and problems for herself. She sounded as though this were the most natural thing in the world. In fact, she even proposed a ruse: a third party would have to be found on whom to pin the blame, the problems, and the teasing. He was entranced by her words, which in his ears could only be declarations of love. There was little chance of finding a third party to suit Angiolina, but after listening to her he thought he could settle tranquilly into his own emotions. She was exactly the way he had wanted her to be: she gave him love without burden or risk.

For the time being, the whole of his life was concentrated on that love: he could think of nothing else, could not work, could not even adequately accomplish his duties at the office. So much the better. For now his life took on an entirely new cast; later, it would be all the more pleasurable to regain his former placidity. Fond of images, he saw his life as a perfectly straight road running through a peaceful valley. From the time he first approached Angiolina, the road began to turn and wind through a varied landscape of trees, hills and flowers. It was only a short stretch, then it dropped back into the valley, to the flat, safe, uneventful road that was made less boring by the memory of that charming, colorful, perhaps even exhausting interlude.

One day she informed him that she had to go to work for a family she knew, Deluigi by name. Signora Deluigi was a kind woman; she had a daughter who was a friend of Angiolina's, an aged husband, and there were no young men in the family. Everybody in the family liked Angiolina. "I like to go because my days there are more enjoyable than in my own home." Emilio could make no objection and even resigned himself to seeing her less often in the evening. She returned home from work so late it was not worth getting together.

For that reason he could now dedicate his free evenings to his friend and to his sister. He still tried to fool them, as he fooled himself, about the importance of his adventure, and went so far as to try to convince Balli that he was pleased Angiolina was busy some evenings so as not to have her around all the time. Balli made him blush when he looked at him with his calm scrutinizing gaze. Not knowing how to conceal his passion, Emilio joked about Angiolina, telling him about certain accurate observations he had made which, it must be said, in no way diminished his affection for her. He laughed about her lightheartedly enough, but Balli, who knew him and could hear the off-pitch tone of his words, let him laugh by himself.

She occasionally affected a Tuscan accent, which resulted in something more English than Tuscan. "Sooner or later," Emilio said, "I will rid her of that pretense which I find so annoying." She always carried her head bent to one side over her right shoulder. "A sign of vanity, according to Gall," Emilio remarked, with the gravity of an experimental scientist, adding, "Who knows whether Gall's observations are not more accurate than is generally believed?" She was gluttonous; she loved to eat, well and copiously. He pitied anyone who had to support her! Here he was, lying in his teeth because he loved to see her eat, just as he loved to see her laugh. He ridiculed all of the weaknesses that he actually enjoyed in her. He was very disturbed one day when, speaking about a woman who was very ugly and very rich, Angiolina exclaimed. "Rich? Then she can't be ugly." Beauty mattered so much to her, yet compared with that other powerful attribute, she belittled it. "A vulgarian," he said, now laughing with Balli.

Between his manner of speaking with Balli and the manner he used with Angiolina, two individuals had begun to take shape in Emilio, but he made no attempt to conciliate them; each lived peaceably with the other. As it happened, he was lying neither to Balli nor to Angiolina. By not confessing his love in words, he felt as safe as the ostrich which believes it has eluded the hunter by not being able to see him. When he was with Angiolina, however, he totally abandoned himself to his emotions. Why diminish the power and pleasure of such emotions by resisting them when he was not at risk? He not only desired her, he loved her! Seeing how defenseless she was, like certain pathetic animals who were born that way, he felt growing within him something akin to paternal affection. Her lack of intelligence was just one more weakness that required his affection and care.

They crossed each other on Campo Marzio just as she was leaving, furious that he had not been where he was supposed to have been. It was the first time that he had ever made her wait, but, showing her his watch, he proved to her that he was not late. Her anger subsided. She confessed she wanted to see him for a particular reason, which was why she had come early. She had to tell him about the strange things that had happened to her. She clung affectionately to his arm: "I cried so much yesterday." And she wiped away tears which he could not see in the dark. She would not tell him anything before they reached the terrace. Arm in arm, they climbed up along the dark avenue. He was in no hurry to arrive. The news he was going to hear could not be all that bad, since it made Angiolina all the more affectionate. He stopped repeatedly to kiss her against the veil of her hat.

He sat her down on the low wall, lightly rested one arm on her knees, and shielded her with his own umbrella to protect her from the penetrating drizzle that had been falling for hours.

"I'm engaged," she said in a voice that tried to sound sentimental but was immediately altered by an irrepressible giggle.

"Engaged!" Emilio muttered, so incredulous at first that he began looking for a reason for her to tell him such a lie. He looked at her squarely and in spite of the dark saw in her face the sentimentality that had vanished from her voice. It must be true. Why else would she lie to him? Now they had the third party they needed!

"Are you satisfied now?" she asked sweetly.

She was far from imagining what was going on in his mind and he, out of embarrassment, did not say the words that were burning his lips. But how could he feign the pleasure she was expecting to see in him! His pain was so intense that she had to remind him of the other times he had relished hearing her talk about their plan. Coming from Angiolina's mouth, it had felt to him like a caress. Moreover, he himself had daydreamed about it, had imagined its fulfillment and the ensuing happiness. But how many other plans had passed through his head without leaving a trace? In his lifetime he had gone so far as to imagine theft, murder, rape. He had felt the courage, the strength, the perversity of the criminal, and had imagined the consequences of those crimes, his impunity first of all. But then, satisfied by the dream, finding the things that he had wanted to destroy unchanged, he calmed down, his conscience at peace. He had committed the crime but had caused no harm. Now, however, the dream had become reality, and although this was what he had longed for, he was surprised, no longer able to recognize his dream because it had looked so different before.

"Don't you want to know who the bridegroom is?"

With sudden resolve, he straightened up. "Do you love him?"

"How can you ask me such a thing!" she exclaimed, genuinely surprised. By way of reply, she kissed the hand that held the umbrella.

"Then don't marry him!" he declared, explaining his statement to himself. Since he already possessed her, he no longer desired her. Why should he have to concede her to others in order to possess her in another manner? Seeing her even more surprised, he tried to convince her: "With a man you don't love you could never be happy."

But she had no such hesitations. For the first time, she complained about her family situation. Her brothers were unemployed, her father was sick. How were they to manage? And it was cheerless in her house; he had seen it in sunlight, when the men were not around. No sooner did they come home than they quarreled with each other and with their mother and sisters. Of course, the forty-year-old tailor Volpi was not the husband she had dreamed of, but in his own way he was good and kind, and with time perhaps she would come to love him. She could not hope for better. "You love me, don't you? And yet, you don't consider the possibility of marrying me." To hear her speak without any trace of resentment toward his egotism moved him deeply.

True. Perhaps she was cutting a good deal. With his customary weakness, unable to convince her yet wanting to go along with her, he managed to convince himself.

She told him about meeting Volpini at the home of Signora Deluigi. He was a very small man. "He comes up to here," she said laughing as she pointed to her shoulder. "Cheerful. He says he's small but his love is big." Suspecting perhaps — oh, how wrongly — that Emilio might be stung by jealousy, she hastened to add: "He's pretty ugly. A face covered with straw-colored hair. A beard that goes up to his eyes all the way to his glasses." Volpini's tailor shop was in Fiume, but he said that after they were married he would allow her to spend one day a week in Trieste. In the meantime, since he was away so much of the time, they could continue to see each other at their pleasure.

"We must be very prudent, however," he urged. "Very, very prudent!" he repeated. If this was such a stroke of luck for her, would it not be wiser if they stopped seeing each other altogether so as not to compromise her? To put his own troubled conscience to rest he would have been capable of any sacrifice. He took Angiolina's hand, pressed it to his forehead, and in that pose of adoration opened his heart to her: "To avoid causing you any harm I would be ready to give you up."

Perhaps she understood. She made no further allusion to the betrayal they had concocted, which may have been why that evening they loved each other more tenderly than ever. For a moment, just that once, she seemed to have attained Emilio's level of emotion. Not once did she strike a sour note; she did not even tell him she loved him. He devoted himself to caressing his own torment. The woman he loved was sweet and defenseless, but she was corrupt. On one side she was selling herself, on the other she was giving herself. He could not forget her impulse to laugh at the beginning of their discussion. If that was how she took the most important step in her life, how would she behave when she was living with a man she did not love?

She was lost! Hugging her tightly with his left arm, he put his head in her lap and, more compassionate than passionate, murmured: "Poor darling!" They remained like that for a long time. Then she lowered her head to his and lightly kissed his hair, intending perhaps that he not notice. It was the sweetest thing she had ever done during their relationship.

After that, things went from bad to worse. The sad drizzle

that had persistently accompanied Emilio's anguish with a gentleness that at times seemed compassionate, at others indifferent, suddenly turned into a violent downpour. A gust of frigid wind coming from the sea overturned the damp atmosphere and now shook them out of the dream that had granted them a moment's happiness. She was seized with panic over getting her dress wet and started to run, after refusing Emilio's arm: she needed both hands to hold the umbrella against the wind. In her struggle against the wind and the rain, she became irritable and refused even to think about their next meeting. "Let us worry now about getting home."

He saw her climb into a carriage of the streetcar, and from the darkness where he was standing, he caught a glimpse of that lovely sulking face in the tram's yellow light, her beautiful eyes busily checking the damage done to her dress by all the water.

four

Often during their relationship there had been such downpours, tearing him from the enchantment to which he surrendered with so much abandon.

Early the next day he went to Angiolina's house. He had no idea whether he was going there to avenge himself with a sarcasm worthy of the way she left him the evening before, or rather to recapture from the rosiness of her face his previous feelings, undermined by his bitter ruminations during the night, feelings he could no longer do without, as he was discovering from the anxiety that made him run all the way there.

Angiolina's mother opened the door, greeting him with the usual courteous words, her face as blank as parchment, her voice painfully loud. Angiolina was getting dressed and would be there shortly.

"How do you feel about it?" the woman asked him abruptly. She began talking to him about Volpini. Surprised that the mother also sought his approval for Angiolina's marriage, he hesitated, so that she, mistaken about the nature of the doubt she saw written on his face, tried to convince him. "You must understand, it is a piece of luck for Angiolina. Even if she is not in love with him, she will have a good life, a happy one, because he is very much in love with her. You should see him!" She gave a noisy little laugh that moved only her lips. One could see her satisfaction.

He ended up feeling flattered to see that Angiolina had made her mother understand how much his approval mattered to her; he gave it in generous words. He was sorry she was not marrying someone else, but in view of the fact that it was for her benefit . . . Her mother gave another little laugh, but this one was more facial than vocal and struck him as ironic. Did she also know about his pact with her daughter? That would not have displeased him either. Why should he worry about those titters directed toward good old Volpini? What was certain was that he was not the butt of the joke.

Angiolina came in all dressed and ready to go out. She was in a hurry because she had to be at Signora Deluigi's at nine o'clock. As he did not want to leave her just yet, they walked together in full daylight for the first time.

"I think we make a handsome couple," she said smiling as she noticed how each passerby looked at them. It was impossible to walk by her without taking notice of her.

Emilio also looked at her. Her white dress, which exaggerated the silhouette of the day — tiny waist, billowing sleeves, like inflated balloons — solicited a glance; it was made for that purpose. Her head, instead of being obscured by all that dazzling whiteness, stood out under its own golden and brazenly rosy luminosity; on her lips a narrow blood-red line glared against her teeth, revealed in a sweet happy smile tossed into the air and caught by the onlookers. The sun played on her blond curls, powdering them with gold.

Emilio reddened. He thought he could read a denigrating judgment in the eyes of every passerby. He looked at her again. There was no doubt, her eyes extended a kind of greeting to every well-dressed man who passed; she did not look at them, but there was a flash of light in her eyes. Something moved in her pupils and continuously modified the intensity and direction of the light. Her eyes sparkled! Emilio fixed on that verb as the perfect description of the movement in those eyes. In those rapid little unpredictable flickers of light he thought he could hear a tiny sound.

"Why are you such a flirt?" he asked, forcing himself to smile.

With an unembarrassed laugh, she replied: "I? I have eyes for looking, I do."

She was therefore aware of the movement of her eyes. Only she was fooling herself by calling it "looking."

A moment later an underling clerk went by, Giustini by name, a handsome young fellow Emilio knew by sight. Angiolina's eyes brightened, and Emilio turned to look at the fortunate mortal who had just passed them. The little clerk had stopped to look at them.

"He stopped to look at me, didn't he?" she asked with a happy smile.

"Why does that please you?" he asked sadly. She did not begin to understand him. Then, she slyly tried to make him believe that she had only wanted to make him jealous, and finally, to reassure him, she shamelessly pursed her red lips, in full sunlight, to mime a kiss. Oh, how little she knew about dissembling. The woman he loved, *Ange*, was his invention, he had created her himself out of an act of will. Not only had she not collaborated in this creation, her resistance prevented him from him proceeding. In the light of day the dream faded.

"Too much light!" he muttered, dazzled by it. "Let us go into the shade."

Seeing his face contorted, she looked at him curiously: "The sun bothers you? I hear there are people who really can't bear it."

How wrong she was to love the sun. As he was leaving her, he asked, "And what if Volpini hears about our stroll through town?"

"Who would tell him?" she said with absolute assurance. "I would tell him that you're a brother or a cousin of Signora Deluigi. He doesn't know anyone in Trieste, so it's easy enough to make him believe anything I like."

When they separated, he wanted to continue analyzing his own impressions and walked on by himself, heading nowhere. A burst of energy made his thinking quick and intense. He set up a problem and immediately solved it. He would do well to leave her at once and never see her again. He could no longer delude himself about the nature of his feelings, because the pain he had felt just before was too closely associated with the shame he felt for her and for himself.

He went looking for Stefano Balli with the intention of making him a promise that would render his decision irrevocable. Instead, the sight of his friend was enough to make him change his mind. Why should he not amuse himself with women the way Stefano did? He remembered what his life would have been without love: on the one hand his subjugation to Balli, on the other his melancholic sister, and that was all. He did not think he was any less energetic now than he had been just before; quite the contrary. Now he wanted to live, to enjoy life at the price of suffering. He would be demonstrating forcefulness by the way he dealt with Angiolina, not by cravenly fleeing her.

The sculptor received him with a coarse greeting: "You're still alive? I'm warning you: if, as would seem from the contrite look on your face, you're here to ask me a favor, you're wasting your time and your breath. You poor bastard!"

Although he was shouting his teasing threats into Emilio's ears, Emilio was relieved of all his doubts. By the mention of help, his friend had given him good advice. Who, in this matter, could be of greater help than Balli? "I beg of you," he pleaded, "I need your advice."

Balli started to laugh. "It's about Angiolina, isn't it? I don't want to know anything about her. She came between us, and she can stay there, but I don't want to be bothered any more by her."

Had Balli been even harsher with him, Emilio would still not have been deterred from getting his advice. His salvation depended on it. Stefano, who was so knowledgeable about such things, would set him on the right path to continue his pleasure without any further suffering. In a twinkling he fell from the height of his earlier heroic intention to the basest abjection. He was perfectly conscious of his weakness and was totally resigned to it. He was crying for help! He would have liked at least to retain the appearance of someone merely asking for an opinion, just to have another viewpoint. By a curious mechanical effect, however, that shouting in his ears made him all the more suppliant. What he needed most was to be coddled.

Stefano finally took pity on him. He flung an arm around him and dragged him toward Piazza della Legna, where his studio was.

"Let's talk about it. If help is possible you know I'll give it to you."

Deeply moved, Emilio spilled out the whole story. Yes, he could see it clearly now. It had become a very serious matter for him, and he described the love he felt, his desperation to see her, talk to her, his jealousy, his suspicion, his incessant torment and his total neglect of everything that was not related to her or to his feelings for her. Then he told him about Angiolina as he now saw her in the light of her behavior on the street, about the photographs on the wall of her room, her commitment to the tailor, and the pact they had made. He smiled as he talked about her. Having brought her to mind, he could see her gaiety, her ingenuous perversity, which made him smile without irritation. Poor girl! Those photographs meant so much to her that she kept them hanging on the wall. She took such delight in being admired on the street that she wanted him to keep track of the glances she received. As he related all this, he realized that there was nothing there to offend anyone who had declared that she was no more than an amusement for him. Granted, he had omitted from his account all his observations and experiences, but for the moment, what had been omitted no longer mattered. He watched Balli anxiously, fearing that he would burst out laughing, and continued his account only because logic drove him on. Having declared that he wanted advice, he had to ask for it. The sound of his own words echoed in his ears as though they came from someone else and brought him to a conclusion. Very calmly, almost as if he wanted Balli to overlook the ardor with which he had spoken until then, he asked. "In view of my not knowing how to behave as I should, don't you think I would do well to end this relationship?" Once again, he stifled a smile. It would be comical if Balli, in good faith, advised him to leave Angiolina.

But Stefano immediately demonstrated his superior intelligence by refusing to advise him. "You understand that I can hardly advise you to be different from what you are," he said with affection. "I knew that this kind of adventure was not for you." Given the way Balli answered him, Emilio thought that the feelings he had found so frightening only a moment before were a common phenomenon and saw in this another reason for reassurance.

Balli's servant, Michele, approached, a man well advanced in years, a former soldier. Standing at attention, he quietly said a few words to his master and then walked off after raising his hat with a broad gesture while keeping his body immobile.

"Someone is waiting for me in my studio," Balli said with a grin. "It's a woman and it's a pity that you can't listen to our conversation. It would be very instructive for you." Then he had an idea: "How would you like the four of us to get together one evening?" He thought he had found a stratagem to help his friend, and Emilio accepted enthusiastically. Naturally! The only way to imitate Balli was to see him in action.

That evening Emilio had an appointment with Angiolina at the Campo Marzio. During the day he had been contemplating the reproaches he would make. But the purpose of her coming was to be entirely his for a few hours. At that hour there were no strollers on Sant'Andrea to steal her attention away. Why spoil pleasure with quarrels? It seemed to him he was being more like Balli by loving gently and enjoying a love that he had almost relinquished that morning in a moment of madness. The only residue of his earlier indignation was an agitation that colored his words and the entire evening, which started out delightfully. They agreed to devote one of the two hours they could spend together to walking away from town and the other to returning. He was the one who made the proposal, hoping to calm down as he walked beside her. It took them almost an hour to reach the Arsenal, an hour of perfect bliss under a limpid night sky, the fresh air cooled by an early autumn.

She sat down on the low wall that bordered the road while he remained standing, dominating her completely. Illumined on one side by the light of a street lamp, her head emerged from the dark background of the Arsenal that stretched along the shore, an entire city, asleep at that hour. "The city of labor!" he remarked, surprised to have come to such a setting for his tryst.

Closed off by the peninsula in front and hidden by the houses in the nocturnal darkness, the sea had disappeared from the panorama. What remained visible were a few houses along the shore as though pieces on a chessboard, and beyond them, a ship under construction. The city of work looked larger than it really was. On the left, the distant streetlamps made it look as though it extended farther out. He recalled that those streetlamps belonged to another large enterprise located on the shore opposite the Muggia valley. Work went on there as well: it was fitting that the one should face a prolongation of the other.

She too was gazing out, and for a moment Emilio's thoughts strayed far from his passion. In the past, he had toyed with socialist ideas, but naturally had not lifted a finger to put them into practice. He had done nothing about them. How remote those ideas were now! He felt remorseful, as though he had betrayed them, because for him the cessation of desires and ideas, his only area of action, was tantamount to apostasy.

His slight malaise quickly passed. She asked about many things, particularly the colossus hanging in midair, and he explained a ship launching to her. In his life as a solitary pedant he had never learned how to relate his thoughts and words to the ears for which they were intended, and some years before, he had vainly tried to emerge from his shell and communicate with a crowd but had to withdraw, exasperated and scornful. Now, instead, how sweet it was to refrain from abstruse words, better still complex ideas, and be understood. As he spoke, he was able to break open his own concept, liberating it from the words from which it was born, and even see a flash of understanding in those blue eyes.

Nonetheless, a terrible dissonance shattered all that harmony. A few days before he had heard a story which had moved him deeply. For about ten years a German astronomer had lived in his observatory on one of the highest peaks of the Alps in the midst of eternal snow. The closest village was a thousand meters below, and from there, a twelve-year-old girl brought him food every day. During those ten years, climbing up and down those thousand meters, the little girl grew big and strong and beautiful, and the scientist asked her to marry him. The wedding had taken place only recently in the village, and for their honeymoon the bride and groom climbed up together to their dwelling in the observatory. In Angiolina's arms the story came back to him. That was how he would have liked to possess her now, a thousand meters away from any other man. That was how — were it possible for him, like the astronomer, to continue dedicating his life to his own goals — he would have been able to bind himself to her, without reservation.

"And you," he asked impatiently, seeing that she had not yet understood why she had been told this story, "would you like to come and stay with me up there?"

She hesitated. It was obvious that she hesitated. One part of the anecdote, concerning the mountain, had immediately been understood by her. He only saw love up there, while she could already feel the cold and the boredom. Looking at him, she understood what response he wanted, and just to humor him said, without a trace of enthusiasm, "Oh, it would be marvelous!"

But he was already deeply offended. He had always thought that once he decided to make her his own, she would joyfully accept any condition that he imposed. Instead, no! That high up she would not have been happy, not even with him, and in the darkness he saw clearly on her face her astonishment that anyone could propose she spend her youth in snow and solitude, her beautiful youth — her hair, her complexion, her teeth, all the things that she so loved to see admired by others.

The roles were inverted. He had proposed — granted, by means of a rhetorical device — to make her his and she had not accepted him. He was really put off! "Naturally," he said with bitter irony, "up there no one would be offering you photographs, nor would you find people in the street stopping to stare at you."

She heard the bitterness, but did not take offense at the irony, feeling that she was right, and began arguing with him. On the mountain it was cold and she did not like the cold. During the winter she was unhappy even in the city. Furthermore, in this life you live only once, and up there life was likely to be shorter and worse, since she could not believe it was very amusing to watch the clouds go by even if they passed beneath one's feet.

She was right, in fact, but how insensitive and unintelligent she was! He made no further attempt to discuss it with her, for how could he have convinced her? He looked away, searching for something to say. He could have insulted her, which would have avenged him and soothed him. But he remained silent and undecided, looking around at the night, at the rare lights on the darkened peninsula ahead, then at the tower that stood at the entrance to the Arsenal, above the trees, bluish gray, a motionless shadow that seemed to be a muddle of colors hanging in midair.

"I'm not saying no," Angiolina said to mollify him. "It

might be marvelous, but . . . " She interrupted herself with the thought that since he was so eager to see her enthused about that mountain, which in any case they would probably never see, it would be silly not to satisfy him. "It could be very nice," she said, and repeated the phrase with growing enthusiasm. But he, even more offended by a lie so transparent that it seemed a joke, did not detach his eyes from the leaden air until she pulled him toward her. "If you want proof, let's go tomorrow, right now, and I will live alone with you forever."

In a state of mind exactly like the one he had been in that morning, he remembered Balli. "Balli, the sculptor, wants to meet you."

"Is that so?" she asked playfully. "I want to meet him, too!" She seemed to want to run at once in search of Balli. "I heard so much about him from a young woman who liked him a lot that I've wanted to meet him for a long time. Where has he seen me that he wants to know me?"

It was hardly new for her to demonstrate her interest in other men in his presence, but how it hurt! "He did not even know that you existed," he said harshly. "He knows only what I told him." He hoped he had vexed her, but on the contrary, she was very grateful that he had talked about her. "But who knows," she said in a comic tone of diffidence, "what you may have told him about me?"

"I told him you were a betrayer," he said, laughing. The word made them both laugh heartily, which instantly put them in a good mood and in harmony. She let herself be held in a long embrace and then, very emotional all of a sudden, whispered in his ear, "*Zhe tem bokú.*" This time he repeated it with sadness: "Betrayer." She laughed again uproariously, then found something better. Kissing him, she spoke against his lips, with a charm he would never forget, asking him over and over in a muted pleading voice that kept changing tone, "Isn't it true that it's not true that I am that awful thing?"

The end of the evening was thus equally delectable. One shrewd gesture on Angiolina's part was all it took to erase every doubt, every hurt.

On the way back, remembering that Balli was to bring a woman with him, he quickly broached the subject. She did not seem displeased by the idea, but nevertheless made a point of inquiring, with an indifference that could not have been faked, whether Balli was really in love with the woman. "I don't think so," he replied in all sincerity, pleased by her indifference. "Balli has a strange way of loving women. He loves them very much, but all of them equally, when he's in the mood for them."

"Has he had very many?" she asked thoughtfully. To this he felt he should lie. "I don't think so."

The following evening the four of them were to meet at the Public Garden. The first to arrive were Angiolina and Emilio. It was not too pleasant to wait outdoors because, even though it had not rained, the ground was damp from the sirocco. Angiolina tried to hide her eager anticipation under a pose of ill temper, but she did not fool Emilio. He was seized by an intense desire to conquer this woman who seemed to him to be slipping away from him. Instead he became tedious, he felt it himself, and she did not fail to make him feel it even more so. Clutching her arm he asked her, "Do you love me at least as much as yesterday?" "Yes," she answered harshly, "but one doesn't say such things every minute."

Balli arrived from the Aqueduct arm in arm with a woman as tall as himself. "How long she is!" Angiolina said, immediately making the only judgment that could be made from that distance.

As he approached them, Balli made the introductions: "Margherita! *Ange!*" He tried to see Angiolina in the dark and brought his face so close that had he pursed his lips he could have kissed her. "*Ange*, really?" Still not satisfied, he struck a match and used it to illuminate the rosy face that lent itself with great seriousness to his scrutiny. Lit up in the darkness, it was adorably transparent. Her large limpid eyes, which the flame penetrated as through the clearest water, glimmered with sweetness and joy. Unaffected, Balli turned the flame toward Margherita's face, a pure pale face, two enormous turquoise eyes, so big and vivacious they made it impossible to look away, an aquiline nose, and on her small head, a mass of chestnut hair. A street urchin's fearless look in her eyes contrasted sharply with the gravity in her face of a suffering madonna. Aside from making herself visible, she took advantage of the match to look at Emilio with curiosity. Then, because the flame had still not gone out, she blew on it.

"Now you all know each other. That thing over there," Balli said, indicating Emilio to Margherita, "you will see in the light." He took the lead with Margherita, who was already glued to his arm. Her tall, lanky body was probably not very attractive, marked as it was by the contradictory characteristics of vivacity and suffering in her face. Her stride was unsteady and too small for her size. She wore a short flame-colored jacket, but on her back, skinny, pathetic, slightly curved, it lost all of its audaciousness. It looked like a uniform worn by a child, whereas Angiolina's drabber color seemed brighter. "Pity," Angiolina murmured with regret, "that lovely head stuck on that shaft."

Emilio wanted to make some comment. He came up to

Balli and said, "I am very impressed by the eyes of your young lady. I would like to know what you think of my young lady's eyes."

"The eyes are not bad," Balli declared, "but the nose is not perfectly shaped. The lower line is unfinished. It needs another swipe of the thumb."

"Is that so!" Angiolina exclaimed, taken aback.

"I could be mistaken," Balli said quite earnestly. "We shall soon see in the light."

When Angiolina thought she was far enough away from her fearsome critic, she muttered irritably: "As though his cripple were perfect."

At the Mondo Nuovo they came into an oblong room, closed off on one side by a partition, and on the other, by glass doors leading to the tavern's spacious terrace. Seeing them, a waiter hastened over, a young man whose clothing and manners indicated a country boy. He stood up on a chair and lit two gas jets that barely brightened the vast room. He stayed up there, rubbing his sleepy eyes until Stefano came over to pull him down, shouting that he would not allow him to fall asleep that high up. The little farmhand descended from the chair holding on to the sculptor and went off fully awake and cheerful.

Because Margherita's foot was hurting her, she sat down at once. Balli was extremely solicitous and urged her not to be so formal and to take off her boot. But she was unwilling. "There always has to be some pain, and this evening I hardly feel it at all."

How different this woman was from Angiolina. Affectionate and decorous, she expressed her love wordlessly, without betraying her meaning, whereas the other one, when she wanted to manifest her sensibility, wound herself up like a machine that requires advance preparation in order to start.

For Balli that would not do. Having told her to take off her boot, he kept insisting on being obeyed until she finally declared that she would take off both boots if he so ordered but that it would serve no purpose since that was not the cause of her pain. During the course of the evening she was obliged to give repeated signs of submission because Balli wanted to demonstrate his system with women. Margherita performed her role admirably. She laughed a lot, but she obeyed. One could hear in her responses a certain ability to think, which made her subjugation all the more suitable as a model.

At first, she tried to start a conversation with Angiolina, who, on tiptoe, was peering into a far-off mirror so as to rearrange her curls. Margherita was telling her about the pain she had in her chest and legs; she could not remember a time when she had not been in pain. Her eyes still fastened to the mirror, Angiolina replied, "Really? Poor thing!" Then suddenly she declared with great simplicity, "I always feel fine." Emilio, who knew her well, stifled a smile on hearing in her words the most complete indifference to Margherita's suffering, and the instantaneous and total satisfaction with her own health. The misfortunes of others only made her more aware of her own good fortune.

Margherita sat down between Stefano and Emilio. Angiolina, last to be seated, took her place opposite Margherita and while still standing threw Balli a strange glance. To Emilio it looked like a challenge, but the sculptor interpreted it better: "Sweet Angiolina," he said unabashedly, "she looks at me in the hope that I will also find her nose beautiful. Useless. Her nose ought to be like this." Dipping a finger in beer, he drew on the table the curve he wanted, a thick line hard to imagine on a nose.

Angiolina looked at the line as if she wanted to memorize

it and touched her nose: "It's better the way it is!" she said quietly, as though she no longer cared about convincing anybody.

"What poor taste!" Balli exclaimed, unable to keep himself from laughing. It was clear from that moment that he found Angiolina very amusing. He continued to say unpleasant things to her but appeared to be doing so to provoke her into defending herself. She too was amused. Her eyes shone with the same benevolence toward the sculptor as did Margherita's. The two woman aped each other, and Emilio, after vainly trying to place a word in the general conversation, was now wondering why he had arranged that meeting.

But Balli had not forgotten why. He stuck to his system, which seemed to be brutality, even toward the waiter. He scolded him for proposing nothing for dinner but veal in every kind of sauce. Resigned to eating veal, he placed his order and as the waiter was about the leave the room, shouted after him, in another comic outburst, "Rascal, mongrel!" The waiter found it funny to be shouted at and carried out his orders with unusual diligence. Thus, after dominating everyone around him, Balli thought he had given Emilio a lesson according to the rules.

But Emilio was incapable of applying a system like that even to the least important things. Margherita did not feel like eating. "Watch out," Balli told her, "this will be the last evening we spend together. I can't stand simpering!" She finally agreed to order along with the others and soon seemed to have acquired an appetite. Emilio mused that Angiolina had never granted him any such mark of affection. In the meanwhile, Angiolina too, after endless hesitations, announced that under no circumstances would she eat veal.

"Didn't you hear?" Emilio asked her. "Stefano can't stand

simpering." She shrugged her shoulders. She did not care about pleasing anyone, and to Emilio it seemed that her disdain was aimed more at him than at Balli.

"This veal meal," said Balli with his mouth full, looking squarely at the other three, "is not exactly what I would call harmonious. The two of you are dissonant together: you black as coal and she blonde as a spike of wheat in June. You seem to have been placed together by an academic painter. The two of us, on the other hand, could be put on a canvas above the title 'Grenadier and wounded wife.' "

Margherita aptly retorted: "It's not for show that we go out together." Balli, serious and brusque even in a gesture of affection, kissed her on the forehead in reward.

With a sudden onset of modesty, Angiolina began contemplating the ceiling.

"Don't play the innocent," Balli said to her irritably. "As though the two of you don't do worse."

"Says who?" Angiolina asked, turning threateningly on Emilio.

"Not I," Emilio protested ineptly.

"So what do you do together every evening? Since I never see him, it must be with her that he spends his evenings. It is only natural that he should also experience love, given the vigor of his youth. Farewell billiards, farewell walks. I hang around all alone waiting for him or I have to make do with the first moron who comes my way. We used to have such good times together! I, the most intelligent person in the city, and he the fifth, since below me there are three empty spots and then he comes next."

Margherita, who had regained her composure after that kiss, looked tenderly at Emilio. "It's true! He talks to me about you all the time. He really loves you."

To Angiolina, however, the fifth intellect in the city seemed of little account. All her admiration went to the one who was first.

"Emilio tells me you have a beautiful voice. Sing something. I'd love to hear you."

"That's all I need. After a meal I rest. I have the slow digestion of a snake."

Only Margherita understood Emilio's state of mind. Looking at Angiolina, her expression grew serious. Then she turned to Emilio, dedicating her attention to him while talking about Stefano.

"He can be brusque, it's true, but not always, and even when he is, he's not threatening. You do what he wants because you love him." Then, her voice still low but modulated into a softer tone, she added, "A man who thinks is entirely different from those who don't." It was easy to understand that by *those others* she meant certain men she had run into, so that he, distracted for a moment from his own tormented confusion, looked at her compassionately. She was right to love in others the qualities that she needed: weak and gentle as she was, she could not have defended herself alone.

Balli, suddenly turning his attention back to Emilio, exclaimed, "How mute you've become!" Then, to Angiolina, he asked, "Is he always like that during the long evenings you spend together?"

Apparently forgetting her hymns of love, she replied peevishly, "He's a serious man."

Balli, with the generous intention of aggrandizing Emilio, wove a teasing biography of him: "As for goodness, he is the first and I am the fifth. He is the only male with whom I have ever gotten along. He is my alter ego, my other self, and . . . he always shares my opinion when I am unable to share his." With this last phrase he had forgotten the purpose that had prompted him in the first place, and in his high spirits squashed Emilio under the weight of his own superiority. All Emilio could do was set his mouth in a smile.

Fearing that the effort he had put into his smile was transparent, he decided that to appear more nonchalant he should say something. There had been some talk — he had no idea on whose part — of having Angiolina pose for a figure Balli had in mind. He was in agreement. "Only the head will be sketched," he told Angiolina, as though he did not know that she would readily have consented to more. But she, without asking for his approval, had already accepted while he was engaged in conversation with Margherita, and abruptly interrupted his remarks — which, anything but spontaneous, had grown into an irrelevant peroration — by exclaiming, "But I already accepted."

Balli expressed his thanks and said that he would surely take advantage of the occasion, but not for a few months because for the moment he was too busy with other work. He scrutinized her at length, imagining the pose in which he would portray her, and Angiolina turned red with pleasure. If only Emilio could have had an ally in his misery. But no! Margherita was not in the least jealous, and she too looked at Angiolina with an artist's eye. Stefano would make something beautiful out of that, she said, speaking animatedly about the ways art had surprised her when she saw rising out of soft clay a face, an expression, a living thing. Balli quickly became brusque again: "Your name is Angiolina? I'll call you Angiolona, or better still Giolona." And from then on he always called her that, its big open vowels the essence of contempt made sound. Emilio was astonished that this unflattering augmentation of her name did not offend

Angiolina, but she never took it badly, and whenever Balli shouted it into her ears, she would laugh as though she were being tickled.

Balli sang on the way home. He had an even voice and a big one, which he modulated with wasted good taste in view of the vulgar ditties he chose to sing. That evening he sang one but dared not say all the words because of the presence of the two women. He nevertheless made them understood through the clever innuendoes transmitted by his voice and eyes. Angiolina was enraptured.

When they parted, Angiolina and Emilio remained standing for a moment as they watched the other couple walk away. "He's blind!" she said. "How can he love a dried out beam that can hardly stay upright?

That evening she did not give Emilio the time to make the reproaches that he had been rehearsing all day. Once again she had the most surprising news to tell him. The tailor Volpini had written to her — she forgot to bring the letter with her — that he would not be able to marry her for another year. One of his partners was preventing it by threatening to dissolve the partnership, thus leaving him without capital. "It seems the partner wants him to marry his daughter, a little hunchback who would look just right beside my future husband. However, Volpini assures me that in a year he will be able to do without the partner and his money, and then he will marry me. Understand?" He had not understood. "There's something else," she said quietly and embarrassed. "Volpini does not want to live for a whole year in his state of desire."

Now he understood, and protested. How could she dream of obtaining from him approval of that kind? On the other hand, how could he object? "What guarantees do you have of his word?"

"Those that I need. He is ready to sign a contract with a notary."

Pausing for a moment he asked, "When?"

She laughed. "Next Sunday he can't come. He wants to make all the arrangements so the contract will be ready for signing in two weeks, and then . . . " she interrupted herself laughing and hugged him.

She would be his! This was not the way he had imagined possessing a woman, but he too hugged her effusively and tried to convince himself of his utter happiness. There was no doubt, he had reason to be grateful to her! She loved him, or rather, she loved him too. So why complain?

Furthermore, this was perhaps the very recovery he wanted. Disgraced by the tailor, then possessed by him, *Ange* would die, and he too would be able to have a good time with Giolona—lighthearted, the way she liked men to be, cavalier and contemptuous like Balli.

five

Until that evening, as Balli said, relations between the two friends had been very cool because of Angiolina. Emilio had rarely sought out his friend and had not even been aware of neglecting him. Whereas Stefano had taken offense and stopped running after Emilio, however attached he continued to be to that friendship, as he was to all his habits. That dinner unsettled Stefano's certainty and raised instead the question that he might be the one who had given offense. Emilio's suffering had not escaped his notice, and when the pleasure of finding himself admired by both women had subsided, a pleasure of considerable intensity but of short duration, his conscience began to nag at him. To silence it, he dashed to Emilio's house at noon the next day in order to sermonize him. A good lecture might help cure Emilio more effectively than the example of his own behavior, and even if it proved ineffectual, it would at least enable him to regain the status of friend and adviser and rid him of the appearance of rival, which he had played for the fun of it in a moment of foolishness.

Signorina Amalia came to the door. The woman aroused in him an unpleasant feeling of pity. In his eyes, one had the right to live only to enjoy fame, beauty, power, or at least wealth; otherwise, no, because one became an odious burden on the lives of others. Why then was that pathetic creature still living? Obviously an error of Mother Nature. When he came to the house and did not find his friend, he often invented some pretext for escaping immediately because that pale face and spent voice depressed him so much. She, however, wishing to live Emilio's life, regarded herself as Balli's friend.

"Is Emilio home?" Balli asked anxiously.

"Please come in, Signor Stefano," Amalia said beaming. "Emilio!" she called out. "Signor Stefano is here." Then she reproached Balli: "It's been so long since we've had the pleasure of seeing you! Have you too forgotten us?"

Stefano started to laugh. "It's not I who neglect Stefano. It's he who has lost interest in me."

Accompanying him to the door of the dining room, she murmured with a smile, "Yes, yes, I understand."

With those few words they had already taken note of Angiolina.

The small apartment consisted of only three rooms reached from the hallway by that one door. Thus when a visitor came to see Emilio in his room, Amalia found herself a prisoner of her own room, which was the last one down the hall. It was not easy for her to make an uninvited appearance, being shyer with men than Emilio was with women. But Balli, from his very first visit to their home, was the exception to the rule. After having often heard him described as rude, she saw him for the first time when her father died. Surprised by his kindness, she immediately felt close to him. He was an exquisite consoler. He knew when to speak and when to remain silent. Discreetly, from time to time, he had known when to indulge her great loss and when to restrain it; on occasion he had helped her find the most suitable, the most satisfying way of expressing it. She had grown used to weeping in his presence, and he came frequently, enjoying his role of consoler, for which he was so gifted. Once that incentive ended he made himself scarce. Family life did not suit him, and moreover, for someone who was attracted only to the beautiful and the immoral, the fraternal affection offered him by that ugly woman was bound to irritate him. This was the first time, in fact, that she ever voiced a reproach, because she found it perfectly natural that he should seek entertainment elsewhere.

In addition to the beautiful marquetry table of dark wood — the only piece of furniture in the house that testified to the family's former affluence — the little dining room contained a worn sofa, four chairs of similar shape but not matching, an armchair, and an antique cupboard. The poverty apparent in the room was reinforced by the meticulous care given to those pitiful pieces.

As he came into the apartment, Balli thought back to the role of consoler that he had enjoyed so much; it was like coming to a place where he himself had suffered, but suffered sweetly. He relished the memory of his own goodness and thought it had been a mistake to have stayed away so long from a place where he felt more than anywhere else that he was a superior man.

Emilio greeted him with particular affability, precisely to camouflage the rancor that smoldered in his heart. He did not want Balli to notice how deeply he had hurt him. He would indeed rebuke him, and harshly, but only after finding a way to conceal his wound. He regarded him exactly as he would an enemy.

"What good wind brings you here?"

"I was passing by and wanted to say hello to your sister, whom I have not seen in a long time. I find her looking much better than the last time I saw her," Balli said, looking at Amalia, whose cheeks were flushed and whose gentle gray eyes sparkled with excitement.

Emilio looked at her and saw nothing. His rancor suddenly turned to rage as he became aware that Stefano had no recollection of what had happened the previous evening and could consequently behave toward him with such non-chalance.

"You had a good time last night, didn't you, and in part at my expense."

What astonished Balli more than anything else about this open display of resentment was its inappropriateness in front of Amalia. It came as a surprise since he had done nothing to offend Emilio. On the contrary, he thought he deserved a paean of gratitude for his intentions. To counter the attack, he instantly lost all notion of his own wrongdoing and felt absolved of any fault. "We'll talk about it later," he said out of deference to Amalia. She left the room even though Balli, who was in no hurry to get into an argument with Emilio, wanted her to stay.

"I don't see what you can reproach me for."

"Oh, nothing of course," Emilio said, finding no better reply than this irony on being confronted directly.

Balli, convinced of his innocence, was more explicit. He said that he had done exactly what he had proposed to do when he offered to give him some lessons. If he too had started bleating with love, how successful would the cure have been? Giolona needed to be treated the way he had treated her, and he was hoping that with time Emilio would learn to imitate him. He did not believe, could not believe that a woman like that should be taken seriously, and he described her with the very words Emilio had used a few days before. She was so like Emilio's portrayal of her that he had been able to see through her at once, all of her.

But Emilio, hearing his own words repeated, remained completely unconvinced by them. He replied that he had his own way of courting a woman and that he would not have known how to behave any differently since it seemed to him that gentleness was the essential condition for attaining pleasure. Which hardly meant that he took the woman seriously. Had he promised to marry her?

Stefano laughed heartily. Emilio had undergone an extraordinary change in little time. Only a few days before — had he forgotten? — he had been so worried about his own state of mind that he was begging for help from anybody he ran into.

"I don't object to your having a good time, but you don't look like the kind of person who knows how to have a good time." Emilio, in fact, looked worn out. His life had never been particularly joyous, but it had become terribly dull ever since his father's death, and his whole being suffered from this new condition.

Discreet as a shadow, Amalia wanted to pass through the room unnoticed. To silence Stefano, Emilio stopped her, but even so, the two men could not stop the discussion they had started. Balli playfully said that he was appointing her the judge of a case about which she was to know nothing. A dispute had arisen between the two old friends. The best thing to do was to resolve it blindly, relying on some God-given judgment that surely had been invented for such cases.

But God's judgment could no longer be blind, since Amalia had already guessed the nature of the case. She gave Balli a look of gratitude, a look of an intensity no one would have thought possible in those little gray eyes. At last she had an ally, and the bitterness that had been weighing on her heart for some time melted in a surge of hope. She was candid: "I've already understood what this is about. You are so right." Her voice, rather than a declaration in his favor, sounded like a plea for help. "One has only to look at him, always preoccupied and depressed, his face etched with his hurry to get out of this house where he leaves me all alone."

Emilio listened to her anxiously, fearing that those laments would degenerate into the usual tears and sobs. Instead, while talking to Balli about her great unhappiness, she remained calm and smiling.

Balli, who saw in Amalia's distress no more than an ally in his quarrel with Emilio, accompanied her words with reproachful gestures directed toward his friend. But Amalia's words no longer accompanied his gestures. Laughing and cheerful, she related how a few days ago she had been out walking with Emilio and had been able to observe how he tense he became as soon as he saw in the distance female figures of a particular stature and a particular complexion: very tall and very blonde. "Did I see right?" she asked smiling, delighted that Balli concurred. "Very tall and very blonde?" There was nothing offensive to Emilio in this teasing. She had gone over to stand close to him, placing her white hand on Emilio's head in a gesture of fraternal tenderness.

Balli added in confirmation: "As tall as a soldier of the King of Prussia's army and so blonde as to be colorless."

Emilio laughed, but he was still beset by the memory of his jealousy: "So long as I can be sure that you don't want her."

"Can you imagine, he's jealous of me, his best friend!" Balli shouted indignantly.

"One can understand why," Amalia said gently, almost begging Balli to be indulgent toward his friend.

"One does not understand why!" Stefano protested. "How can you say one understands such an infamy?"

She did not reply, but held to her opinion with the look of conviction of someone who knows what she is saying. She believed she had thought this through very carefully and had thus intuited her poor brother's state of mind, but her perception had come instead from her own sentiments. She was all red in the face. Certain tones of that conversation echoed in her soul like bells clanging in a desert; farther and farther they traveled, covering vast empty spaces, measuring them, instantly filling them all and making them sensitive, endowing them generously with joy and pain. She remained silent for a long while. She forgot they had been discussing her brother and thought about herself. Oh, what a strange, wonderful thing! She had talked about love at other times, but differently, without indulgence, because one shouldn't. How seriously she had taken the injunction that had been dinned into her ears since childhood. She had detested, despised those who disobeyed it, and had suppressed every one of her own impulses to rebel. She had been cheated! It was Balli who was the epitome of virtue and strength, Balli who talked about love with ease, for whom love had never been a sin. How many times he must have loved! With that sweet voice and those smiling blue eyes, he always loved everything and everyone, even her.

Stefano stayed for dinner. Somewhat flustered, Amalia had announced that there would be little to eat, but on the contrary, Balli was surprised to discover that one ate very well in that house. For years Amalia had spent a good part of her day at the stove and had become an excellent cook, to satisfy Emilio's delicate palate.

Stefano had stayed most willingly. It seemed to him that he had been the loser in the discussion with Emilio, and he looked forward to retaliating, pleased that Amalia had agreed with him, excused him, defended him, taken his side entirely.

For him and for Amalia that dinner was sheer delight. He was talkative, telling them about his early years, which had been filled with remarkable adventures. Whenever the penury that forced him to resort to questionable expedients threatened to turn into misery, help always turned up. He related in minute detail an adventure that had saved him from hunger and had allowed him to earn a tip for finding a lost dog.

That's how it always was. Once he had finished his studies, he pounded the pavements of Milan and was on the point of accepting a job he had been offered in a commercial company. For a sculptor, it was hard to start a career. As a novice, he would quickly have died of starvation. Passing in front of a building one day in which the works of a recently deceased artist were being exhibited, he went in to make his final farewell to sculpture. There he found a friend and together they began to demolish mercilessly the works on display. Instigated by the bitterness of his desperate situation, Balli found everything mediocre, meaningless. He spoke loudly and passionately; that critique was to be his final work as an artist. In the last room, in front of a piece that the defunct maestro had been unable to complete because of the malady that had befallen him, Balli came to a sudden halt, amazed that he could no longer pursue his critique in the same vein he had taken until then. That plaster model represented the head of a woman with a vigorous profile, the firm lines roughly modeled yet forcefully expressing pained contemplation. Balli's voice rose with emotion. He had discovered in the late sculptor that there had always been an artist in him, right from the first sketch, but that academism had inevitably intervened to destroy the artist by making him forget his first impressions, his first emotions, and remember only impersonal dogma: the perils of art!

"Quite so!" said a bespectacled old man standing near him, who nearly poked his nose into the plaster model. Balli continued his praise, speaking movingly about the artist, who had died in old age and carried his secret with him to his grave, except for that one instance when death itself had prevented him from concealing it.

The old man stopped looking at the plaster model and turned to examine the critic. It was by pure chance that Stefano introduced himself as a sculptor and not as a commercial inspector. The old man, a rich eccentric, like a character in a fairy tale, commissioned him first to do a bust of him, than a funerary monument, and in the end remembered him in his will. From that meeting, Balli had work for two years and money for ten.

Amalia said, "How wonderful it must be to know people who are so intelligent and so kind."

Balli protested. He described the old man with heartfelt antipathy. That pretentious Maecenas had hovered over him relentlessly, requiring him to produce a given amount of work every day. A true philistine bereft of any taste of his own, he could appreciate art only when it was explained and demonstrated to him. Every evening Balli was so exhausted from working and talking, it seemed to him at times that he was stuck in the very job of commercial inspector from which he had escaped by sheer luck. When the old man died, he wore mourning for him, but in order to lament him more cheerfully, he did not come near clay for months on end.

How wonderful Balli's life was! He did not even have to be grateful for the blessings that heaven showered on him. Wealth and happiness were the natural consequences of his destiny. Why should he be surprised by them or grateful for rewards sent by providence? Beguiled, Amalia listened to this tale, which only proved to her how very different life could be from the one she had known. It was natural that life should be hard for her and her brother, and just as natural that for Balli it should turn out to be blissful. She admired

Balli's happiness and loved the strength and certainty in him that were the first elements of his good fortune.

Emilio, on the other hand, listened with resentment and envy. Balli seemed to be bragging about his good fortune as though he had earned it. No happy event had ever fallen Emilio's way, not even something unexpected. Even misfortune had been announced to him in advance, making itself clearer as it approached; he had plenty of time to look it in the face and when it hit him — the death of his loved ones, poverty — he was all ready for it. That was why his suffering lasted longer but was less acute, and why his many misfortunes had never shaken him out of his sad inertia, which he attributed to his hopelessly dull and unchanging destiny. He had never inspired a powerful emotion, neither love nor hate. An old man like the one unjustly despised by Balli had never intervened in his life. Jealousy flooded his heart to the point that it extended to the admiration Amalia was lavishing on Balli. Conversation at the table became extremely lively once he too participated in it. He struggled to win Amalia's attention.

But he did not succeed. What did he have to talk about that could rival Balli's fantastic autobiography? Nothing but his present passion, and since he could not talk about that, he was quickly relegated to the position of second fiddle, his by destiny. Emilio's efforts produced nothing more than an idea or two that only served to ornament the monologue of his friend who, though unconscious of it, sensed the contest and became all the more inventive, colorful, and spirited. Never had Amalia been the object of so much attention. Although she listened avidly to the confidences made to her by the sculptor, she was not deluded: they were indeed intended to seduce her, and she felt completely his, but no hope for the future flitted through the mind of this dreary creature. It was the present that made her rapturous, those minutes that made her feel desirable, important.

They all went out together. Emilio would have preferred to be alone with Balli, but Amalia reminded him of his promise the day before to take her out for a stroll. She was not ready for that festive occasion to end so soon. Stefano seconded her. As he saw it, Emilio's devotion to Amalia could counteract Angiolina's influence over him; he no longer remembered that only a few minutes before he had tried to insinuate himself between brother and sister.

She was ready in flash and had even found the time to rearrange her thin hair—more mottled than a precise color—into curls on her forehead. Putting on her gloves, she invited Balli to step out with a smile that begged him to find her attractive.

Outside, she looked even drabber than usual, dressed all in black, a small white feather stuck in her little hat. Balli joked about the feather. He nevertheless said he liked it and managed to hide his displeasure at having to walk through town alongside that homely little woman whose perverse taste of putting up a white signal only emphasized her closeness to the ground.

The air was balmy, but the sky, covered by a dense white mist, like a white cape, was really wintry. The long bare branches still unpruned, and the ground, whitish in that diffused and overcast light, made Sant'Andrea look like a snowy landscape. With no way of rendering the softness of the air, a painter trying to reproduce the scene would have set down this erroneous impression.

"Between the three of us," Balli remarked, "we know the whole city." Along the promenade they had been forced to slow their pace. In that vast somber landscape with the enormous white sea as background, the crowd, all festive and noisy and official, was anything but somber; it was more like an ant colony.

"You're the one who knows everyone," Amalia said, remembering that she had often come to that promenade without having to tire herself greeting people. Every one they passed saluted Balli warmly and respectfully, and people even waved to him from carriages. She felt very much at ease beside him and enjoyed that triumphal walk as though some part of the reverence directed to the sculptor were intended for her.

"What a pity if I hadn't come!" Balli said, responding to an elderly lady who was leaning out of her carriage to see him with a carefully measured greeting. "All these people would have gone home disappointed." They were certain to find him on the promenade on Sunday, which he observed, as regularly as a factory worker, with Brentani, who was otherwise locked up in an office all week.

"*Ange!*" Amalia murmured with a discreet titter. She had recognized her from Emilio's description and from his agitation.

"Don't laugh!" Emilio warned her heatedly, confirming Amalia's assumption. He also saw something new: the tailor, Volpini, a thin, unremarkable little man, made even more so by the splendid feminine figure beside whom he walked, his stride lengthened by determination and vanity. "He's the same color as Angiolina," Balli laughed. Emilio disagreed. How could he compare Volpini's straw color with the gold of Angiolina? He turned and saw Angiolina lean over and talk to her companion, who looked up, not at all humpbacked as it turned out. They were surely speaking about the three of them.

Only much later, when they were back in the center of town and about to leave each other, did Amalia, who had suddenly fallen silent as her habitual solitude loomed close once more, in order to say something and break the silence that already lay over her, ask who was the man with Angiolina. "Her uncle," Emilio replied with much gravity after a moment's hesitation, while Stefano gave him an ironic look on seeing his embarrassment. His sister's innocent gaze made him feel ashamed. How surprised Amalia would be to learn what kind of woman her brother's great love was, the love which had already made her suffer so much.

"Thank you," Amalia said, taking leave of Stefano. How delicious the memory of those hours would have been if at that moment she had not had the misfortune to notice that Balli was unable to answer her because his mouth was paralyzed by a yawn.

"You were bored. I thank you all the more."

So humble, so kind, Stefano thought with emotion, suddenly overcome with fondness for her. He explained that in his case a yawn was a nervous response. He would prove to her that he was not bored by their company: they would soon find him to be a nuisance.

He kept his word. It would be hard to say why he climbed those stairs every day to have coffee at the Brentanis'. Jealousy, probably. He was trying to hang on to Emilio's friendship. But Amalia could not begin to guess all that. She thought he came to see them more often out of fondness for her brother, a fondness from which she too benefited because some of it devolved on her.

Between sister and brother there were no more disputes. Emilio, given his blindness, was in no way surprised by this. He felt that his sister stood behind him, that she understood him better, and what was more, that her new benevolence extended to his passion. When he spoke about it, Amalia's face lit up; it glowed. She tried to make him talk about love and never warned him to be on his guard or to leave Angiolina. Why should he leave Angiolina when she was happiness incarnate?

One day Amalia asked to meet her and later reiterated her wish on several occasions. But Emilio took care not to grant it. She knew nothing about Angiolina except that she was very different from her, stronger, more vigorous, and Emilio was delighted to have created in her mind an Angiolina very different from the real one. In his sister's presence, he would cherish that image, embellish it, adding all the qualities he would have liked Angiolina to possess, and when he noticed that Angiolina herself was collaborating in that artificial construction, he was overjoyed.

Hearing about a woman who had conquered all the prejudices of class and property in order to be with the man she loved, Amalia whispered into Emilio's ear, "She's like Angiolina."

"Oh, if only she were like that!" Emilio thought, while arranging his face in an expression of concurrence. Later he convinced himself that she was like that woman, or at least that she would be like her if she had grown up in another environment, and he would end up smiling. Why should he suppose that Angiolina would let herself be stopped by prejudices? Seen through Amalia's ennobling vision, his love for Angiolina swathed itself at times in all sorts of illusions.

It was rather Amalia who resembled that woman who had broken down every obstacle. She felt an enormous power in her long white hands, great enough to break the strongest chains. But there were no chains in her life; she was completely free. No one asked that she be decisive, or strong, or loving. How would she ever release the immense force trapped inside that frail organism?

In the meantime, stretched out in the old armchair, Balli

sipped his coffee and experienced a great sense of well-being as he remembered how at that time of day, he used to engage in the dreadful habit of meeting his artist friends at the caffè for discussions. How much more enjoyable it was here, in the company of those two gentle souls who loved and admired him!

Equally disastrous was Balli's intervention between the two lovers. During the course of his brief acquaintance with Angiolina, he had assumed the right to pelt her with insults, which she tolerated smilingly, not at all offended. At first, he was satisfied with saying them to her in Tuscan, with its aspirated and softened consonants, all of which sounded to her like caresses. But even when his insults fell on her in good Triestino dialect, hard and coarse, she did not get angry. She felt — as did Emilio — that they were spoken without any malice intended; it was just his way of speaking, an innocuous way of moving his mouth. And that was the worst of it. One evening, Emilio, at the end of his patience, finally asked Balli not to join them any more. "It pains me too much to hear her vilified like that."

"Is that so?" Balli asked, his eyes wide with amazement. Forgetful as always, he had once again thought that to cure Emilio he had to behave that way. Once he was convinced of the contrary, he stayed away from the lovers for a while.

"I don't know how to behave any other way with a woman of that kind."

At that, Emilio felt ashamed and rather than admit to such weakness, he resigned himself to enduring his friend's presence.

"Bring Margherita some time."

Their so-called "veal dinner" repeated itself many times, the scenario much like the first time: Emilio condemned to silence, Margherita and Angiolina on their knees before Balli.

One evening, however, Balli did not shout, did not order people around, did not solicit adoration, and for the first time was the companion Emilio would have wanted.

"How you must feel loved by Margherita!" he said on the way back just to be pleasant. The two women were walking a few steps away from them.

"Alas," Balli said quietly, "I'm afraid she loves many others the way she loves me. She's a very kind soul." Emilio almost fell over. "Not another word!" Balli added, seeing that the two women had stopped to wait for them.

The next day, during a moment when Amalia had to go to the kitchen, Balli related that by accident, a postman's mistake, he had discovered that Margherita had given an appointment to someone else, "another artist in fact," he growled. "That upset me very much. It is outrageous to be treated like that. I set out to make inquiries, and when I thought I had discovered my rival, I found that there were two of them, which made the whole thing much more innocent. And so for the first time I stooped to find out about Margherita's family and learned it consisted of a mother and a bevy of very young sisters. Understand? Margherita has to provide for the education of all those girls." Then Balli, his voice deep with emotion, concluded, "Imagine, from me she refused to take a penny. I want her to confess, to tell me everything. I will kiss her one last time, I will tell her that I don't hold it against her, and I will leave her with the fondest memories." Then, puffing on his cigarette, he suddenly calmed down, and when Amalia returned, he quietly sang Otello's line, "*Pria confessi il delitto e poscia muoia!*" let her first confess her crime and then die.

That same evening Emilio told Angiolina about Margherita. She felt a surge of joy that she could not make herself repress and instantly realized that she owed Emilio an apology for her reaction. But it was hard. How dreadful for him to see the sculptor obtain with mockery and laughter what he could not achieve with all his suffering!

At the time, he was also going through a period of strange illusions concerning Angiolina. A dream, the kind that came to him when he was wide awake, made him believe it was he who was corrupting the girl. For from the beginning of their relationship, those first evenings he spent with her, he had started to lecture her about honest women and their rewards. He had no way of knowing what she had been like before she became his pupil. How could he not have understood that an honest Angiolina would have meant an Angiolina who was his? He went back to the same lecture he had interrupted but this time changed his tone. He quickly discovered that complex abstract theories were useless with Angiolina. For days on end he pondered the right method for reeducating her. In his dream he caressed her as though he had already made her worthy of him. He tried to make reality conform to his dream. The most effective method was to make her feel that respect was so desirable she would want to acquire it for herself. Which was why he now found himself forever on his knees before her, just the right position to be knocked down effortlessly the day Angiolina found it opportune to give him a kick.

six

One evening, at the beginning of January, Balli was walking all by himself along the Aqueduct in the foulest of moods. He missed the company of Emilio, who had gone with his sister to visit someone, and Margherita had not yet been replaced.

The sky was clear despite the sirocco that had been blowing across the city ever since morning. The wretched carnival, beginning that evening with a masked ball, could not possibly hold out against that damp cold. "Oh, to have a dog now to bite those calves!" he thought, seeing two bare-legged *Pierettes* pass by. Because it was so lackluster, the carnival aroused in him a moralist's ire. Later, much later, given his attraction to sensuality and colorful events, he too would take part in it, forgetting all about his ire. But for the moment, he reminded himself, he was watching the prelude of a dreary comedy. A vortex was beginning to form which, for a few moments, would tear the worker, the dressmaker, and the poor tradesman out of their quotidian boredom and pull them into suffering. Bruised and lost, some would return to their old life, which would now seem all the duller, while others would never see another Lent.

He yawned again; even his own thinking bored him. "You can smell the sirocco," he thought, and looked again at the bright moon that stood above the mountain as though on a pedestal.

His glance focused on three figures coming down the Aqueduct. They caught his attention because he suddenly noticed that all three were holding hands. A small squat man was in the middle, and two women, two slender silhouettes, were on either side of him. There was something ironic about the pose that gave him an idea for a sculpture. He would dress the two women in the robes of ancient Greece and the man in a frock coat. The women would be laughing wildly like bacchantes, while the man's face would be lined with boredom and fatigue.

As he drew closer to the figures, the vision of his project suddenly vanished. One of the women was Angiolina, the other a certain Giulia, an unattractive girl Angiolina had introduced to Balli and to Emilio. He did not know the man who passed him only a few steps away, head high, all smiles, looking venerable in his long brown beard. It was not Volpini; Volpini was sandy-haired.

Giolona's warm loud laughter rang out. The man was surely there for her, and it was only because of her that he had taken Giulia's hand. Balli was firmly convinced of this without being able say why. His great powers of observation proved so entertaining that he forgot how bored he was. "Now that's an original occupation; I'll become a spy!" He followed them, keeping to the shadows of the trees. Giolona laughed a lot, almost without a stop, while Giulia, in order to participate in the conversation, had to lean over since her two companions on her right most often ignored her.

Very soon there was no more need for great powers of observation. A few steps from the caffè, they stopped at the Aqueduct. The man let go of Giulia, who discreetly moved away, and took both of Angiolina's hands in his. He seemed to be asking something of her and repeatedly brought his shaggy beard close to her face. From afar, he seemed to be kissing her. Then the three reunited and entered the caffè.

They sat down in the first room near the entrance but in such a way that all Balli saw was the man's head. That, however, was in full light. A dark olive face framed by a beard so heavy it almost reached his eyes, but the shiny yellow head was bald. "The umbrella vendor of via Barriera!" Balli laughed. Emilio Brentani's rival was an umbrella vendor! But so much the better, for a tradesman of that ilk might cure Emilio. Balli felt he could make the event look so ridiculous that Emilio would laugh about it and not be hurt. Balli had not a doubt about how witty he would be.

Since the umbrella vendor kept looking to one side, Balli, wanting to be a conscientious spy, had to ascertain that Angiolina was on that side. And so he entered the caffè. It was indeed she, sitting with her back to the wall. Giulia, seated opposite her, totally isolated, was sipping a clear syrupy liqueur from a small glass. Despite her great attention to her drink, she was less distracted than the other two. It was she who noticed Balli and sounded the warning. Too late. He had been able to observe that the two hands were once again clasped under the table and he was struck by the affectionate way Angiolina looked at the umbrella vendor. Emilio was right: those eyes did indeed sparkle as though something were burning in their flame. Balli envied the umbrella vendor. How much better off he would be in that man's place instead of where he was!

Giulia greeted him. "Good evening!"

He became indignant at the realization that she expected him to join them. He had tolerated her for one evening to be with Emilio and Angiolina. Acknowledging Angiolina with a quick nod, he walked out slowly. She almost crumpled in her chair in order to appear further removed from her companion and watched Balli with huge pleading eyes, ready to smile at him if only he did so first. But he did not and, turning away without responding to the umbrella vendor's greeting, he crossed the threshold.

"How expressive we are!" he mused. "She begged me not to tell Emilio about this meeting and I replied that I would tell him the minute I saw him."

He glanced back at the umbrella vendor. Between his bald head and his hairy face was a look of utter contentment. "Oh, if only Emilio had seen it!"

"Good evening Signor Balli," he heard spoken respectfully behind him. He turned around. It was Michele. He appeared at just the right moment.

On a sudden impulse Balli told him to go find Emilio Brentani: if he was at home, to bring him back at once, and if not, to wait until he returned. Michele barely took the time to hear the order before running off.

Waiting impatiently, Balli leaned against a tree facing the caffè. He would manage to keep Emilio from assaulting the umbrella vendor or Angiolina. His hope was to keep him calm and liberate him from that attachment once and for all.

Giulia came to the door and looked around carefully, but since she was in the light and Balli was in the shade, she could not see him. Balli remained immobile, not really caring about concealing himself. Giulia went back in and later emerged accompanied by Angiolina and the umbrella vendor, who no longed dared hold his loved one's hand. They directed their quickened steps toward Caffè Chiozza. They were running away! As far as the Chiozza, Balli's task was easy, because Emilio had to arrive by that street. But when they turned right, in the direction of the station, Balli found himself in an awkward situation. Impatience made him belligerent. "If Emilio doesn't get here in time I will fire Michele!"

Up to a certain point he was helped by his excellent eyesight.

"Ah, you scoundrels!" he muttered angrily, seeing that the umbrella vendor felt secure enough to take hold of Angiolina's hand again. But soon after, he lost sight of them in the shadows projected by the tall houses, so that when Emilio finally arrived on the scene, Balli, knowing it was too late to catch up to them, greeted him with one word "Pity! You missed a spectacle that would have been salutary for you." Then he started to sing "*Sì, vendetta, tremenda vendetta . . .*" and, in the hope that the trio might have stopped to await them, dragged Emilio with him to the station.

Emilio had understood at once that this concerned Angiolina. He agreed to walk with Balli, asking him questions as though he did not have the slightest suspicion of the truth. Then he understood: his throat tightened when he saw how ridiculous the situation was. Oh, to be rid of that, first and foremost! He stopped resolutely. He wanted to know what was going on or he would not take another step. He wanted to hear the whole story with total honesty. It was about Angiolina, wasn't it? "Whatever you have to tell me cannot possibly surpass what I already know," he laughed. "So let's stop this comedy."

He was very pleased with himself, especially when he saw that he immediately obtained from Balli what he wanted. Growing serious, Balli told him how he had happened to run into Angiolina and caught her in the act. The situation could not have been clearer had it been a bedroom. "That man was there for Angiolina, not Giulia. Or rather, Angiolina was there for him. How she stroked his hands and how she looked at him! It wasn't Volpini, you know." He interrupted himself to look at Emilio and see whether perhaps the calm emanating from him came from the assumption that the man who betrayed him was Volpini.

Emilio heard him out, pretending to be surprised by the news. "Are you sure?" he asked conscientiously. He knew that Volpini was not in Trieste and therefore had not thought of him at all.

"Of course! I know Volpini and I also know the other one. The umbrella vendor from Barriera Vecchia. The one with the cheap umbrellas, the colored ones." This was followed by a detailed description of the umbrella vendor in the yellow light of the gaslamps and of Angiolina's eyes. Bald, but so dark and hairy! "He's a monstrosity of nature, because no matter what light he's in, he remains dark." Concluding his account, Balli said: "Since there is no reason to feel compassion for you, I only feel it for that poor Giulia. The umbrella vendor does not have a friend like me on whom to unburden the sad finales of his romantic adventures. She was the mistreated one! She had to make do with a little glass of dessert wine, while Angiolina had herself ceremoniously served a hot chocolate and a plateful of buns."

Emilio appeared to take great interest in all the clever observations of his friend. He no longer even felt the need to pretend indifference; it had almost crystallized in his initial effort. He would have been able to go to sleep with that vapid smile and that serenity sitting on his face like a mask. Pretense of that kind went far below the epiderm. Vainly, he looked for something in himself besides her and found nothing but tremendous fatigue. Nothing else! Perhaps boredom with himself, with Balli, with Angiolina. And he thought "When I'm alone, I'll surely feel better than I do now."

Balli said, "Now let's go home and sleep. You already know where to find Angiolina tomorrow. You will say a few words of farewell and be done with it, the way it happened with me and Margherita."

It was a good idea but perhaps unnecessary. "Yes, I'll do that," Emilio said, adding with sincerity, "but maybe not tomorrow." He wanted to sleep late tomorrow.

"Now that's a worthy friend," Balli said admiringly. "In a single evening you have regained all the esteem you lost with the foolishness of these past months. Will you walk me home?"

"Part of the way," Emilio said yawning. "It's late and I was already on my way to bed when Michele came for me." He obviously regretted that untimely summons.

He was still unsettled when he was alone again. What was left for him to do that evening? He started walking home, intending to go to bed.

But when he reached the Caffè Chiozza, he stopped to look in the direction of the station, the quarter of the city where Angiolina was making love with her umbrella vendor. "Still," he thought, and he formulated both the idea and the words, "it would be nice if she came by here and I could tell her right now that between us everything is finished. Then everything would really be finished and I would be able to go home and sleep soundly. She has to come this way!"

He leaned against a road sign, and the longer he waited, the greater his desire to see her that very night.

To be prepared, he even thought about the words he would say to her. Kind words. Why not? "Goodbye, Angiolina, I wanted to save you and you mocked me." Mocked by her, mocked by Balli! Powerless rage flooded his heart. At last he relaxed, and all the fury and commotion pained him less than the indifference to which he had been condemned just before by Balli, a prisoner of his own character. Kind words to Angiolina? Absolutely not! Few, cruel and glacial! "I knew perfectly well what you are. I'm not at all surprised. Ask Balli. Goodbye."

He started walking to calm himself because the thought of those icy words made him burn with shame. They were not offensive enough! They offended only him. He began to feel dizzy. "In cases like this, one kills," he thought, "one doesn't talk." The fright caused by his own thoughts quieted him. He would be no less ridiculous if he killed her, he told himself, as though he really had thought of murder. He had not, of course, but once he was reassured about that, he rather enjoyed the idea of being avenged by Angiolina's death. That kind of vengeance would make him forget all the pain she had caused. Then he would be able to weep for her. He was so moved by the thought that tears came to his eyes.

With Angiolina he would have to follow the same method he had used with Balli. Both of his enemies had to be treated the same way. To her, he would say that he was leaving her not because of her betrayal, which he had expected all along, but because of the degrading individual she chose as his rival. He had no desire to place his lips where the umbrella vendor had placed his. So long as it was Balli, Leardi, or even Sorniani, he could close an eye, but the umbrella vendor! In the dark he tried out the grimace of disgust that would accompany those words.

Any of the words he imagined hurling at her always produced a convulsion of laughter. Was he going to continue talking to her like that all night long? It was therefore urgent that he talk to her right away! He remembered that Angiolina would probably return home by way of via Romagna. Walking quickly, he might still catch up with her. No sooner had he finished thinking all this than he broke into a run, overjoyed to have taken a decision that would put an end to the doubt clouding his mind. At first the rapid movement gave him some relief. Then he slowed down because a new idea gave him pause. If they were going back to Angiolina's from that side of town, would it not be more likely to find them by going up via Fabio Severo from the Public Gardens and then down via Romagna, thus meeting them head on? He had no hesitation about running and would have attempted that enormous circuit, but just then he thought he saw Angiolina passing in front of Caffè Fabris in the company of Giulia and a man who had to be the umbrella vendor. Even at that distance he could recognize the graceful way she had of skipping when she wanted to charm him. He stopped running because he had all the time in the world to catch up with them. He also had time to plan what he was going to say to her without getting flustered. Why complicate it with an excess of details and strange thoughts? It was just the usual kind of adventure, and in a few minutes it would be ended in the simplest way.

When he reached the slope of via Romagna, he no longer saw the three people, who must already have gone by. He increased his pace, seized by a doubt that made him as breathless as the incline. What if it was not Angiolina? How would he control his constantly revived agitation during an entire night?

Although they were now only a few steps away from him in the dark, he still believed them to be the three people he was looking for. So that for a moment he was calm. It was so easy to be calm when you knew you were about to go into action!

The group looked like the one Balli had described to him. A fat man walked between two women, holding the arm of the woman Emilio had taken for Angiolina but who, seen close up, had none of her characteristic movements. He looked her in the face with the calm and irony he had prepared so carefully. It was a great surprise to see the unfamiliar face of a dried-out old hag.

A painful delusion. Not wishing to take abrupt leave of the group on which he had hinged so much hope, he thought of asking them whether by chance they had seen Angiolina and was already planning how he would describe her. It was too embarrassing! One word out of his mouth and all of them would immediately have guessed everything. He continued walking quickly and before long broke into a run. In front of him he saw a long stretch of white street and remembered that when he turned the corner, he would see another equally long, and then yet another. Interminable! But he had to get rid of his uncertainty and for the moment, the uncertainty whether Angiolina was on that street or elsewhere.

Once more he turned over what he would say to her that night or the next morning. With great dignity (the more agitated he became, the calmer he thought he was), he would tell her that to be rid of him she had only to say one word, just one. He did not have to be ridiculed. "I would have withdrawn at once. I did not have to be driven away by an umbrella vendor." He repeated this sentence a number of times, modifying a word here or there and trying to perfect the tone of his voice, which grew increasingly ironic and cutting. He stopped when he realized that his efforts to find the right expression were making him shout out loud.

To avoid the deep mud in the middle of the road, he walked on the shoulder, on gravel, but he stumbled on the uneven surface, and to keep from falling, he scraped his hands on the rough wall beside the road. His physical pain only increased his desire for vengeance. He felt more humiliated than ever, as though that near fall were another one of Angiolina's ploys. In the distance he thought he saw her again. A reflection, a shadow, a movement, everything took on the shape and demeanor of the phantasm that eluded him. He started to run, hoping to catch up with her, not calm and ironic as he had been on the slope of via Romagna, but firmly intent on becoming violent with her. Happily, it was not she. In his misfortune, Emilio felt as though all the violence he had been about to unleash on her was now directed to himself, leaving him breathless and without hope of reason or control. He bit his hand like a lunatic.

He was now halfway through his long itinerary. Angiolina's house, tall and solitary, a barracks, its white face lit up by the moon, was shuttered and shrouded in silence. It looked abandoned.

He sat down on a low wall and tried to find reasons for calming himself. Seeing him like that one would have thought that he had just learned about the betrayal of a loyal woman. He looked at his wounded hands. "These wounds were not there before," he thought. She had never treated him like that before. Perhaps all that torment and all that pain heralded his recovery. But then he thought with anguish, "If I had possessed her, I would not be suffering this much." If he had wanted to, really been determined, he could have had her. Instead, his sole intention had been to infuse their relationship with an idealism that ended up making him look ridiculous in his own eyes as well.

He stood up, calmer but more exhausted than when he had sat down. It was all his fault. He was the weird one, the sick one, not Angiolina. And this humiliating conclusion accompanied him all the way home.

After waiting once more to scrutinize a woman who had Angiolina's figure, he finally found the courage to close the door behind him. It was over for that evening. What he had hoped for until then had no further chance of success.

He lit the candle, moving slowly to delay as long as possible the moment when he would be lying in his bed with nothing left to do and no way to fall asleep.

He thought he heard someone talking in Amalia's room. At first it seemed to be a hallucination. It did not sound like agitated cries, but more like peaceful conversation. He opened the door just a crack and was convinced. Amalia was talking to someone: "Yes, yes, that's exactly what I want," she said in a perfectly clear steady voice.

He ran to his room for the candle and returned. Amalia was alone. She was dreaming. She was on her back, one of her slender bare arms bent under her head, the other resting beside her side on the gray blanket. Her waxlike hand was exquisite. As soon as the light touched her face she fell silent and her breathing became more labored. She made several attempts to change her position, apparently no longer comfortable.

He brought the candle back to his room and prepared for bed. His thoughts had finally taken a new direction. Poor Amalia! Life did not hold much happiness for her, either. Her dream, which must have been pleasant in so far as could be determined from her voice, was none other than a natural reaction to the sadness of reality.

Soon after, those same tranquil words, enunciated almost syllable by syllable, echoed once more from the next room. Half naked, he returned to the door. There was some connection between the separated words, but (who could doubt it?) she was speaking to someone she really loved. Both the tone of her voice and the sense of her words conveyed great tenderness and deference. Twice she said that the other person — her imaginary interlocutor — had intuited her wishes: "Will we really do that? I never dreamed of such a thing!" Then a pause, interrupted by indistinct sounds that nonetheless indicated the dream was continuing, and again other words that continued to express the same idea. He stood there eavesdropping for a long while. Just as he was about to leave, a complete sentence stopped him: "On a honeymoon, everything is permissible."

Poor thing! She was dreaming about marriage. He was ashamed to have intruded into his sister's secrets that way and closed the door. He would try to forget what he had heard. His sister must never suspect that he knew anything about those dreams.

Once in bed his thoughts did not return to Angiolina. For a long while he continued to hear the words that had come to him from the next room, muted, calm, tender. Exhausted, his mind emptied of all emotions, he felt almost happy. As soon as his relationship with Angiolina was ended, he would be able to devote himself entirely to his sister. He would live up to his obligation.

seven

He woke up in broad daylight after only a few hours' sleep, and immediately recalled the events of the previous evening, but not the pain. He could therefore delude himself into believing that the cause of his anguish was not his betrayal by that woman but the impossibility of avenging himself then and there. She would soon discover his wrath and his renunciation. Once his rancor was vented, his strongest remaining bond to her would dissolve.

He left the house without a word to his sister. Before long, he would return to her and cure her of the dreams he had spied on.

A light wind was blowing. Near the Public Gardens both the wind and the climb tired him. But that was nothing compared to the exhaustion and pain of the night before. In the bright clear light of morning he was enjoying the physical exercise out-of-doors.

He was not thinking about what he would say to Angiolina. He was too sure of his arguments to need any preparation, too certain of knowing how to hurt her, too certain of leaving her. Angiolina's mother came to the door. She led him into her daughter's room adjoining the one where she was getting dressed, and then, as she usually did, offered to keep him company.

This new delay, though a matter of only a few minutes, exasperated him. "Did Angiolina came home late last night?" he asked with a vague intention of making inquiries.

"She was with Volpini at the caffè until midnight," the

old woman answered in one breath. The words sounded glued together in that nasal voice.

"But didn't Volpini leave yesterday?" he asked, surprised by the complicity between mother and daughter.

"He was supposed to leave, but he missed the train and should have left by now."

He did not want the old woman to suspect that he did not believe her, and so he remained silent. The story had become very clear; there was not a chance of fooling him and raising doubts in his mind. The lie they invented had been foreseen by Balli.

In front of the mother he had no trouble greeting Angiolina with the look of a satisfied lover. He felt genuinely satisfied. Now that he had finally caught her, he would not give in to his usual habit of immediately clarifying and simplifying things. This time she would be doing the talking. He would let her flounder in her lies in order to catch her *in flagrante*. When they were alone, she went to the mirror to arrange her curls and, without looking at him, began telling him about the evening in the caffè and Balli's surveillance. Her lighthearted laugh and rosy freshness infuriated Emilio even more than her lies.

She told him that Volpini's unexpected return had really annoyed her. Seeing him again, her reaction had been more or less: "Don't you ever get tired of bothering me?"

She said all this to make Emilio happy. Instead, he felt that compared to Volpini, he was the more ridiculed of the two. To fool him must have taken considerable effort: of her many ruses and deceptions he had probably discovered only a small part. Since Volpini good-naturedly let himself be taken in, it took little to fool him. And if Angiolina's escapades also amused her mother, as it seemed, then he was the likely butt of their hilarity, whereas Volpini was feared for the time being.

He was seized by one of those violent attacks of rage that made him grow pale and tremble. But she went on babbling, as though she were trying to confuse him, which gave him time to compose himself.

Why despair, why rail against the laws of nature? Angiolina was already corrupt in her mother's belly. The ugliest thing about her was her complicity with her mother. Since she too was a victim of universal laws, she did not deserve to be blamed. In the end, his old faith in determinism was reborn. Nevertheless, he could not give up his desire for revenge.

Angiolina was finally obliged to take note of his strange behavior. She turned to him. "You haven't even kissed me," she said in a tone of reproach.

"Never will I ever kiss you again!" he replied calmly, looking at those pink lips he was renouncing. Finding nothing else to say, he stood up, although he did not have the remotest intention of leaving, since that brief statement was hardly sufficient. It would take more than that to compensate him for so much suffering. What he did want her to understand from his statement was that he intended to leave her. That, in fact, would be the most dignified way of putting an end to their degrading relationship.

Guessing everything that was going in his mind and assuming he would not let her defend herself, she commented drily, "It was wrong of me to tell you that the man was Volpini. It wasn't. That was what Giulia asked me to say. That man was there for her. Since she often accompanied us, it seemed right that for once I would accompany her. It's unbelievable how much he's in love with her! Even more than you with me."

She stopped. From the expression on his face she could

see how little he believed her. She fell silent, mortified to have told two such glaring lies. She placed her hands on the back of a nearby chair and clutched it with all her might. Her face was completely drained of all expression, and she persisted in staring at a gray spot on the wall. That was doubtless how he looked when he was pained.

At that, he felt strangely obliged to prove to her that he really knew everything and that in his eyes she was hopelessly degenerate. Just before he would have been satisfied with few words, but Angiolina's pitiable embarrassment made him loquacious. He was aware of experiencing intense pleasure. From an emotional point of view, it was the first time that Angiolina had ever wholly satisfied him. Standing there mutely, she was the very image of a lover convicted of betrayal.

A moment later, however, the conversation turned almost comical. Hoping to hurt her, he reminded her what had been ordered at the caffè at the umbrella vendor's expense. "Giulia, a glass of some clear liqueur, you, a cup of chocolate and a pile of pastries."

Outraged, she heatedly defended herself, and her face flushed over this opportunity to restore her slandered virtue. At last she was accused of a vice she did not have, and Emilio understood that Balli must have been mistaken about that detail.

"Chocolate! I can't stand it! Chocolate, me? I had a glass of I don't know what and didn't even drink it." Her denial could not have been more forceful had she been affirming her absolute innocence. A certain note of regret nonetheless crept in, as though she were sorry that she had not eaten more, in view of the fact that her abstemiousness had not sufficed to save her in Emilio's eyes. She had made that sacrifice for him.

He made a violent gesture to end the pretense that was spoiling his final farewell. "That's enough!" he said with contempt. "Enough! I will say only this to you. I gave you my love and for that alone I had the right to be treated differently. When a young woman allows a young man to love her, she is already his and ceases to be free." This declaration — made in a sudden switch from the intimate *tu* to the formal third person *lei* — may have been feeble, but it was very accurate as a lover's reproach, too accurate. For the truth was that he had no right to make any claim other than having told her he loved her.

Realizing, thanks to his analytical mind, that in a situation of this kind words might fail him, he immediately pulled out what he knew was his trump card: abandonment. A little while earlier, relishing Angiolina's distress, he had thought he would not leave her until much later. He had hoped for a very different scene. Now he saw an imminent danger. He himself had alluded to his lack of rights. It was highly likely that when he had run out of arguments, she would agree with him and ask him: "What did you ever do for me that entitles you to make me bend to your will?" He circumvented that danger. "I am leaving you," he said gravely. "When I have regained my composure perhaps we can see each other again. But for the foreseeable future, it is better for us to remain apart."

He left, but not without admiring her for the last time, noticing her pallor, her eyes wide as though with fear, and perhaps her indecision as to whether she should find some other lies to retain him. Walking along with unchanged resoluteness, he nevertheless sorely regretted not having seen more of her distress. The sound of her anguish on seeing him leave still rang in his ears, and he continued listening to it so as to engrave it all the deeper into his memory. He had to hold on to it. It was the finest gift she could have given him.

Ridicule no longer assailed him. At least not in Angiolina's eyes. She could be whatever she chose to be, but for years to come she would remember the man who had loved her, not just to caress her, but with all his soul, and so much so that the first offense to his love wounded him so deeply that he gave her up. Who could tell? Perhaps a memory like that could serve to elevate her? The anguish in Angiolina's voice had made him forget once more all of his scientific conclusions.

It was hard for him to enclose in an office the agitation that was churning in him. He went home intending to go to bed. In the repose of his bed and the silence of his room he would be able to continue enjoying the scene with Angiolina as it might have unfolded. Given the excitement of that day, he thought he might confide in his sister. But then he remembered what he had discovered the night before. Sensing her remoteness from him, and her preoccupation with her own desires, he told her nothing. The time would surely come when he would once again surround his sister with his solicitude, but for another day or two of life, he wanted to devote himself to his own passion. The thought of locking himself up in the house and exposing himself to Amalia's queries was intolerable. He changed his plan.

He did not feel well, he told his sister, but fresh air would make him feel better, he hoped.

She did not believe that he was really sick. Until then she had always intuited the different phases of Emilio's sentimental life. This time, for once, she was mistaken and believed he had taken the day off in order to spend it with Angiolina. That was because he had a satisfied look on his face that she had not seen in a long time. She asked no questions. Many a time she had tried to get him to confide in her, after which she became resentful because he had repulsed her offers.

When Emilio was outside again, alone, still hearing Angiolina's anguished moan, he was tempted to race back to her. What would he do all day, unoccupied except for his agitation which, though not painful, was nothing but an intense desire, an impatient expectation, as though every moment was supposed to bring him something new, a new hope such as Angiolina had never given him in the past?

He could not possibly go to Balli and hoped he would not run into him. He was afraid of him. In fact, the only painful sensation he felt was that fear. He told himself it came from the knowledge that he was incapable of imitating Balli's equanimity when Balli had felt obliged to leave Margherita.

He walked toward the Corso. Angiolina might come that way when she went to work at the Deluigi's. He had not had a chance to ask where she was going, but she clearly was not staying home. Meeting her in the street he would have given her a reserved but pleasant greeting. Had he not told her that once he calmed down he could become her friend? Oh, if only that calm came soon, along with the moment when he might be near her again!

He looked around to see whether she was within sight.

"Well, hello, Brentani! How are you? You're still alive? No one ever sees you!" It was Sorniani, sprightly as ever but yellow as ever, sickness written all over his face except for his vivacious eyes. Whether they expressed vitality or anxiety, one couldn't tell.

When Brentani turned to him, Sorniani examined him with as much attentiveness as surprise. "Are you sick? You look strangely pale." This was not the first time that Sorniani told him he looked sick, Obviously, he saw reflected on other faces something of his own jaundiced complexion.

Emilio was happy to look sick. He could complain about something other than his misadventure, since about that he could not talk.

"It seems I have a stomach problem," he said with feeling. "That bothers me less than the depression it causes."

He remembered having heard that stomach ailments caused depression. He gleefully began describing his depressive state because hearing himself talk about it, he could analyze it better. "It's so strange. I could never imagine that without being aware of it, a physical indisposition can turn into a moral state. My indifference to everything depresses me. If all these houses on the Corso started to dance, I wouldn't even look. And if they threatened to fall on top of me, I'd let them fall." He broke off when he saw a woman approaching who looked like Angiolina. "It's a nice day today, isn't it? The sky must be blue, the air soft, the sun bright. I understand it but I don't feel it. I see gray and feel gray."

"I have never been sick," Sorniani said with undisguised smugness. "In fact, now I think I am permanently cured." Then he talked about various medicines that were supposed to produce miracles.

Emilio suddenly felt a desperate need to get rid of that bore who didn't even know how to listen. He extended his hand without saying a word and started to walk away. Saying goodbye without taking his hand, Sorniani asked, "How is your love life?"

Emilio pretended not to understand. "What love life?"

"That . . . what's her name? The blonde. Angiolina."

"Ah yes," Emilio replied vaguely. "I don't see her any more."

"You did well!" Sorniani exclaimed with conviction, moving in closer. "That's not a woman for a man like you who, what's more, are not in the best of health. She drove

Merighi crazy and besides, she fooled around with half the city for sure."

The expression "fooled around" offended Brentani. If that little yellow runt had not described Angiolina's expansive love life quite so accurately, he would have paid no attention to his gossip, but in the present situation it all sounded credible. He protested, saying that although he did not know her very well, he considered her a serious person. He succeeded in his purpose of needling Sorniani who, turning even paler — his stomach surely played some part in his malady — gave his rash provoker an earful.

Angiolina serious? Even before Merighi came on the scene, she must already have started her experiences with males. Barely an adolescent, she could be seen trotting around the old part of the city at indecent hours in the company of boys — she liked them beardless. Merighi arrived in time to take her to the new part, which later remained her center of activity. She paraded on the arm of the richest young men, always with the yielding tenderness of a newlywed. This was followed by a list of names Brentani already knew, from Giustini to Leardi, all of them in the photographs proudly displayed on Angiolina's bedroom wall.

Not one new name. Sorniani could not have invented anything that precise. A terrifying question made the blood rush to his face. Was Sorniani going to list himself in his impassioned recital? He continued listening to him with growing anxiety, his right fist clenched, ready to strike.

But Sorniani interrupted himself to ask, "Are you feeling sick?"

"No," Emilio answered, "I'm just fine." He stopped to wonder whether it was worth encouraging him go on with his chatter.

"But it's obvious that you must be sick. You've changed color a number of times."

Emilio relaxed his hand. There was no need to punch Sorniani. "You're right, I don't feel very well."

Punch Sorniani! Great act of vengeance! It was himself he ought to punch. Oh, how he loved her! He confessed it to himself with a yearning he had never felt before. Coward! he said to himself, recognizing that he would go back to her, and as quickly as possible. That morning he had been full of resolution and determination to be avenged. He had berated her and then walked out. Very clever! All he had done was punish himself. Every one of them had possessed her, but not he. So that the only ridiculous one among them was he himself. He remembered that in a few days Volpini would be arriving to collect the advance that had been contracted. And that was when he chose to get excited about things he had always suspected? What would Angiolina do after she had given herself to the tailor? It was only natural that after giving herself to him in order to deceive him more easily, she would deceive him with someone else, since Emilio had chosen just that moment to leave her. For him, she was lost. The future passed before his eyes as though it were taking place right there, on the Corso. He saw her emerge from Volpini's arms, disgusted, and immediately seek compensation for her revulsion. She would deceive him, and this time with good reason.

It was not just his nonpossession of her that provoked his despair. Until then, he had reveled in the memory of the anguished sound he had torn from her. But what did that mean in the life of a woman who in the arms of others would experience very different kinds of pleasure and pain? There was no turning back. To resist the temptation, all he needed was to remember what Balli would have said.

He told himself that without that severe judge at his side, his dignity would be of little concern, now that he understood that his attempt to raise her up had only bound his every thought, his every desire, all the more abjectly to Angiolina.

Some time had elapsed since his conversation with Sorniani, but the upheaval caused by the man's words had still not abated.

What if she made an attempt at reconciliation? In that case, his dignity would not have prevented him from welcoming her with open arms. But not the way it was before. He would immediately go to the heart of the matter, that is, possession. Enough romanticizing! "I know you were possessed by all those men," he would shout, "and I love you all the same. Be mine and tell me the truth so that I have no further doubts." The truth? Even when he imagined the coarsest candor, he still idealized Angiolina. The truth? Could she tell the truth, did she know how? Even if only a part of what Sorniani told him were true, lying was so innate in that woman, she could never be rid of it. He was forgetting how clear-sighted he had been at other times, that is, his strange collusion in seeing Angiolina as she was not; it was he who had created the lie. "How could I not have seen that the only thing that made me ridiculous was the lie!" he told himself. "By knowing everything and telling it to her face, there is no more ridicule. One is free to love however and whomever one likes." It was as though he were saying all this to Balli.

The wind had died down and the day was really spring-like. In another state of mind, a day of freedom like that would have filled him with joy. But what kind of freedom was it if he could not see Angiolina?

Even so, pretexts could have been found to go to her house at once. If nothing else, he could always produce some new admonishments. For instance, he had never suspected the existence of those beardless boys who preceded Merighi, about whom Sorniani had talked to him earlier that day. "No!" he said out loud. "Weakness like that would have me in her thrall. Patience! Ten days, two weeks and she will make the first move." Patience! But in the meantime, what would he do with himself that first morning?

Leardi! That handsome young man, blond and strong, with the complexion of a girl on a virile body, was walking down the Corso, serious as always, wearing a light-colored coat perfectly suited to that mild winter day. Brentani and Leardi barely greeted each other, both of them extremely haughty, though for very different reasons. Emilio, faced with that elegant young man, reminded himself that he was a writer of some repute. Leardi, on the other hand, thought that he could look down on Brentani because Brentani was not as well dressed, and because he never met him in any of the city's grand houses where he, Leardi, was welcomed with open arms. But he would have liked this superiority of his to be acknowledged by Brentani as well, and so he replied courteously to the greeting made to him. Seeing Brentani approach with his hand outstretched, Leardi responded with more cordiality than surprise.

Brentani had yielded to a sudden impulse. Since he was not free to see Angiolina, the best he could do was to attach himself to someone who in his mind was perennially associated with to her. "You too are taking advantage of this lovely weather to go for a stroll?"

"I'm just out for a short walk before lunch," Leardi said, thereby accepting Brentani's company.

Emilio talked about the fine weather, his own indisposition, Sorniani's illness. He then commented that he did not care much for Sorniani because of all his boasting about his success with women. Words flowed from his mouth. He had the strange feeling of being with someone who mattered greatly in his life, and he wanted every one of his words to secure that person's friendship. He looked at Leardi anxiously after mentioning Sorniani's successes. Leardi did not bat an eyelash. Emilio had expected an arrogant smile. That kind of smile in response to his remark would have been tantamount to a confession of his own affair with Angiolina.

Leardi was no less loquacious. He wanted to show Brentani how cultivated he was. He complained that on the Corso one always saw the same faces; it was deplorable that life in Trieste was so dull and unartistic. The city did not suit his taste.

As he listened, Brentani was seized with a terrible need to make Leardi talk about Angiolina. Listening almost mechanically in the hope of catching a sound that might evoke Angiolina's name, all he heard of what Leardi was saying was isolated words,. He looked for an opportunity to mention it so as to talk about her. It was just his luck not to find one. Exasperated by the nonsense Leardi was babbling, ever so slowly in order to let him savor it all the more, Emilio abruptly interrupted him. "Look, look," he said in a tone of surprise as his eyes followed the elegant figure of a woman who bore no resemblance whatever to Angiolina. "That is Signorina Angiolina Zarri."

"Certainly not!" Leardi contradicted, annoyed at having been interrupted. "I have seen her full face. That's not her."

He was off again, on the subject of half-empty theaters and society women with little wit, but Brentani had already decided not to suffer his lecture any longer. "You know Signorina Zarri?"

"You know her too?" Leardi asked genuinely surprised.

For Brentani it was a moment of agonizing doubt. He was not sure that he could find a ruse to make a man like Leardi talk. But since he was so desperate to unmask any lie that could prevent him from seeing Angiolina in her true colors, could he not turn to Leardi in total sincerity and appeal to him for the whole truth? The only reason he opted for reserve was his antipathy to Leardi. "Yes, a friend introduced her to me a few days ago."

"I was a friend of Merighi's. I knew her very well many years ago."

Suddenly very calm and in control of his facial expression, Brentani winked: "Very well, eh?"

"Oh no," Leardi solemnly replied. "How could you think such a thing?" He played his role very well, limiting himself to this expression of surprise.

Brentani understood Leardi's tactic and did not insist. He behaved as though he had forgotten his indiscreet query of a moment before and with much gravity said: "Tell me about that story with Merighi. Why did he leave her?"

"Because of financial difficulties. He wrote me that he had been forced to break his promise to Angiolina. As it happens, I heard only a few days ago that she is engaged again, to a tailor it seems."

It seems? Oh, one couldn't give a finer performance than that. But to do it that well, to be obliged to tell a tale so artfully constructed, which must have been an effort and a nuisance (why did he talk about Angiolina only when he was forced to?), he must still have good reasons, such as very recent relations with that woman.

Leardi was already launched on some other subject, and soon after, Emilio left him. In order to get away, he again had recourse to the pretext of a sudden malaise. Seeing him so distressed, Leardi believed him and even demonstrated such friendly compassion that Brentani was obliged to show his gratitude. What he really felt was hatred! He would have liked to follow him, at least for that one day: sooner or later he would find him with Angiolina.

A wild rage made him grit his teeth, and immediately afterward he reproached himself for it with bitterness and irony. Who could know with whom Angiolina would deceive him that day? Perhaps with someone he did not even know. How superior Leardi was to him, that idiot without a thought in his head! That kind of equanimity was the true science of life. "Yes indeed," Brentani thought, and it seemed to him that he was saying something that was as embarrassing to the elite of humanity as to himself. "The proliferation of images in my brain is the cause of my inferiority." For if Leardi had thought Angiolina was deceiving him, he would not have known how to visualize it in images as three-dimensional, as vivid, as animated as he did when he imagined her with Leardi. Only in them did he discover the nudity he had barely glimpsed before, nudity in which the lowliest stevedore found instant satisfaction and relief. A brief act, a brutal one, the travesty of every dream, every desire. As fury darkened the dreamer's vision, it vanished, leaving in his ear the prolonged echo of a resonant laugh.

At lunch Amalia could not help but notice that something was upsetting Emilio. He scolded her angrily for not having the meal ready. He was hungry and in a hurry. Then he suffered the torment of having to eat after his shameful outburst. And once he had eaten, he sat in front of his empty plate in a state of indecision. Finally he made up his mind: that day he would not go looking for Angiolina, in fact, he would never go near her again. The greatest remorse he felt just then was over his rudeness to his sister. She looked sad and pale. He would have liked to ask her forgiveness. But he did not dare. He was convinced that if he said anything pleasant, he would burst out crying like a child. He ended up saying gruffly, but with the evident intention of mollifying her: "You should go out. The weather is unusually beautiful." She did not reply and left the room. That made him furious: "Don't I have enough trouble? She should have understood by now the state I am in. My affectionate invitation should have been enough to make her treat me kindly and not bother me with her resentment."

He felt tired. He lay down in his clothes and immediately fell into a slumber that did not erase the memory of his misfortune. He raised his head once to wipe his tear-filled eyes and thought bitterly that those tears were being squeezed out of him by Amalia. Then he forgot everything.

When he awakened, night was falling in one of those melancholy sunsets of a beautiful winter day. He sat on his bed, still undecided. In earlier years he used to study at that hour. Now the books on his shelves offered themselves to him in vain. All those titles announced things of the past, dead things; they would never suffice to make him forget for even one moment the life and the pain that stirred in his heart.

He looked into the adjoining dining room and saw Amalia near the window, bent over her embroidery frame. He made an attempt at cheerfulness and said affectionately, "Have you forgiven me for my outburst this afternoon?"

She raised her eyes for a moment to say gently, "Let's not talk about it any more," and went back to her work.

He was prepared for reproaches and was disappointed to see her so calm. Was everyone around him calm except himself? He sat down beside her, admiring the way the silk thread followed the design. He tried unsuccessfully to find something else to say.

But she was not asking for anything. She had ceased suffering from the yearnings for love that had so troubled her existence and that, at first, she lamented so much. Once again, Emilio asked himself, "Why on earth did I leave Angiolina?"

eight

Balli decided to cure Emilio once and for all. That very evening he came to dinner at Emilio's house. He started out by not showing any interest in knowing what had happened. Only after Amalia left the room did he ask, while puffing on his cigarette and staring at the ceiling: "Did you make her understand with whom she was dealing?"

With a touch of pride, Emilio said he had, but then he felt embarrassed to say anything else in that same tone of voice.

Amalia soon returned. She related the altercation she had with her brother at lunch. She said it was very wrong to blame a woman because lunch was not ready. She depended on the heat of the stove, and the thermometer had not yet been introduced into kitchens. "On the other hand," she added smiling affectionately at her brother, "I can't hold it against him. He came home in such a mood that if he hadn't found some scapegoat, it might have harmed him."

Balli did not seem to associate the bad mood of the person under discussion with the events of the previous evening. "I too was in a bad mood today," he said, trying to keep the conversation from turning serious.

Emilio protested that he had been in a very good mood. "Don't you remember how cheerful I was this morning?"

Amalia had related their quarrel with humor. It was evident that she had talked about it only to entertain Balli. She had forgotten all about her resentment and no longer seemed to remember that Emilio had apologized to her. He was deeply hurt.

When the two men were alone in the street, Balli said, "Look how free we both are now. Isn't that much better?" He leaned affectionately on his friend's arm.

But his friend did not see it that way. He understood that he was obliged to appear similarly affectionate and said, "It certainly is better this way. But I will only be able to appreciate this new state after much time has elapsed. For the moment, I feel very lonely, even near you." Although he had not been asked, he recounted his visit that morning to via Fabio Severo. He did not mention having been there during the night as well. He talked about the anguished sound in Angiolina's voice. "That was the only thing that moved me. It was hard to leave her at the very moment I felt I was loved."

"Hold on to the memory," Balli told him, with uncharacteristic seriousness, "and never see her again. Along with that sound of anguish, always remember the state you were in because of your jealousy and any desire to be with her again will quickly pass."

"Even so," Emilio confessed with total candor, touched by Balli's warmth, "I have never suffered more jealousy than now." Stopping to look Balli squarely in the face, he said gravely, "Promise me that you will always tell me what you hear about her, but that you will never go near her, never. And if you should meet her in the street, you will tell me right away. I want a solemn promise."

Balli hesitated only because it seemed strange to him to have to make a promise of that kind.

"I am sick with jealousy, but only jealousy. I am even jealous of others, and of you above all. I could bear the umbrella vendor, but I could never bear you." There was nothing frivolous about his tone. He was trying to arouse Balli's compassion to be sure of securing his promise. If Balli refused, he had already decided he would instantly race back to

Angiolina. He did not want his friend to take advantage of a situation that in large part had been created by him. He looked at Stefano, his eyes flashing menacingly.

Balli readily guessed what was going through Emilio's mind and felt genuinely sorry for him. He therefore made him the solemn promise Emilio had requested. Then he told him, for the sole purpose of distracting him, that he regretted never being able to approach Angiolina. "On the assumption that it would please you, I had been thinking for some time about getting her to sit for a preliminary drawing." For a moment he had a dreamy look, as though he were visualizing the pose.

Emilio was alarmed. Childishly, he reminded Balli of his promise made only a few moments before: "You've already made the promise. Go look for your inspiration somewhere else."

Balli laughed heartily. Then, moved by yet another proof of the depth of Emilio's passion, he said. "Who could have foreseen that an adventure of this kind would take on such importance in your life! If it weren't so painful, it would be laughable."

Emilio then lamented his sorry fate but with so much self-irony that he cleared himself of all ridicule. He said that everybody who knew him surely knew what he thought about life. In principle, he saw it as devoid of any serious meaning. In fact, he had not trusted what little happiness came his way; he had never believed in it and had never really looked for happiness. But how much harder it was to extricate oneself from torment! In a life without serious meaning, even an Angiolina became serious and important.

During that first evening, Balli's friendship was enormously helpful to Emilio. The compassion Emilio sensed in his friend greatly reassured him. First of all, he could be sure, for the moment at least, that neither Stefano nor Angiolina would go looking for each other. In addition, his was the kind of docile nature that craved affection. Ever since the previous evening he had been looking for someone to lean on. It may have been his lack of a confidant that so often gave his agitation free rein to tyrannize him mercilessly. He might have been able to control it had he been given the chance to explain and to think rationally, and been forced to listen as well.

He returned home much calmer than when he had left. A stubbornness rose up in him on which he rather prided himself, as though it were a strength. He would not go near Angiolina unless she begged him. He could wait. Their relationship would not and should not be revived through any act of submission on his part.

Sleep, however, eluded him. In his futile attempts to attain it, his agitation increased as it had the evening before. His excited imagination constructed an entire scenario of Balli's betrayal. Balli was surely betraying him. Just before, Stefano had confessed to thinking about having Angiolina pose for a drawing. Now, taken by surprise in his studio, sketching her half naked, he apologized to Emilio, remembering his confession. In reprisal, Emilio hurled scalding words of hatred and contempt at him. They were very different from the words he had used with Angiolina, because in this case he had every right: an old friendship, to begin with, then that solemn promise made to him. And how complex his sentences were! They were finally addressed to someone who could understand what he was saying.

He was torn from his dream by Amalia's voice echoing softly and resonantly from the next room. Relieved to have been shaken out of his nightmare, he jumped out of bed and placed himself where he could eavesdrop. For a long while he heard words that made no sense to him, except that they expressed much tenderness. Nothing more. Once again, the dreamer wanted something that others also wanted. Emilio had the impression that she wanted more than was being asked of her; she wanted others to make demands on her. It was really a dream of submission. Was it the same as the night before? The poor woman had created a second life for herself; the night granted her what little happiness the day denied her.

Stefano! She spoke Balli's name. "She too!" Emilio thought bitterly. How could he not have noticed earlier? Amalia perked up only when Balli came. In fact, he now recognized that she had always shown the sculptor the same kind of submissiveness that she was offering in her dream. When her gray eyes fell on the sculptor they gleamed with a new kind of light. No, there was no doubt about it. Amalia was also in love with Balli.

It was unfortunate that when he went back to bed, Emilio was unable to fall asleep. He remembered with disgust how Balli swaggered about the infatuations he inspired and how, with that self-satisfied smile of his, he said that the only success he had not had was as an artist. In the prolonged half-sleep that finally overcame him, he dreamed absurd dreams. Balli had taken advantage of Amalia's submissiveness and, making light of it, had refused to honor his obligation. The dreamer, once he was fully conscious, did not make light of his dream. Between a man as immoral as Balli and a woman as naive as Amalia, anything was possible. He decided to take upon himself Amalia's recovery. He would begin by keeping away from their house this man who, albeit inadvertently, had become the bearer of misfortune. If not for Balli, his relationship with Angiolina would have been so much nicer, uncomplicated by all that bitter jealousy. Even the separation would now be easier.

Emilio's office life was hellish. It took all his strength to focus his attention on his work. Any pretext sufficed to leave his desk and devote a few more minutes to coddling and indulging his heartache. His mind seemed made for that alone, so that when he no longer had to concentrate on other things, his mind automatically returned to its favorite pastime, filling up like an empty vessel and making him feel like someone who had managed to lift an intolerable weight from his shoulders. The muscles relax, stretch, and return to their natural position. When finally the clock struck the hour that allowed him to leave his office, he felt almost happy, though not for long. At first, he wallowed voluptuously in his regrets and in desires that became increasingly clear and justified. His pleasure lasted only until he stumbled onto jealous thoughts that made him tremble with pain.

Balli was waiting for him on the street. "Well, then, how are things going?"

"So-so," Emilio replied, shrugging his shoulders. "I had a dreadfully difficult morning."

Seeing him pale and downcast, Stefano thought he could guess what Emilio meant by "difficult." He had taken the tack of being very gentle with his friend. He proposed going home with him for lunch and going for a walk together in the afternoon.

After a hesitation that escaped Balli's notice, Emilio accepted. For a second he had considered the possibility of refusing Balli's offer and telling him, then and there, what he already knew he would have to tell him. It would be an act of cowardice not to save his sister for fear of losing a friend. By doing what he had in mind, he could see nothing but a proof of courage. That he did not do it just then was because of a lingering doubt that he could be mistaken about Amalia's sentiments. "Yes, do come!" he said to Balli, repeating the invitation yet again. Whereas Stefano attributed the repetition to gratitude, Emilio understood he had done so for the pleasure provided by this opportunity to dispel all his doubts at once.

During the meal, he was indeed able to obtain all the certainty he needed. How Amalia resembled him! It seemed to him he was seeing himself dining with Angiolina. Her desire to please made her so awkward that it robbed her of all naturalness, to the point of opening her mouth to say something and then on second thought closing it. How she hung on Balli's every word! She may not even have heard what he was saying. An involuntary reaction provoked her laughter or her gravity.

Emilio tried to distract her, but he was not heard. He was not even heard by Balli, who, perhaps unaware of the feelings he inspired in her, had fallen under a kind of spell, manifested by the intellectual exuberance aroused in him whenever he held sway over someone. Emilio examined and evaluated his friend with clinical objectivity. Balli had completely forgotten the purpose of his visit. He was telling stories Emilio had heard before. It was obvious he was talking solely for Amalia's benefit. They were the same anecdotes he had already related to the silly woman, about his sad but joyful bohemian life whose gaiety and freedom so enchanted Amalia.

When Emilio and Stefano went out, the bitter rancor toward his friend that had been festering in Emilio swelled to bursting. Something Balli said had been the proverbial straw: "Did you see what a delightful hour we spent together?"

Emilio wanted to respond with an insult. A delightful hour? Not for him! He would remember that hour with the same revulsion he felt about the hours spent with Balli and Angiolina. During that meal, in fact, he had experienced the same old agonizing jealousy. To begin with, he held against his friend the fact that he had not noticed his silence. Balli had been so inattentive to him that he could imagine Emilio had enjoyed himself. But worse still, how could he not have noticed that in his presence Amalia was afflicted with an almost pathological confusion and agitation that at times made her stammer? He was so lucid about his own feelings that he was afraid Balli would think he was using Amalia to avenge himself for Balli's behavior with Angiolina. The first thing he had to do was avoid betraying his resentment; he had to sound like a good pater familias who was acting to protect his loved ones.

He began with a lie, making it sound like a casual remark. That very morning, he said, an old relative stopped him to ask if it was true that Balli was engaged to marry Amalia. That was not all he wanted to say, but he felt relieved to have said that much. He was on the right track to make Balli understand that he was neither the superior person nor the best of friends he thought he was.

"Really?" Balli exclaimed, genuinely surprised and laughing artlessly.

"Yes, really," Emilio replied, making a grimace that tried to be a smile. "People are so malicious it can even make one laugh." He had said that because he found Balli's laughter objectionable. "You can understand that a little respect is in order, since it does not amuse *us* that people talk this way about poor Amalia." That plural *us* expressed an attempt to disclaim any personal responsibility for what he was saying. At the same time, his voice had risen in the heat of his emotion. He would not let Balli take lightly a subject that was roiling him.

Stefano did not know how to react. In his entire life he had not often been wrongly accused. He felt as innocent as a newborn. The respect he felt and had always shown the

Brentani family, along with Amalia's homeliness, should have placed him above suspicion. He knew Emilio extremely well and did not believe he could get upset about a remark made by some aged relative. But he had discerned in Emilio's tone a violence, and something even stronger, hatred perhaps, that startled him. He immediately hit on the truth. For some time now, he reflected, all Emilio's thoughts, his whole existence, had been centered on Angiolina. Could the violence and hatred in Emilio's voice be attributed to his jealousy over Angiolina, even though he spoke only of Amalia?

"I did not think that at our age, mine, that is, and the signorina's, we could be thought capable of such silliness." He sounded embarrassed. The subject upset him as well.

"What can I say? People are like that . . . "

But Balli, who did not believe for a minute in those "people," replied angrily, "Forget it! I have already understood what this is all about. Let's talk about something else."

They remained silent for a while. Emilio was reluctant to speak for fear of compromising himself. What had Balli already understood? His own secret, his resentment, or rather, Amalia's secret? He looked at his friend and saw that he was more upset by his remarks than he could have imagined. Stefano's face was very flushed and his troubled blue eyes stared off into space. He suddenly looked hot, for he pushed his hat back in order to bare his high forehead. It was obvious that he was angry and that all of Emilio's subterfuges to conceal his rancor behind lofty family reasons had been futile.

Emilio was seized with the childish panic of losing his friend. If he broke off with both Angiolina and Balli, he would be unable to keep an eye on them and, sooner or later, they would surely get together. With this in mind he resolutely placed an affectionate hand on Balli's arm. "Listen,

Stefano. You must understand that if I spoke to you the way I did, I had to be motivated by compelling reasons. It is a great sacrifice for me to give up your frequent visits to my house." The fear of not arousing his friend's compassion aroused his own emotions.

Balli immediately calmed down: "I believe you," he said, "but I beg of you, don't ever mention your relative again. I find it very strange that you want to discuss serious matters with me and feel the need to tell me such lies. Now, talk to me honestly." Having recovered his equanimity, he felt a renewal of the friendly interest he had always taken in Emilio's affairs. What new misfortune was threatening that unfortunate man?

What a good friend Balli was! Emilio was ashamed of himself. He had been wrong to doubt him. He wanted to dispel whatever shadow his words had cast in his friend's heart. As for Amalia's secret, there was no hope of protecting it any longer. "I am very distressed," he declared, in the hope of heightening the sympathy he had already perceived in Balli's remarks. He did not mention his discovery that his sister was dreaming out loud about Stefano, but only spoke of the changes that took place in Amalia as soon as Balli crossed the threshold of their house. When he was not around, she seemed to be ailing, tired, distracted. Something had to be done to cure her.

Balli had only to hear a confession of this kind from Emilio's lips to believe it completely. He even suspected that Amalia had confided in her brother. At that moment she seemed uglier to him than ever before. The charm conferred on her ashen face by her presumed gentleness had vanished. Now she seemed aggressive to him, forgetful of her looks and her age. How incongruous passion would be on that face! Here was a second Angiolina come to disturb his habits, but an Angiolina that turned his stomach. His affectionate compassion for Emilio grew stronger, as Emilio had hoped it would. Poor devil! Now in addition he had a hysterical sister to look after.

It was he who apologized for being irascible. As always, he was sincere: "If not for this new circumstance, which I could never have guessed, this would have been the last time we saw each other. You understand, I thought that because of your fixation over Angiolina, you were unable to forgive me for the interest I aroused in her, and so you tried to find some pretext for quarreling with me."

Emilio suddenly felt very uneasy. Balli had just explicated to him the very essence of his wicked action. He protested so vehemently that Balli felt obliged to apologize for his suspicion, but in his own eyes his vehemence was a sham. For a moment his thoughts turned to Amalia: "How curious that Angiolina should be playing a part in his sister's destiny!" He consoled himself with the thought that in time he would make it up to her, first of all by making Balli understand what an admirable person Amalia really was, and then by lavishing his own affection to her.

But how was he going to give her proof of that affection in his present condition? That evening, like the preceding one, he sat motionless for a long time at the table on which he had expected to find a letter from Angiolina. He stared at the table as though his staring could make it produce the letter. His desire for Angiolina had grown more intense. Why? Even more than the day before, he felt how sad and pointless a game it was to stay away from her. Oh, adorable Angiolina! She gave no one reasons for remorse.

Later, when he heard from the next room the clear resonant voice of that other dreamer, his remorse became searing. What harm could have come from letting Amalia continue those innocent dreams that constituted all there was to her existence? The truth is that his remorse turned into boundless sympathy for himself, making him weep copiously, which in turn brought him great relief. So that night, remorse provided him with a good night's sleep.

nine

How superior Amalia was to him! She expressed surprise the following day when Balli did not appear, but with such indifference that it would have been hard to discern any trace of disappointment.

"Could he be sick?" she asked Emilio, and he recalled that whenever she spoke to him about Stefano it was always with great nonchalance.

He was nonetheless convinced that he had not been mistaken. "No," he replied, lacking the courage to say more. He was overcome with compassion at the thought that hanging over this fragile little creature was an imminent and unsuspected agony similar to the one he was experiencing. And it was he who was going to deliver the blow. It had already left his hand but was still suspended in midair; before long it would fall on that gray head with enough force to bow it. And that gentle face would lose the serenity it wore with such inconceivable stoicism. He would have liked to take his sister in his arms and begin consoling her before the pain began. But that he could not do. He could not even pronounce his friend's name without embarrassment. Between brother and sister there was now a barrier — Emilio's doing — but he was unaware of this. Once again he promised himself that he would be there for his sister when she needed to be consoled, as she surely would. Then, all he would have to do is open his arms. Of that, he was certain. Amalia was made of the same stuff as he, in that when she was unhappy, she would turn to anyone near her. And so, he let her wait for Balli to come.

Emilio would have found that kind of waiting intolerable. It took genuine heroism to ask nothing more than the usual: "Is Balli not coming?" A third glass stood on the table, set for Balli. It was immediately replaced in a corner of the cupboard that Amalia used as a sideboard. The glass was then followed by the cup intended for Balli's coffee, and once that too was replaced, Amalia locked the cupboard. She was extremely calm and moved very slowly. Only when she turned her back to him did he dare look at her carefully, and then his imagination led him to perceive suffering in every sign of physical weakness. Had her shoulders always drooped like that? Had her scrawny neck not grown thinner over the past few days?

She came back to the table and sat down beside him. "There!" he thought, "that composed look means she has decided to wait another twenty-four hours." How he admired her! He would not have been able to wait a single night.

"Why doesn't Signor Balli come here any more?" she asked the next day after putting the glass back.

"I think he doesn't find us entertaining enough," Emilio said after a brief hesitation, determined to say something that could make Amalia understand Balli's attitude. She did not seem to attribute much importance to this observation, and very attentively put the glass back in its habitual corner.

In the meanwhile, he had decided not to leave her hanging any longer. When he saw three coffee cups on the table instead of two, he said, "You can spare yourself the trouble of preparing coffee for Stefano. He will probably not be coming here for some time."

"Why?" she asked, holding the cup and turning ghastly pale.

He did not have the courage to speak the words he had

already prepared: "Because he doesn't want to." Was it not better to help her get over her delusion, thereby allowing her to gain gradual control of her pain, rather than force her to betray herself by confronting her with a revelation she was not yet ready to receive? He told her that he thought Balli could no longer come at that hour because he was working frenetically.

"Frenetically?" she repeated, turning to the cupboard. The cup fell from her hand without breaking. She picked it up, carefully cleaned it and put it back in its place. She then sat down beside Emilio. "Another twenty-four hours," he thought.

The next day Emilio could not prevent Balli from accompanying him to the door of his house. Stefano absently looked up at the first-floor windows but then quickly lowered his gaze. He must have seen Amalia in one of the windows, but he did not greet her! After a moment, Emilio also risked an upward glance, but if she had been at the window, she must have moved back. He wanted to reproach Stefano for not greeting her, but he had no way of verifying what had happened.

Deeply troubled, he went upstairs to Amalia. She had surely understood.

She was not in the kitchen. She came soon after, walking quickly, and stopped to fuss with the door, which would not stay closed. She appeared to have been crying. Her cheeks were red and her hair was wet. She had evidently rinsed her face to wipe away all trace of her tears. She asked him nothing, but all through the meal he constantly felt a question looming. Obviously agitated, she could not find the courage to speak. To explain his own agitation he told her that he had slept badly that night. Balli's glass and cup had not reappeared on the table. Amalia was no longer waiting.

But Emilio was. It would have been a relief for him to see her weep, hear some sound of her suffering. He would not have that satisfaction for some time. He came home every day primed for the pain of seeing her cry, hearing her confess her despair, but instead found her quiet, downtrodden, in perpetual slow motion, like someone worn out with fatigue. She took care of the house with what seemed to be her habitual meticulousness and talked to Emilio about it as in the past, when the two young siblings, once they were orphaned, had tried to improve their modest home.

It was a nightmare to face such mute sadness. And how dreadful that suffering must have been, doubtless aggravated by all kinds of suspicions. Emilio was afraid she might even manage to guess the truth; he felt threatened by the need to explain what he had done, which now seemed incredible even to him. At times her gray eyes cast a suspicious interrogating glance at him. Ah, those eyes did not flinch. They looked at things seriously and steadily, seeking the cause of so much pain. He could not stand it any more.

One evening when Balli was not free — he was probably with some woman — Emilio decided to stay home with his sister. But then he found it tedious to be near her in the silence that so often fell between them, condemned as they were to repress what was uppermost in their thoughts. He took his hat to go out.

"Where are you going?" she asked, absently tapping her plate with her fork while her head rested on her arm. That was enough to quell his courage to leave. He was being called to order. If together those hours were so painful, what was it like when Amalia was alone?

He put his hat back and said, "I wanted to take my despair out for a walk." The nightmare vanished. What an inspiration that had been: if he could not talk about her anguish, he could at least distract her with the tale of his own. She immediately stopped her tapping and turned to look him in the face to see what her anguish looked like on someone else.

"Poor dear," she murmured, seeing him pale, suffering, distressed for reasons she could not begin to fathom. Then, encouraging him to confide in her: "When did you see her last?"

With almost gleeful expansiveness, he began telling her. He had not seen her at all. When he was out, not wishing to be seen, that is, not stopping on those streets he knew she had to pass at certain hours, he nonetheless waited for her. But he never saw her. It almost seemed as though, ever since he left her, she avoided being seen around town.

"That may indeed be the case," Amalia said, wholly and devotedly intent on analyzing her brother's misfortune.

Emilio laughed out loud. He said Amalia had no idea what stuff Angiolina was made of. Eight days had passed since he had left her, and he was absolutely positive that he had been completely forgotten. "I beg of you, don't laugh at me," he asked, even though he saw that she was nowhere near laughing at him. "That's how she is." At that, he launched into a biography of Angiolina. He talked about her flightiness, her vanity, everything that contributed to his unhappiness. Amalia continued to listen to him silently without registering any surprise. Emilio thought she might be examining his emotions to discover analogies with her own.

In this way they spent an enjoyable quarter of an hour. It was as though everything that had separated them suddenly disappeared, or rather brought them together, for he had talked about Angiolina not to unburden himself of the love and desire that until then had made him chatter so volubly, but solely for his sister's pleasure. He felt deep affection for Amalia; it seemed to him that, listening to him, she had formally pardoned him.

His effusion led him to say something that made the evening end in a very different way. Having come to the end of his story, he asked without hesitating: "And what about you?" Not only had he not hesitated, he had not even taken the time to think. After resisting for so long the desire to ask his sister to confide in him, in that moment of abandon he gave in. He had experienced such relief from confiding in her, it seemed to him perfectly natural to invite Amalia to make similar confidences.

But Amalia did not see it that way. She looked at him with terror-stricken eyes. "I? I don't understand!" Even if she really had not understood, she could have guessed everything from the embarrassment written all over him on seeing her so dismayed. "You must be out of your mind!" She had understood, but was evidently unable to figure out how Emilio had managed to divine the secret she had been guarding so jealously.

"I was asking if you . . . " Emilio stammered, equally dismayed. He was searching for a lie, but in the meantime Amalia had found the most obvious explanation and came out with it in so many words.

"Signor Balli has talked to you about me!" she shouted. Her suffering had found words. Blood rushed to her face from the violence of her indignation and her mouth arched tensely. For a moment she became forceful. In this she was just like Emilio. One could understand how the conversion of her pain into fury had galvanized her. No longer was she a woman abandoned without a word; she was a woman scorned. But forcefulness was not in her nature and did not last long. Emilio swore that Balli had never talked about Amalia in any way to suggest that he thought she was in love with him. She did not believe him, but the shred of a doubt that he had raised in her mind undid her control, and she began to cry.

"Why doesn't he come here any more?"

"For no particular reason," Emilio said. "He will surely come in a few days."

"He will not come!" Amalia shouted, regaining in their exchange her earlier forcefulness. "He doesn't even greet me." Her sobbing prevented her from speaking in longer sentences. Emilio rushed over to embrace her, but his pity offended her. She rose brusquely, tearing herself loose, and ran to her room to calm herself. Her sobs turned into shrieks and, soon after, ended completely. When she came back, she was capable of speaking, except for an occasional suppressed sob. She had stopped in the doorway.

"I don't even know why I'm crying this way. The silliest thing can send me into this kind of frenzy. There must be something wrong with me. I did nothing that could have given that gentleman the right to behave as he has. You're sure of that, aren't you? Well then, that is enough for me! And besides, what could I possibly have done or said?"

She sat down and started to cry again, but more softly.

Clearly, Emilio's first obligation was to exonerate his friend, and he tried but failed. Being contradicted upset Amalia all the more.

"Let him come!" she cried. "If he doesn't want to see me, he doesn't have to. I won't let him see me."

Emilio thought he had hit on a good idea.

"You want to know the reason for the change in Balli's attitude? Someone asked him in my presence if he was getting engaged to you."

She looked at him uncertain whether to trust him. Nor did she fully understand, so that to ascertain the meaning of his words she repeated them: "Someone said to him that he was going to get engaged to me?" She burst into a loud laugh, but only with her voice. So he was afraid to be compromised and forced to marry her? But who could have put an idea like that in his head, a head that usually did not seem to be among the stupider ones? Was she a schoolgirl to fall hopelessly in love over a couple of words and a glance? She granted — her admirable willpower allowed her to go so far as to sound genuinely indifferent — that Balli's company was not displeasing to her, but she had not imagined it could be so dangerous. She wanted to laugh again, but broke into tears.

"I don't see any reason to cry about this," Emilio timidly remarked. He would now have liked to terminate the confidences that he had so thoughtlessly encouraged. Words did not heal Amalia; they only sharpened her pain. In this, she did not resemble him.

"I don't have any reason when I am treated this way? He flees as though I were running after him." Once again she raised her voice, but because of the effort immediately fell back exhausted. Emilio's words had come as a total surprise because, after so much time, she had still not found the right attitude to take. Once again she tried to attenuate the impression the scene must have made on Emilio.

"It's my weakness that causes my agitation," she said, taking her head in both her hands. "Haven't you already seen me cry for more trivial reasons?"

Without saying so to each other, each of them thought back to the evening when she had burst into tears simply because Angiolina was taking away her brother. They looked at each other gravely. That time, she thought, she really had cried over nothing, and precisely because then she had not yet experienced the irremediable heartbreak she was now suffering. He, on the other hand, saw how similar that scene was to this one, and felt a new burden weighing on his conscience. This evening was clearly the continuation of that earlier one.

Amalia had come to a conclusion. "Isn't it your duty to defend me? It seems to me that you can no longer be a friend to someone who has offended me for no reason."

"He hasn't offended you," Emilio protested.

"You can think what you like! But either he returns to this house or you have to turn your back on him. As for me, I promise you that he will find no change in my demeanor. I will make an effort to treat him differently from what he deserves."

Emilio had to admit that she was right and, not considering that the situation was important enough to break off relations with Balli, said he would make him understand that he was expected to be seen in their house once again.

Not even this satisfied the gentle Amalia.

"You consider an insult to your sister a bagatelle? You can behave however you like, but I too will do as I see fit." Her tone was icily threatening and contemptuous. "Tomorrow I will apply at the agency across the street for a position as a housekeeper or a servant." She spoke so coldly that the seriousness of her intention could not be doubted.

"Did I say I don't want to do what you want?" Emilio asked fearfully. "Tomorrow I will talk to Balli, and if he does not come home with me tomorrow, I will see him less often."

That "less often" did not go down well with Amalia. "Less often? As you like." She got up and, without saying good night, went into her room, where the candle that she had brought when she first sought refuge there was still burning.

Emilio thought she continued to be resentful because that made it easier for her to gain control of herself. The moment she relented enough to say a word of thanks or of simple agreement, she would become emotional all over again. He would have liked to go to her, but he surmised that she was getting undressed, and so from outside her door he wished her a good night. She replied with cold indifference in a barely audible voice.

Amalia was right, in fact. Balli had to come to the house at least once in a while. The sudden cessation of visits was indeed insulting. Clearly, to help Amalia recover, it was first of all necessary to eradicate the insult. He went out in the hope of finding Balli.

He had no sooner stepped outside the door than he was faced with the most powerful distraction. By an uncanny coincidence, he walked right into Angiolina. How quickly his sister, Balli, his own remorse vanished from his thoughts! He was was amazed to discover that in those few days, he had forgotten how the color of her hair gilded her whole face, how blue those eyes were that now looked at him questioningly. He greeted her curtly: for all that he wanted his greeting to be cool, it turned out brusque. At the same time, he looked at her in a way that might have frightened her had she had not been so surprised and upset.

Yes, she was upset. She returned his greeting, confused and blushing. Her mother was with her, and after a few steps, she turned toward her in order to look back at the same time. He understood from her glance that she was expecting him to accost her, which was precisely what gave him the courage to accelerate his pace and go right by them.

He walked for some time with no destination, just to calm himself. Perhaps Amalia had seen clearly and his rupture with Angiolina had been a severe lesson for her. Perhaps she loved him now! As he walked, he had the most wonderful daydream. She loved him, she ran after him, she clung to him, yet he continued to flee her, to rebuff her. What balm to his emotions!

When he came back to reality, the memory of his sister aggrieved him once more. In those few days his life had become so sad that the thought of Angiolina, until then a source of anguish for him, was now a not entirely enjoyable refuge from the knowledge that he had embittered his sister's life.

That evening he did not find Balli. Late in the evening he came across Sorniani, who was coming from the theater. After greeting him, Sorniani immediately began telling him that he had seen Angiolina and her mother in the first balcony. She was absolutely stunning, in a yellow silk gown and a small hat, of which one saw only two or three large roses in the gold of her hair. It was the first performance of *The Walkyrie*, and Sorniani was surprised that Emilio, known for having written on avant-garde music in the past — what had he not done in his lifetime? — had not been there to see it.

Confused and upset as she had appeared, she had nonetheless gone off to the theater, and with rather expensive tickets. Heaven only knew who paid for them! Another utterly vain dream.

He told Sorniani that the following evening he too would be going to the Communale, although he had no such intention. He had lost his only chance to go to the opera when it might have given him pleasure. Angiolina would not have gone the following evening even if her ticket were paid a second time. Wagner and Angiolina! It was amazing enough that they had met even once.

He spent a sleepless night. He was restless and could not find a position comfortable enough to lie still. To calm himself he got out of bed, remembering that he might find some diversion in his sister's room. But Amalia no longer dreamed; she had even lost her happy dreams. A number of times he heard her turn in her bed, apparently as uncomfortable for her as his for him.

Toward morning, she heard him at the door of her room and asked what he wanted.

He had gone back there hoping to hear her talk in her sleep and learn if at least once in twenty-four hours she derived some kind of pleasure.

"Nothing," he replied, disappointed to hear that she was awake. "I thought I heard you moving and I wanted to know if you needed something."

"I don't need anything," she answered gently. "Thank you, Emilio."

He felt that he had been forgiven, and experienced such sweet, such intense atonement that tears came to his eyes.

"Why aren't you sleeping?" he asked.

The moment was so joyful he wanted to savor it, to prolong it and intensify it by communicating to his sister his own troubled emotions.

"I just woke up. What about you?"

"I have been sleeping very badly for some time now," he replied, still assuming that it was a consolation for Amalia to know how tormented he also was. Then, remembering his exchange with Sorniani, he announced that for distraction he had decided to see *The Walkyrie*. "Would you join me?"

"With pleasure," she replied. "So long as it doesn't cost you too much."

Emilio insisted. "It's not that often." His teeth were chattering from the cold, but he had found such contentment on that spot that he was reluctant to leave it.

"Are you in your nightshirt?" she asked, and hearing that he was, ordered him back to bed.

He went reluctantly, but once there, he immediately found the position he had been seeking all night long and slept uninterruptedly for a few hours.

With Balli there was no problem reaching an understanding. In the morning Emilio found him walking behind the dogcatcher's wagon, all upset over the fate of those pitiful creatures. He was genuinely moved, but the reason he went in search of such emotions—so he said—was because his fondness for animals heightened his artistic sensibility. He paid little attention to what Emilio was saying, his ears deafened by the howling of the dogs—the most excruciating sound in all of nature when caused by pain as unexpected as that of a sudden constriction around the neck. "You can hear in it the fear of death," Balli said, "and at the same time, an immense, powerless indignation."

Emilio bitterly remembered that Amalia's lamentations also conveyed surprise and immense powerless indignation. The presence of the dogcatcher facilitated his purpose. Balli heard him distractedly and declared he had no objection to coming to his house that very day.

Only when he came for Emilio at his office at noon did he begin having a few vague doubts about his decision. He was already convinced that Amalia had confided to her brother that she was in love with him, and that Emilio had thought it wise to keep him away from the house. Now, however, Emilio wanted him to return because Amalia did not understand why he had made himself scarce. "It must be to save face," he thought with his habit of finding an easy explanation for everything.

They were already on their way to the house when

another question occurred to Stefano: "What if your sister bears me a grudge?"

Emilio, secure in the assurances his sister had given him, reassured him. "You will be welcomed as in the past."

Balli said nothing. But now he would behave differently so as not to delude her and find himself once again the object of her unwanted affections.

Amalia was prepared for everything but that. She had planned to be friendly but cool, and here it was he who was setting the tone of their relations. She had no choice but to acquiesce and passively follow his lead; she could not even betray any resentment. He treated her like some young lady he had just met, with all the requisite courtesy and the most respectful indifference. Gone were the sparkling monologues in which Balli let himself go completely, revealing how much higher he esteemed himself than anyone around him, and with such unbridled immodesty that he could only enjoy the company of people totally devoted to him, since the mere suggestion of irony left him speechless and breathless. That day he did not talk about himself at all, but about other things instead, and at that laconically. In her surprise at his remoteness, Amalia barely listened. He told them how bored he had been at the performance of *The Walkyrie*, where half the audience tried to make the other half think they were enjoying it. Then he talked about the boredom of that interminable carnival season with still a month to go. In the light of all the boredom around him, he began yawning repeatedly. Naturally, transformed like that, he too was boring. Where was the wonderful vivacity that Amalia had enjoyed so much because it had seemed expressly intended for her pleasure?

Emilio sensed that his sister must be suffering and tried to encourage some sign of interest on Stefano's part. He talked about Amalia's unhealthy pallor and threatened to call Doctor Carini if her color did not improve soon. Doctor Carini, a friend of Balli's, was mentioned for the express purpose of prompting Stefano to comment on Amalia's health as well. But Stefano, with childish stubbornness, made a point of not contributing to the subject, and Amalia responded to her brother's affectionate words with a brusque remark. She felt the need to be brusque with someone and could not with Balli. Soon after, she went to her room and left them alone.

Outside, Emilio returned to the subject of his ill-conceived remarks, trying to explain them and to absolve Amalia of any involvement. He admitted that he had been irresponsible. He had surely been mistaken about Amalia's feelings and gave his word of honor that she had never said a word in that regard. Balli pretended to believe him, declaring it was, in any case, useless to go over that subject again since he had long ago forgotten about it. As usual, he was very pleased with himself. He had behaved as was necessary to restore Amalia's serenity and to avert any trouble with his friend. Emilio said no more, seeing that he was wasting his breath.

That same evening, brother and sister went to the opera, Emilio hoping that this unusual distraction would be all the more distracting for his sister.

But not at all! Her eyes did not brighten once during the performance. She hardly saw the audience. Her thoughts were so concentrated on the injustice done her that she was unable to notice all those lively, elegant women who, at other times, had interested her so much that merely talking about them gave her pleasure. Whenever the opportunity arose, she had always asked for a description of their attire, whereas now, she did not even look at them.

A certain Signora Birlini, a wealthy lady who had been a

friend of Amalia's mother, sitting in a nearby box, recognized Amalia and greeted her. In the past, Amalia had taken pride in the affection shown her by a few wealthy ladies. Now, it was with effort that she managed a smile to respond to the warmth communicated to her, and she quickly lost all interest in the blonde woman who had obviously been pleased to see Amalia present at the performance.

But Amalia was not present. She let herself be lulled in her thoughts by that strange music whose details escaped her but whose boldness and power felt threatening to her. Emilio distracted her from her thoughts for a moment by asking her how she liked a motif that kept recurring in the orchestra.

"I don't understand," she replied.

As it happened, she had not heard a note of it. But once absorbed by the music, her terrible heartache took on new color and greater significance, all the while becoming simpler, purer, because it was now cleansed of all humiliation. Small and weak, she had been overcome; who could have expected her to fight back? Never before had she felt so much at peace, so free of anger and so inclined to weep copiously but without sobbing. Since she could not do so, her relief remained incomplete. She was wrong to have said that she had not understood the music. That magnificent resonant wave expressed all of human destiny. She watched it rush down the incline, guided by the various levels of the floor. At times it was only a single cascade, at others it was broken into a thousand smaller ones, all of them tinted by the variegated lights and reflections; a harmony of colors and sounds that held the epic destiny of Sieglinde, but hers as well, petty as it was, the end of one stage of life, the withering of a bud. Her destiny deserved no more tears than anyone else's, only as many, and the ridicule that had suffocated her had no place in that expression, however all-inclusive it was.

Emilio was intimately familiar with the genesis of those sounds, but he could not get as close to them as Amalia did. He believed that his love and his pain would soon be transformed into artistic genius. Not so. For him, heroes and gods were moving across the stage, and they were taking him far away from the world in which he had suffered. During the intermissions he searched vainly in his memory for what could have warranted such a change. Was it perhaps that art was healing him?

When he left the theater at the end of the performance, he was so excited by this hope that he did not notice how much more depressed his sister was than usual. Deeply inhaling the cold night air, he said that the evening had done him a lot of good. But while he was describing with his habitual verbosity the strange peace that had pervaded him, a profound sadness came over him. Art had given him no more than a brief respite, and would be unable to repeat it, because now, certain fragments of the music had adapted themselves perfectly to certain of his own emotions; if nothing else, to his compassion for himself, for Angiolina, for Amalia.

In the excitement of the moment, he would have liked to regain his composure and extract new confidences from Amalia. He was forced to recognize that their mutual confessions had been useless. She continued to suffer mutely, not even admitting that she had ever allowed him to suspect anything. Their pain, however similar its origin, clearly did not bring them any closer together.

One day, he chanced to see her out for a stroll, walking slowly, in the middle of the afternoon. She was wearing a dress she had probably not worn in ages, for Emilio had never seen it. It was made of a stiff fabric, in shades of light blue, that puffed out her emaciated little body.

She was startled to see him and was ready to follow him

home. What sorrow could have driven her to seek diversion in that stroll! He could easily commiserate, remembering how often his own frustrations had also driven him out of the house. But what insane hope could have prompted her to put on an outfit like that? He was firmly convinced that dressed like that, she had hoped to please Balli. How could Amalia have had such an idea? In any case, if she ever really did, it was the first and the last time, for she then went back to her usual attire — gray, like her face and her fate.

ten

His pain, like his remorse, grew fainter and fainter. The components of his life remained the same, but they had become muted, as though seen through an opaque lens that deprived them of light and intensity. A heavy serenity and a heavy lassitude fell over him. He could see quite lucidly how grotesque his exaggerated emotions had become, and so with apparent sincerity he reported to Balli, who had been watching him with considerable anxiety: "I am cured."

The assumption was not unreasonable, since he could not remember with any degree of accuracy what his state of mind had been before knowing Angiolina. The difference was so minimal! He had yawned less and had not experienced the pained embarrassment that afflicted him in Amalia's presence.

The weather, moreover, was dismal. For weeks, not a ray of sun had been seen, so that in his thoughts of Angiolina, her lovely face and the glowing tints of her blond hair became associated with an azure sky and brilliant sunlight — all of which had disappeared from his life at the same time. He had nonetheless come to the conclusion that his separation from Angiolina was very salutary for him. "It is better to be free," he said with conviction.

He also tried to put to good use his newly acquired freedom. He felt, and regretted, that he was inactive, and remembered how years before, art had animated his life, keeping him from the inertia that he fell into after his father's death. He had written his novel, the story of a young artist whose health and talent had been ruined by a woman. In the young man he had portrayed himself, his innocence and his gentleness. He had imagined his heroine in the style of the time: part woman, part tigress. Of the feline, she had the movements, the eyes, and the sanguinary temperament. Although he had never had an intimate relationship with a woman, that was how he envisioned her. No animal as complicated as that could have been born and survived. But with what conviction he had described her! He experienced her pain and her joy, feeling at times in himself that same hybrid mix of tiger and female.

He took up his pen again and in a single evening wrote the first chapter of a novel. He was on a new artistic path that he wanted to follow: he was writing truth. He recounted his meeting with Angiolina, described his own feelings — starting with the most recent ones, violent and irate — his first impression of Angiolina spoiled by her base and perverse soul, and finally, the magnificent landscape that had surrounded the prelude of their idyll. Tired and irritated, he stopped working, satisfied to have set down a whole chapter in one sitting.

The next evening he went back to work, having in mind a few ideas that should have been enough for a string of pages. First, however, he reread what he had written: "Amazing!" he murmured. The man bore no resemblance to him whatever, and the woman retained something of the woman-tigress of his first novel without her vitality. He realized that the truth he was attempting to relate was less credible than the dreams he had fabricated as reality. At that moment he felt despairingly sluggish and was overcome with anguish. He put down his pen, shoved everything into a drawer, and told himself that he would begin again later, perhaps even the very next day. That was enough to quiet him, but he never returned to his manuscript. He wanted to spare himself the pain; he lacked the courage to examine his own inaptitude and try to overcome it. He could no longer think with a pen in hand. Whenever he felt like writing, his brain seemed to atrophy; he would stare at the blank page as in a trance while the ink dried on his pen.

A desire to see Angiolina again took hold of him. He did not decide to go and find her; he merely told himself that now there would be no danger in seeing her again. Quite the contrary. If he wanted to keep to the precise words he had said to her when he left her, he should go to her at once. Was he not secure enough to shake her hand like a friend?

He communicated his thoughts to Balli, in these words: "I would merely like to see whether I could be in better control of myself if I started up with her again."

Balli had too often made fun of Emilio's passion not to believe now in his complete recovery. Moreover, for the past few days he himself had felt a keen desire to see Angiolina again. He had conceived of a figure with her traits and her style of dress. He told Emilio about it and Emilio promised that with his first words to her, he would ask her to pose for him. There was no doubt about his recovery. By then, he was not even jealous of Balli any more.

It turned out that Balli had been thinking about Angiolina no less than Emilio himself. He had been forced to destroy a cast on which he had worked for six months. He too was in a fallow period and could find no other idea than the one that had struck him when Emilio first introduced him to Angiolina. One evening, as he was leaving Emilio, he asked: "You still haven't approached her?" He did not want to be the one to reconcile them, but he did want to know if Emilio had renewed acquaintance with Angiolina without informing him. That, he would have considered treachery!

Emilio's stability continued to grow. Everybody was encouraging him to do what he wanted, but as it happened, he wanted nothing. Absolutely nothing. He would have gone back to Angiolina just to see if he could talk and think with fervor. The animation he could not find in himself had to come from without; his hope was to live the novel he had been unable to write.

Inertia kept him from going to see her. He would have liked someone else to make the effort of reconciling them; he even thought of asking Balli to do so. How much simpler and easier everything would have been if Balli had found his model on his own and had then passed her on to Emilio as his mistress. That was something to think about. He hesitated only because he did not want Balli to play too important a role in his life.

Important? Oh, Angiolina was still very important to him. If for no other reason, when compared to the rest: everything else was so meaningless that she towered over it all. He thought of her constantly, the way an old man thinks of his youth. How young he had been that night when, to regain his sanity, he would have had to commit murder! If he had sat down to write instead of flinging himself into the streets and then, just as fruitlessly, into his lonely bed, he would certainly have found the path of art that he later sought in vain. Now it was all gone forever. Angiolina was still alive, but she could no longer restore his youth.

One evening, near the Public Gardens, he saw her walking in front of him. He recognized her by her gait. She was holding up her skirts to protect them from the mud, and in the dim light of a street lamp he saw the gleam of her black patent leather boots. He was instantly stirred. He remembered how at the end of his amorous anguish he had thought, if only he could possess that woman, he would be healed. Now, instead, he thought, "I would be revived!"

"Good evening, signorina," he said with as much composure as he could muster, given the palpitating desire aroused by that pink baby face and those huge eyes with their sharply defined contours that seemed freshly chiseled.

She stopped, took the hand that had been extended to her, and replied cheerily and naturally to his greeting: "How are you? It's been a long time since we last saw each other."

He replied, but was distracted by his own thoughts. Perhaps he had been mistaken to appear so composed, and worse still, not to have thought about how to behave in order to get where he wanted without delay — to the truth, to possession. He walked beside her holding her hand, but after that initial exchange between people who are pleased to have met, he remained silent and hesitant. His completely sincere elegiac tone of the past would be out of place now, but excessive indifference would also keep him from attaining his goal.

"Have you forgiven me, signor Emilio?" she asked, stopping to take his other hand as well. The impulse was superb and the gesture most unusual for Angiolina.

What he found to say was: "You know what I will never forgive you? The fact that you made no attempt to get in touch with me. Is that how little I meant to you?" He was sincere, having realized that his attempt at play-acting was pointless. Sincerity might be more effective than pretense.

Stammering in her embarrassment, she assured him that she had planned to write to him tomorrow. "But, then, what have I done?" She did not remember that she had just apologized a moment before.

Emilio thought it opportune to appear dubious. "Am I

supposed to believe you?" Then he added, reprovingly, "With an umbrella vendor!"

The words made them both burst into laughter. "Jealous!" she exclaimed, squeezing the hand she was still holding, "jealous of that awful man!" If indeed he was right to have broken off with Angiolina, he was certainly wrong to use that stupid story of the umbrella vendor as a pretext. The umbrella vendor was not the most formidable of his rivals. And for that reason, he had the strange feeling that he could only blame himself for all the misery that had befallen him since his rupture with Angiolina.

She remained silent for a long time. It could not have been intentional, because that would have been too subtle a gambit for Angiolina. She was silent because she probably could not find anything else to say in her defense. And so, they continued to walk in silence side by side in that strange, dark night, under a cloud-covered sky, blanched in one spot by a ray of moonlight.

They arrived at Angiolina's house and she stopped, presumably to take leave of him. But he persuaded her to go on: "Let's keep walking, just like this, without talking." As might be expected, she granted his wish and continued to walk beside him in silence. And he fell in love with her all over again, as of that moment, or rather, as of that moment, he became aware of it. The woman walking beside him was the one his interrupted dream had ennobled, ennobled also by the cry he had torn from her when he left her, which for so long had entirely personified her, ennobled by art as well, since at that point his desire made Emilio feel that a goddess walked beside him, capable of the noblest sounds and words.

Past Angiolina's house, they found themselves on a dark and deserted street closed off on one side by a hill and on the other by a low wall that bordered the fields. She sat down on it and he leaned against her, trying to recapture the position he had enjoyed so much in the past, during the early days of their love. Only the sea was missing. In the humid gray landscape around them, Angiolina's blondeness shone radiantly, the only warm, bright note.

It had been so long since he felt those warm lips against his own that his reaction was overwhelming. "Oh, my dear sweet darling!" he murmured kissing her eyes, her neck, and then, her hand, her clothing. She graciously let him go on, and her graciousness was so unusual that he was moved, first to tears, then to sobs. It seemed to him that it was only up to him to prolong such happiness for the rest of his life. Everything was resolved, everything was explained. His life could no longer hold anything but that one desire.

"You really love me that much?" she murmured, moved and astonished. She too had tears in her eyes. She told him that she had seen him in the street, pale and downcast, his face lined with his obvious suffering, and her heart had clenched in compassion. "Why didn't you come sooner?" she asked him reprovingly.

She leaned against him in order to step down from the wall. He did not understand why she was truncating that delicious reconciliation which he would have liked to prolong indefinitely.

"Let's go to my house," she said resolutely.

Reeling with excitement, he hugged her and kissed her, not knowing how to show her his gratitude. But Angiolina's house was far away, and as they walked, Emilio was back to his old self, with his doubts and his diffidence. What if that moment bound him forever to that woman? Slowly climbing the stairs, he abruptly asked, "What about Volpini?"

She hesitated and stopped. "Volpini?" Resolutely, she descended the few stairs that separated her from Emilio.

She came up close to him, buried her face in his shoulder with an affectation of modesty that reminded him of the old Angiolina and her melodramatic seriousness, and said to him: "Nobody knows, not even my mother." One by one, all the old tricks reappeared, her dear mother included. She had given herself to Volpini because he had insisted, had made it a condition for continuing their relationship. "He sensed that I didn't love him," she whispered, "and wanted me to prove that I did." In recompense, she had received no guarantee other than the promise of marriage. With her usual indiscretion, she mentioned the name of a young lawyer who had advised her to content herself with the promise, because in a situation like that, seduction was punishable by law.

Thus entwined, they never seemed to reach the top of the stairs. Every stair made Angiolina more like the woman he had fled. Now she was finally talking and yielding. Now at last she could be his because — as was being said over and over again — it was for him that she had submitted to the tailor. He could never escape that responsibility even if he left her.

She opened the door and directed him through the dark hallway to her room. From another room could be heard the nasal voice of her mother: "Angiolina, is that you?"

"Yes," she answered, suppressing a chuckle. "I'm going right to bed. Good night, mama."

She lit a candle and took off her cape and hat. Then she gave herself to him, or more precisely, she took him.

Emilio discovered the significance of possessing a woman long desired. During that memorable evening the deepest part of his being seemed to have undergone two mutations. The disconsolate inertia that had driven him to find Angiolina again had vanished. But also vanished was the fervor that had made him sob with both happiness and sadness. The male in him was now satisfied, but other than that, he really felt nothing. The woman he had possessed was the woman he despised, not the one he loved. Ah, the liar! This was not the first nor — as she tried to make him think — the second time she was in bed with a man. There was no point to getting upset about it since he had always known it. But the fact of possessing her had extended his powers of judgment over this woman who had yielded to him. "I will never dream again," he said to himself as he left the house. And a moment later, looking back at the house illumined by the pale rays of the moon: "I may never come here again." It was not a decision. Why make one? It was all too unimportant.

She had accompanied him as far as the outside door of the house. She had not noticed his coolness because he would have been mortified to betray any. Quite the contrary, out of consideration, he had asked to meet her the following evening, but she had to refuse because she was going to be busy all day until late in the evening with Signora Deluigi, who had asked her to make a ball gown for her. They agreed to meet two days later: "But not in this house," Angiolina said, quickly flushing with anger. "How could you even imagine such a thing? I have no desire to expose myself to the risk of being killed by my father." Emilio promised that he would find a room for their next tryst. He would leave a note for her the next day telling her where.

Possession? Truth? The lie was continuing as shamelessly as before and he found no way of extricating himself. In their last kiss, she sweetly begged him to be discreet, particularly with Balli. Her reputation was important to her.

With Balli, Emilio was indiscreet at once, that very evening. His indiscretion was motivated by his determination to react to Angiolina's lies. He ignored her plea, surely intended to fool him rather than keep others in the dark.

Furthermore, it gave him great satisfaction to be able to tell Balli that he had possessed that woman. It was a profound satisfaction, an important one; it cleared all the clouds from his mind.

Balli listened to him like a doctor reaching a diagnosis: "I think I can be quite certain about your recovery."

At that moment, however, Emilio felt a need to confide and told him about the indignation that Angiolina provoked in him: she was still trying to make him believe that she had given herself to Volpini in order to be his. His tone suddenly grew too impassioned: "She is trying to deceive me even now. It pains me so much to find her always the same that I lose any desire to see her again."

Balli saw right through him. "You too are always the same. Not a word you say suggests indifference." Emilio protested energetically, but Balli remained unconvinced. "You made a mistake, a big mistake, to have taken up with her again."

During the night Emilio came to the conclusion that Balli was right. His indignation, a frustrated anger that needed to vent itself, kept him awake. He could no longer delude himself into believing that this was the indignation of a decent man offended by an indecency. He knew only too well that state of mind: he had fallen back into it, and it was just like the one he had experienced before the episode of the umbrella vendor and before the possession. Youth restored! He no longer dreamed of murder, but his shame and his torment made him wish he could annihilate himself.

Added to his old torment was the weight of his conscience, remorse that he had bound himself all the more to that woman, and fear that his own life would be compromised. How else to explain the tenacity with which she held him responsible for her relations with Volpini, if not an intention to hook him, compromise him, suck out the little blood he had in his veins? He was bound forever to Angiolina by the aberration of his own emotions, his senses—in his lonely bed, his desire was reawakened—and by the very indignation that he attributed to loathing.

That indignation was the origin of his sweetest dreams. Toward morning his profound distress had turned into a concern for his own destiny. He did not fall asleep, but rather lapsed into a strange state of apathy that left him with no notion of time or place. He imagined he was sick, seriously sick, incurably so, and Angiolina came to take care of him. She seemed to have the composure and sobriety of a good nurse, gentle and dispassionate. He heard her move in the room, and every time she came close to him, she brought him cooling relief, touching his burning forehead with a cool hand, or kissing him on the eyes and on the brow with delicate kisses that were meant to be imperceptible. Did Angiolina know how to kiss like that? He turned heavily in bed and came to. True possession would be the realization of that dream. And only a few hours earlier he thought he had lost the capacity to dream. Youth had returned. It was flowing through his veins more potently than ever, and rescinded whatever resolution his senile mind had made.

He got up early and went out. He could not wait. He had to see Angiolina right away. In his impatience, he ran to hold her in his arms again and instructed himself not to talk too much. He did not want to demean himself by making declarations that would give a wrong idea of their relationship. Possession did not confer truth. But possession itself, unembellished by dreams or words, was the truth, pure and carnal.

Instead, Angiolina, with admirable determination,

wanted no part of it. She was already dressed to go out and, what was more, had already told him she did not intend to dishonor her home.

In the meantime, he observed something that made him deviate from his own intentions. He became aware that she was scrutinizing him, curious to see whether his love for her had been increased or diminished by his possession of her. She betrayed herself with an ingenuousness that was touching; she must have known men who were repelled by the woman they had slept with. It was easy for him to show her that he was not one of them. Resigned to the fasting she imposed on him, he had to make do with the kisses that had nourished him in the past. But before long, kisses were not enough and he found himself murmuring into her ear all the tender words he had learned during his long-suffering heartache: "*Ange!* My angel!"

Balli had given him the address of a house where they rented out rooms. He told her about it. So as not to make a mistake, she made him accurately describe the house and the exact placement of the room, which caused him no little embarrassment, since he had never seen it. He had been too engrossed in his kisses to be observant, but once on the street he realized, to his astonishment, that it was only then that he knew exactly where he had to go to find that room. There was no doubt about it! It was Angiolina who had given him directions.

He went there directly. The owner of the room was named Paracci, a repulsive hag wearing filthy garments, under which could be discerned a generous bosom, a vestige of youth amidst a flaccid old age, her head sparsely covered with a few strands through which a porous red scalp shone. She welcomed him with extreme courtesy and, instantly striking a bargain, told him that she rented only to people she knew well, therefore to him.

He wanted to see the room. Followed by the crone, he entered through the door on the stairs. Another door, always kept closed—this the Paracci woman declared as though swearing an oath—connected it with the rest of the apartment. Rather than furnished, it was cluttered with a huge bed, seemingly clean, two large armoires, a table in the middle, a sofa and four chairs. There would not have been space for one more stick of furniture.

The widow Paracci stood there looking at him, her hands on her ample flaring hips, a smile on her face—an ugly grimace that exposed her toothless mouth—like someone awaiting a compliment. Indeed, there was in the room an apparent effort at decoration. At the head of the bed stood a Chinese parasol, and on the wall—there too!—were assorted photographs.

A cry of surprise escaped his lips on seeing alongside the photograph of a half-nude woman, a girl he had known, a friend of Amalia's, who had died some years before. He asked the crone where she had found those photographs, and she replied that she had bought them to decorate the wall. He stared fixedly at the gentle face of that poor girl who had posed so stiffly before the camera, perhaps the only time in her life, to become an ornament for that sordid room.

Nevertheless, in that sordid room, in the presence of that squalid old hag who was looking at him, delighted to have acquired a new client, love flooded his thoughts. It was precisely such an environment that made it all the more exciting to envision Angiolina arriving there to offer him the love he longed for. With a fevered thrill he thought, "Tomorrow I will have the woman I desire!"

He had her, but never had he loved her less than that day. His anticipation had worried him; he thought he would be incapable of any pleasure. About an hour before leaving for the appointment, he decided that if he did not find the pleasure he expected, he would inform Angiolina that he no longer wished to see her, and with the specific words: "You are so dishonest you revolt me." The words had come to him as he looked enviously at Amalia because he saw her as unhappy but serene. And it occurred to him that for Amalia love still held the grandeur and purity of divine desire; whereas once gratified, petty human nature became ugly and demeaned.

But that evening, he was satisfied. Angiolina had kept him waiting more than half an hour — a century. He thought he felt nothing but anger, an impotent anger that augmented the loathing he claimed she provoked in him. He thought he would slap her when she showed up. No excuses were possible since she herself had told him that she was not going to work that day and would therefore be on time. Was it not because of her certainty that she would not be late that she had not wanted to make an appointment for the previous evening? And now she had made him wait, first an entire day, and then so many minutes.

But once she arrived, he marveled at his good luck, having despaired of ever seeing her again. He whispered reproaches against her lips and her neck which she did not bother to contest, since they sounded like a prayer, an adoration. In the half-light, the widow Paracci's room was transformed into a temple. For a long time not a word broke into the dream. Angiolina gave far more than she had promised. She had unpinned her long hair and he found himself on a pillow of gold. Like a child, he pressed his head into it to smell the color. She was an obliging partner — on that bed he found no cause for complaint — and sensed with remarkable intuition what he wanted. There, everything turned into gratification and delight.

Only a short while later, however, the memory of that scene made him grit his teeth with fury. For a moment passion had freed him from his confining costume of observer, but had not prevented his memory from engraving every detail of that scene. Now he could he say that he really knew Angiolina. Their lovemaking had left him with indelible memories, on the basis of which he could reconstruct what Angiolina had not expressed but, on the contrary, had studiously concealed. With cold reason alone he could not have made the deduction. Now, however, he knew, with indisputable certainty, as though she had told him so herself, that she had known other men who had given her greater pleasure. A number of times she had said, "Enough now. I can't any more." She had tried to sound admiring but had not succeeded. He could divide the evening into two parts. During the first she had made love to him; during the second she had forced herself not to push him away. When she left the bed she could not conceal her impatience with being there. And so, naturally — it did not take unusual powers of observation to see through her — seeing his reluctance, she pushed him out of bed, playfully telling him, "Let's go, my great big lover." Big lover! The ironic words must have been in her mind for a good half-hour. He had read them on her face.

As always, he needed to be alone in order to sort out his observations. For the moment, he could see that she no longer belonged to him. It was the same kind of awareness as that evening with Angiolina in the Public Gardens while they were waiting for Balli and Margherita — an excruciating sensation of wounded pride and unbearable jealousy. He wanted to be rid of her but could not leave her without having first tried to win her over again.

He accompanied her to the street and then, despite her insistence that she was in a hurry, persuaded her to return home by the route he had taken the evening she had been seen with the umbrella vendor. Via Romagna was exactly the same as it had been that unforgettable night, its bare trees silhouetted against a moonlit sky, the ground thickly carpeted with mud. The one great difference was having Angiolina beside him. But she as so far away! For the second time, on that same street, he looked for her.

He described to her the way he had torn through those streets. He told her how his desperation to see her had made her appear to him a number of times, how a slight injury from a fall had made him cry, because that was the drop that had made the cup run over. She listened to him, flattered to have inspired so great a passion, and when he became emotional, lamenting that all his suffering had still not granted him as much love as he felt he deserved, she protested vehemently, "How can you say such a thing?" She kissed him to clinch her protest. But she then made a mistake, as she always did when she had second thoughts: "Didn't I give myself to Volpini in order to be yours?" And Emilio lowered his head in conviction.

Volpini, without knowing it, was only poisoning the pleasures that, according to Angiolina, he had procured for him. Instead of anguishing over Angiolina's indifference, after hearing the mention of Volpini, Emilio became fearful of her and the plans he suspected her of making. At their next meeting, his first words were to ask what guarantees she had received in exchange for her submission to Volpini. "Oh. Volpini can't do without me," she said with a smile. For a moment even Emilio was reassured, convinced that a guarantee like that was good enough. He himself, far younger than Volpini, could not do without Angiolina.

During their second tryst in the widow's room, the observer in him was not distracted for a second. His reward was a dreadful discovery: during the time that he had exercised so much effort to stay away from Angiolina, someone had taken his place, someone who did not seem like any of the men he knew and distrusted. It was not Leardi, or Giustini, or Datti. Someone who taught her new mannerisms: coarse language, amusing at times, vulgar puns. It must have been a student, because she handled with considerable aplomb a few Latin words given obscene meanings. It was not that unfortunate Merighi, who could surely could not guess that he was still being exploited; according to her, he was the one who had taught her even those few words of Latin. As though she were capable of knowing any Latin and not showing it off until then! No, the one who taught her Latin had to be the same one who also taught her those bawdy Venetian songs. She sang them out of tune, but just to know them by heart she must have heard them many times over, in view of the fact that she was unable to reproduce a single note of Balli's ditties, which she had heard more than once. It had to be a Venetian, because a number of times she prided herself on imitating the Venetian accent, which, presumably, she had not known earlier.

Emilio felt him close by, that mocking voluptuary. Up to a certain point he had managed to re-create him, then he lost him and never managed to discover his name. Among Angiolina's photographs there was not one new face. This new rival evidently did not make a habit of giving away his portrait, or perhaps Angiolina thought it more politic not to hang up any more photographs, which she had been collecting all her life, since not even Emilio's had been added to the wall.

He was absolutely positive that if he were to come across that individual, he would recognize him from certain gestures that she had surely learned from him. The worst part of it was that merely from his repeated query regarding where she had learned a given gesture or expression, she could surmise his jealousy: "You're jealous!" she would say with remarkable perception, seeing him serious and quiet. Yes, he was jealous. He suffered when, in a moment of indecision, she ran her hands through her hair as a man would, or in surprise, would exclaim, "Thar she blows!" or, seeing him downcast would ask, "Are you *poisoned* today?" He suffered as though he were face to face with his elusive rival. Worse still, with a lover's overheated imagination, he thought he heard reproduced in Angiolina's voice certain ponderous and imperious tones that came from Leardi. Sorniani too must have taught her something, and even Balli had left traces of himself, in her faithful mimicry of his characteristic affectation of stunned surprise or admiration. As for himself, he did not recognize himself in any of her expressions or gestures. With bitter irony he thought, "Perhaps for me there is no more room."

His most hated rival remained the one he could not discover. It was strange that she made a point of not naming the man who must have been in her life only recently, whereas she normally delighted in boasting about her triumphs, even to the admiring glances she caught in the eyes of men who crossed her path only once in the street. All of them were madly in love with her. "I am all the more to be commended," she asserted, "for having stayed home the whole time you remained away, especially considering the way you treated me."

Sure! She wanted to make him believe that during the entire period of his absence she did nothing but think about him. Every evening, the family aired the question of whether she should write to him or not. Her father, who took very much to heart the honor of his family, would not hear of it. Seeing Emilio start to laugh at the idea of that family council, she cried out, "Ask my mother if you don't believe me!"

She was a stubborn liar despite the fact that she did not possess the art of lying. It was easy to catch her in a contradiction. But when a contradiction was demonstrated to her, she blithely returned to her first assertion since logic meant nothing to her. And perhaps this very simplicity was enough to absolve her in Emilio's eyes.

It could not be said that she was particularly skilled in wickedness; moreover, it seemed to him that whenever she deceived him, she took care to let him know it.

There was no way of determining the reasons for his indissoluble attachment to Angiolina. Any little grief that had come into his drab life, divided between home and office, was easily canceled compared with her. Of all the griefs she caused him, the greatest was not being findable when he needed to be near her. Often, driven from the house by his sister's grim face, he raced to the Zarris', knowing full well that Angiolina did not like him to appear too often in that house, which she so fiercely defended from dishonor. Rarely did he find her there, but her mother very kindly invited him to wait for her, since Angiolina was expected momentarily. She had been called five minutes earlier by some ladies who lived nearby — a vague gesture designated east or west — to try on a dress.

His waiting was intolerable, but he nonetheless stayed on for hours, fixedly scrutinizing the hard face of the old woman, because he knew that returning home without seeing his loved one would have left him irremediably restless. One evening, at the end of his patience, even though the mother, courteous as always, tried to retain him, he finally left. On the staircase he passed a woman, apparently a servant, her head covered with scarf that also hid part of her face. He made way for her, but when she tried to sidle by him, he recognized her by her movements and her figure. Her obvious attempt to escape his notice was what aroused his suspicion. It was Angiolina. Seeing her again, he immediately felt better and was undisturbed by her explanation of the neighbors who had called her, or her indication of a completely different direction from the one indicated by her mother, or even by the surprising fact that she was not angry with him for having come to her house once again and compromised her. That evening she was warm and tender as though she were seeking forgiveness for some wrongdoing, but in his euphoria, he was incapable of suspecting any wrongdoing.

He became suspicious only when, on another occasion, she came to meet him in that same outfit. She told him that returning home late after having been with him, she had been seen by some acquaintances and was afraid of being caught leaving the Paracci house, which did not enjoy high repute; that was why she disguised herself that way. What ingenuity! She did not see that in her babbling she was confessing to him that even the time he met her on the stairs of her house, she had good reason to disguise herself.

One evening, she arrived at their rendezvous an hour late. So that she would not have to knock on the door and risk attracting the attention of the other tenants, he had made a habit of waiting for her on the twisted, filthy stairs, leaning on the banister bent over in order to catch sight of her when she was still at a distance. If someone appeared, he would rush into the room, which meant that all his running around only increased his agitation. In any case, it would have been impossible for him to remain still. That evening, when he had to stay in the room in order to let people pass on the landing, he repeatedly flung himself on the bed, only to get up at once and dawdle away the time by making this choreography as complex as possible. Later, rethinking the state he had been in during that wait, it seemed unbelievable to him. He must have been reduced to crying out in his agony.

When she finally appeared, the sight of her was not enough to calm him, and he scolded her furiously. She paid no attention and thought she could quiet him with a few caresses. She flung the scarf away and put her arms around his neck. Her wide sleeves left them bare, and he felt their burning heat. Her eyes were gleaming and her cheeks were flushed. A horrible suspicion flashed though his mind. "You have just been with some man," he shouted. "You're crazy!" she replied, and without seeming unduly offended, began explaining the reasons for her lateness. Signora Deluigi had not let her go, she had to run home to disguise herself that way, and there her mother had made her do something before she left. Enough reasons to explain a ten-hour delay.

But Emilio was left without the shadow of a doubt; she had just come from the arms of someone else, and he came to the realization that the only way to save himself from such ignominy was through an act of superhuman control. He must not get into that bed, he must repulse her at once and never see her again. But now he knew what *never again* meant. It meant pain, relentless regret, interminable hours of agitation, others of agonizing dreams, followed by inertia, emptiness, the death of imagination and desire — a condition more painful than any other. He was afraid. He pulled her toward him, and his only vengeance was: "I am not worth much more than you."

Now it was she who became angry. Tearing herself loose, she said decisively: "I have never allowed anyone to treat me this way. I'm leaving." She tried to retrieve the scarf but he stopped her. He kissed her and embraced her, begging her to stay. He was not cowardly enough to take back what he had said to her by making a declaration to that effect, but seeing her so decided, and still under the shock of the mere thought of such a finale, his admiration went out to her. Feeling completely vindicated, she yielded. But only by degrees. She stayed, declaring that this would be their last meeting. Only at the moment of separating did she agree to fix, as she usually did, the day and hour of their next meeting. Now that she was totally vindicated, she no longer remembered the origin of their dispute, nor did she make any further attempt to regain his trust.

He continued to hope that his complete possession of her would finally subdue the violence of his emotions. Instead, he went to each assignation with the same intense desire and the same urge to reconstruct the *Ange* that was destroyed each time. His discontent led him to seek refuge in the sweetest dreams. Angiolina had thus given him everything: the possession of her body and—since that was their source —the dreams of a poet.

In his dreams she was so often a nurse that he tried to continue his dream even when he was with her. Holding her tightly in his arms with the fierce longings of the dreamer, he told her: "I would like to fall sick so that you can nurse me." "Oh, wouldn't that be wonderful!" she said, for there were times when she might have acceded to any of his wishes. Naturally, that was all she had to say for any dream to vanish.

One evening when he was with Angiolina, he had an idea which, for that one evening, provided a powerful remedy for his suffering. It was a dream that he had and that he elaborated with Angiolina beside him, in spite of her proximity. The reason they were so unhappy was because of the vileness of the current state of society. He was so certain of this that he could even imagine himself capable of some heroic act in the service of socialism. The whole of their misadventure was the result of their poverty. His argument presupposed that she sold herself and did so because of her family's misery. But this she did not understand, so that his words sounded to her like a caress, and he seemed to be blaming only himself.

In another kind of society he would have been able to live with her, openly, without first making her submit to the tailor. He was embroidering the same lies as Angiolina's, to make her responsive and to lead her into ideas that would allow them to dream together. She asked for explanations and he was enchanted to give them to her and thus give voice to the dream. He told her what a hideous struggle had erupted between rich and poor, the haves and the have-nots. There could be no doubt about the outcome of the struggle which would bring freedom to all, to them as well. He told her about the elimination of capitalism and the short workday that would be required of every one. Men and women would be equals, and love would be a gift they shared.

She asked for other explanations, which began to trouble the dream, and then concluded: "If everything were shared, there would not be enough for anyone. Workers are envious, they are lazy, they won't accomplish anything." He tried to enter into a discussion with her but then gave up. This child of the working class was defending the rich.

It seemed to him that she had never asked him for money. What he could not deny, even to himself, was that once he became aware of her neediness and accustomed her to receiving money instead of trinkets or chocolates, she expressed much gratitude while always affecting much embarrassment.

And this gratitude was renewed with similar fervor whenever he gave her a gift. So that, when he felt the need for her to be docile and amorous, he knew only too well what to do. This need was felt so often that his means were soon depleted. In her acceptance, she never failed to protest, and in view of the fact that her acceptance never went beyond the meager gesture of extending her hand while her protest was fulsome, he remembered the latter more vividly than the former, and continued to believe that even without those gifts their relationship would be the same.

The penury of Angiolina's family must have been extreme. She had made every effort to keep him from making surprise visits to her house. Those unexpected visits did not please her at all. But all the threats of not finding her there, of his being thrown down the stairs by her mother, her brothers, her father, came to naught. When he had the time late in the evening, he was sure to drop in, even though it was often the old lady Zarri who kept him company.

His dreams were what dragged him there. He kept hoping to find Angiolina changed, and continued to come breathlessly in the hope of erasing the impression — always disappointing — of their previous meeting.

Then she tried another tack. She told him that her father would not leave her in peace and that only with great effort had she prevented him from making a scandal. All she had been able to extract from him was the promise that he would abstain from violence, but he insisted on having his say. Five minutes later Zarri came into the room. To Emilio it seemed that the old man, tall, gaunt, unsteady on his feet, needing to sit down as soon as he entered, knew that his arrival had been announced. His first words sounded as though they had been prepared to make an impression. He spoke slowly and awkwardly but imperiously. He said it was his duty to direct and protect his daughter, who needed his care, because if not for him she would have no one else, since her brothers — he did not to want speak ill of them — were little concerned with the affairs of the family. Angiolina seemed vastly pleased by his lengthy prologue, and, with an abrupt announcement that she was going to get dressed in the next room, walked out.

The old man immediately lost all his self-importance. Turning his head to watch his daughter leave, he raised a pinch of snuff to his nose. This was followed by a long pause during which Emilio contemplated the words he would use to answer the accusations that would be made against him. Angiolina's father then looked straight ahead and examined his own shoes at great length. It was by sheer chance that he raised his eyes and saw Emilio again. "Ah, yes," he said, like someone stumbling upon a mislaid object. He repeated his opening statements but less forcefully; he was very distracted. Then, with great effort, he tried to gather his thoughts in order to proceed. He looked at Emilio a number of times, always trying to avoid meeting his glance, and began to speak only after deciding to examine the empty snuff box in his hands.

There were bad people who were harassing the Zarri family. Hadn't Angiolina told him? That was wrong of her. Well, there were these people who were always trying to find fault with the Zarri family. One had to be on one's guard! Did Signor Brentani know *Tic?* If he knew him he would come to the house less often.

At this point the sermon degenerated into a warning to Emilio not to expose himself — a young man like him — to so many dangers. When the old man raised his eyes to look at Emilio again, Emilio understood at once. In those strange blue eyes beneath a silver mane madness hovered.

This time the lunatic kept his eyes fastened to Emilio's.

"It's all very well that *Tic* lives up there, in Opicina, but down here he rains beatings on the legs and backs of his enemies." He added darkly, "Here at home he even beats our little girl." The family had another enemy: *Toc*. That one lived in the center of the city. He didn't beat; he did worse. He took away from the family all the jobs, all the money, all the bread.

At the height of his fury, the old man started to shriek. Angiolina rushed in and understood at once what was going on. "Go away," she said to her father irritably, pushing him out.

The old man stopped at the threshold, hesitating: "He," he said, pointing to Emilio, "didn't know anything about either *Tic* or *Toc*."

"I'll tell him myself," Angiolina replied, by then laughing heartily. Then she shouted, "Mama, come and get Papa." She closed the door.

Emilio, terrified by the insane eyes that had stared at him so intently, asked, "Is he sick?"

"Oh," Angiolina said contemptuously, "he's a lazy lout who doesn't want to work. On one side there is *Tic*, on the other *Toc*, and that way he doesn't leave the house and makes us women work like slaves." All of a sudden she burst into an open-throated guffaw and told him how the whole family, to humor the old man, pretended to feel the beatings that came from *Tic*'s house. Years before, when the old man's mania had barely begun, they were living in a fifth-floor apartment on the Lazzaretto Vecchio; *Tic* lived on the Campo Marzio and *Toc* on the Corso. So they moved, hoping that in some other quarter the old man would find the courage to go out again, but what happened was that *Tic* went to Opicina and *Toc* to via Stadion.

Letting him kiss her, she said "You got off easily. It was your good luck that just then he remembered his enemies."

And so they became all the more intimate. By then Emilio had discovered all the secrets of the house. Angiolina felt that nothing about her could repulse Emilio and once she came out with a memorable remark: "I tell you everything as though you were my brother." She knew he was entirely hers, even if she did not take advantage of it, because it was not in her character to exploit power or to use it in order to prove it, but rather to enjoy it so as to live better and more happily. She ceased having any consideration for him. She arrived late for her appointments even though at every meeting she found him burning with rage, his eyes flaming, violent. She became increasingly coarse. When she tired of his caresses, she pushed him away so roughly that he said, with a smile, he was afraid sooner or later she would start beating him.

He could not be sure, but it seemed to him that Angiolina and the Paracci woman, the one who rented the room to them, knew each other. The old woman looked at Angiolina with an almost maternal expression, admiring her blond hair and lovely eyes. Angiolina later said she had indeed gotten to know her only then, but she betrayed her familiarity with every nook and cranny of the house. One evening, when she arrived much later than usual, Paracci heard them fighting and intervened strongly in Angiolina's favor. "How can anyone chastise an angel like that?" Angiolina, who never refused a compliment, whatever its origin, stopped to listen and said with a smile, "Did you hear that? You should learn from that." He had indeed heard and he was dumbfounded by the vulgarity of the woman he loved.

Convinced by then of the futility of trying to improve her in any way, he felt at times the desperate need to lower himself to her level, or lower. One evening she shoved him away. She had been to confession and for that one day did not want to sin. He was less desirous of possessing her than of being, at least once, ruder than she was. He grabbed her violently, fighting to the end. When, out of breath, he began to regret his brutality, he had the pleasure of catching an admiring glance from Angiolina. For that entire evening she was unreservedly his: she was the dominated woman who loves her master. He decided there would be other evenings like that, but he could not make them happen. It was hard to find a second occasion to look that brutal and violent to Angiolina.

eleven

Fate had clearly ordained that Balli would always intervene to make Emilio look worse in Angiolina's eyes. It had been decided for some time that Emilio's mistress would pose for the sculptor. For work to start, all that was needed was for Emilio to remember to inform Angiolina.

Since it was easy to understand the motive for so much forgetfulness, Stefano decided not to mention it again. For the time being he felt unable to produce any idea other than the figure for which Angiolina was to pose. Just to keep himself busy with this image that pleased him so much, he set up his armature and covered it with clay, modeling the outlines of a nude figure. He wrapped the whole thing in a damp cloth and thought, "A funerary shroud." Day after day he looked at the nude, visualized it dressed, and re-covered it with its rags, carefully moistening them.

The two friends did not discuss the matter. Hoping to arrive at his goal without having to make a formal request, Balli said to Emilio one evening: "I can't seem to work any more. I would be in despair if I didn't have that figure in mind."

"I forgot again to talk to Angiolina about it," Emilio said, but without feigning the surprise of someone suddenly aware of an involuntary omission. "You know what you can do? When you see her, talk to her yourself. You will see how eagerly she obliges you."

There was so much bitterness in that last sentence that

Balli felt sorry for him and spoke no more about it. He knew himself that his intervention between the two lovers had not been very successful, and he wanted no further involvement in their affairs. He could not come between them as he naively had a few months earlier to help his friend; Emilio's recovery would have to come with time. His lovely image, so long contemplated, the only one at present that could get him back to work, was being stifled by Emilio's incurable idiocy.

He tried to get himself started with another model, but after a few sittings gave up in disgust. Abrupt abandonments of ideas, toyed with over long periods, were not uncommon in Balli's career. This time, he held Emilio responsible, rightly or wrongly. There was not a doubt in his mind that if he had the model of his dreams, he would be able to begin again with energy, if only to destroy the figure a few weeks later.

He restrained himself from telling all this to his friend, but he indulged him for the last time. It was useless trying to make Emilio understand how important Angiolina had become for him too; that would only have aggravated the poor man's disease. How to make Emilio understand that the artist's imagination had fastened on that subject precisely because in the purity of those lines he had discovered an indefinable expression, not directly inspired by those lines — somewhat awkward and vulgar — which a Raffaello would have suppressed, but which he was eager to copy, accentuate?

When they walked together through the streets, he did not talk about his wish, but Emilio gained no benefit from this solicitude because that wish, which his friend did not dare express, loomed greater in his mind than it really was and made him jealous, cruelly so. By that time, Balli was as desirous of Angiolina as he was himself. How could he defend himself against a rival like that?

He could not defend himself! He had already revealed his jealousy, but he would not talk about it; it would have been too foolish to appear jealous of Balli after having tolerated the rivalry of the umbrella vendor. That embarrassment disarmed him. One day Stefano stopped by for him at his office, as he often did, to accompany him to his house. They had been walking along the seafront for a while when they saw coming toward them Angiolina, shimmering in the noonday sun that played on her blond curls and on her face, slightly contorted from squinting in the bright light. Thus Balli found himself face to face with his masterpiece, which he saw in every detail while disregarding the contour. She was advancing with her determined stride that took nothing away from the grace of the vertical figure. That was how youth incarnate and dressed would move under the light of the sun.

"Now look here!" Stefano exclaimed emphatically. "You're not going to prevent me from producing a masterpiece just because of your insane jealousy."

Angiolina replied to their greeting with a seriousness that had recently become a mannerism; all of her seriousness was concentrated in her greeting, and even that must have been learned from someone only recently. Balli stopped and waited for a sign of agreement from his companion. "So be it," Emilio said mechanically, hesitantly, still hoping Stefano would see how dearly it cost him to agree. But Balli saw only his model who was about to slip through his fingers. He tore after her the second Emilio gave his consent.

That was how Balli and Angiolina finally got together. When Emilio caught up with them he found they were already in full agreement. Balli did not beat about the bush, and Angiolina, flushed with excitement, immediately asked when she should come. The following morning at nine o'clock. She accepted, remarking how fortunate that the next day she did not have to go to the Deluigi's. "I will be punctual," she said, taking leave of them. Since she was in the habit of blurting out the first words that came to mind, and a stream of them, it did not occur to her that her promise to be punctual might upset Emilio because it emphasized the difference between an appointment with Balli and one with him.

Now that he had committed the offense, Balli's thoughts returned to his friend. He was instantly conscious of having hurt Emilio and affectionately asked his forgiveness: "I couldn't do otherwise, even though I knew it would displease you. I don't want to take advantage of your pretended indifference. I know this upsets you. You are wrong, absolutely wrong, but I know that does not make me right either."

With a forced smile Emilio replied: "In that case I really have nothing more to say to you."

It seemed to Balli that Emilio was being more severe with him than he deserved. "Which means that to be forgiven by you I have no other choice but to tell Angiolina not to come? All right, if that's what you want, I'll even do that."

The offer could not be accepted because the poor girl — Emilio knew her as though he had made her himself — loved even more anyone who rejected her, and he had no wish to give her additional reasons for loving Balli. "No," he declared more affably "let us leave things as they are. On the contrary, I trust you," he added with a laugh. "But only you."

Stefano assured him with great fervor that he deserved that trust. He promised, he swore: the day he was distracted from his work during Angiolina's sittings, even for a moment, he would send the girl away. Emilio was weak enough to accept his promise and even make him repeat it.

The next day Balli came to Emilio to report on the first sitting. He had worked like a demon and had no complaints about Angiolina, who, despite her uncomfortable pose, had held out as long as she could. She still had not understood the pose, but Balli did not give up hope of succeeding. He was more passionate than ever about his project. For eight or nine sittings he would not even have the time to exchange a word with Angiolina. "If I should find myself hesitating in a way that would make me stop, I promise you that we will only chat about you. I'm willing to bet that she will wind up loving you with all her heart."

"At worst, and that would not be so bad, talking about me will bore her so much that she won't love you either."

For two days he was unable to see Angiolina, so it was not until Sunday afternoon in Balli's studio that he saw her again. He found them hard at work.

The studio was little more than a huge depot. The barrenness of its original purpose had been maintained, since Balli did not want it to be plush. The irregular pavement had been left just as it was when bales of goods were deposited there, except for a large carpet in the center, which, in the winter, protected the feet of the sculptor from contact with the floor. The walls were roughly plastered, and here and there, on stands, were figures of clay or plaster, stacked rather than grouped, not at all intended to be viewed. Certain comforts, however, were not neglected. The temperature was kept warm by a pyramidal stove. A large number of chairs and armchairs of various shapes and sizes made the studio look less like a storeroom because of their elegant lines. No two were alike, since Balli wanted whatever he rested on to conform to the shape of the project he had in mind. In fact, he always thought he was still missing some chair shapes he might need. Angiolina was posing on a trestle covered with soft white cushions. Balli, standing on a chair next to another trestle that turned, was working on his barely modeled figure.

Seeing Emilio, he jumped down to greet him warmly. Angiolina also left her pose and sat up on the white cushions. She seemed to be resting in a nest. She greeted Emilio very sweetly. They had not seen each other in a while. She found him a bit pale. Was he perhaps not well? Emilio was infinitely grateful to her for so many demonstrations of affection. She probably wanted to show him her gratitude for leaving her alone with Balli.

Stefano stood before his creation. "Do you like it?" Emilio examined it. On an amorphous base rested a kneeling, almost human figure, both shoulders clothed, evidently Angiolina's in shape and position. Insofar as it went, the figure had something tragic about it. It seemed to be buried in the clay and making superhuman attempts to free itself. Even the head, where a few thumbstrokes had hollowed the temples and smoothed the forehead, looked like a skull meticulously covered with earth so as not to scream.

"You can see how it's coming into existence," the sculptor said, with a caressing glance at his creation. "The whole idea is already there. All that's missing is the form."

But the idea could be seen only by him. It was subtle, almost imperceptible. Out of that clay a supplication was to emerge, the supplication of someone who for one moment believed and might never believe again. Balli also explained the form he wanted. The base would remain rough, but the figure would become increasingly refined as it rose up to the hair, which would be arranged in the coquettish style of the most expert modern hairdresser. The hair was intended to negate the prayer expressed by the face.

Angiolina went back to her pose and Balli to his work. For half an hour she held her pose most conscientiously, imagining that she was praying — as she had been instructed by the sculptor — so as to have a supplicating expression on her face. The expression did not satisfy Stefano, and unseen by Emilio, he made a grimace of disgust. That slut did not have a clue how to pray. Instead of filling her eyes with piety, she cast them upward saucily. She was flirting with God Himself.

Angiolina's fatigue became apparent from her sighs. Balli remained completely unaware of it, having reached a critical point in his work: he kept that poor head bent over her right shoulder without mercy.

"Very tired?" Emilio asked Angiolina, and since Balli could not see him, he stroked her and supported her chin. She moved her lips to kiss his hand without breaking the pose.

"I can hold out for another little while."

Oh, how wonderful she was, sacrificing herself that way for a work of art. If he were the artist, he would regard that sacrifice as a proof of love.

Soon after, Balli granted her a short break. He did not feel any need for one himself and in the meanwhile busied himself with the base. In his long canvas coat he had a priestly look. Seated beside Emilio, Angiolina watched the sculptor with ill-concealed admiration. He was an attractive man, with that elegant beard of his, graying but with glints of gold; strong and agile, he jumped off the stand and climbed up again without shaking the statue and was the image of competence in that rough smock above which rose his stylish collar. Even Emilio admired him, despite the suffering it caused him.

They soon went back to work. The sculptor crushed the head some more, unconcerned that he might be making it lose the little shape it had. He added clay to one side, took some off the other, giving the impression that he was working from the model, since he often looked at her. But Emilio did not see that the clay was reproducing any traits of Angiolina's face. Emilio told him so when Stefano stopped working, and the sculptor showed him how to look at it. For the moment there was no resemblance, unless one viewed the head from a particular angle.

Not only did Angiolina not recognize herself, she was displeased that Balli thought he had portrayed her face in that shapeless thing. But Emilio now saw the very obvious resemblance. The face seemed to be sleeping, immobilized in a tight wrapping; the eyes, not yet molded, seemed closed, but one could sense the living breath that would soon give life to that face.

Balli wrapped the figure in a damp cloth. He was pleased with his work and was all excited about it.

They went out together. Balli's art was really the only point of contact between the two friends. Talking about the sculptor's idea, they felt reconciled and, for the duration of that afternoon, a warmth reentered their relationship, from which it had been absent for some time. For that reason, the one least entertained was Angiolina, feeling like a fifth wheel. Balli, who did not like to be seen in her company in daylight, wanted her to walk in front of them, which she did, with stiff contempt, her little nose in the air. Balli kept talking about the statue while Emilio's eyes followed her movements. During all those hours, there was no cause for jealousy. Balli was lost in his reverie, and when he did take notice of Angiolina, it was only to keep her at a distance without teasing her or insulting her.

It was cold. The sculptor suggested going to a tavern for a glass of warm wine. Inside it was crowded and filled with an acrid odor of food and tobacco, and so they decided to stay in the courtyard. At first, fearful of the cold, Angiolina protested, but when Balli said it was a most original thing to do, she wrapped herself up in her cape and was enchanted to see herself admired by the people who came out of the warm room and by the waiter, who served them while racing back and forth. Balli was insensitive to the cold and kept looking at his glass as though he were discovering his own idea in it. Emilio busied himself with warming Angiolina's hands, which she had let him hold. It was the first time she allowed him to fondle her in Balli's presence, and Emilio reveled in it. "What an adorable creature!" he murmured, even managing to kiss her cheek, which she pressed against his lips.

The evening was clear and blue. The wind whistled above the tall building that shielded them against it. Aided by the warm aromatic drink, which they imbibed copiously, they held out in the bracing temperature for almost an hour. For Emilio it was another unforgettable episode of his love affair: that dim, blue courtyard, with the three of them at one end of a long wooden table, and Angiolina, definitely relinquished to him by Balli, a more than acquiescent lover.

On the way back, Balli told them he had to go to the masked ball that evening. The thought of it bored him to death, but he had made the appointment with a friend, a doctor, who, eager to attend the ball, said he needed the respectable companionship of a man like the sculptor so that his patients would be more inclined to forgive his presence in such a place.

Stefano would have preferred to go to bed early in order to get back to work the next day with a clear head. He shuddered to think of all those hours spent at that bacchanal.

Angiolina asked him if he had a box for the season and wanted to know exactly where it was located.

"If you come in disguise," Balli said laughing, "I hope you will look for me."

"But I've never been to a masked ball," Angiolina protested forcefully. Then, after thinking about it as though she had just discovered that there were such things as masked balls, she added, "I would love to go." It was decided on the spot: they would go the charity ball that was taking place a week hence. Angiolina jumped with joy and seemed so genuinely delighted that even Balli smiled at her complaisantly, as one would at child to whom one gave much pleasure with little effort.

When the two men were alone, Emilio admitted that the sitting had not been an unpleasant experience for him. As they were parting, Balli turned the sweetness of the day into bile: "So you were pleased with us? You must understand that I did my best to make you happy."

That meant he owed Angiolina's effusiveness to Balli's instructions; how humiliating! This was a new and powerful reason for jealousy. He planned to inform Balli that he had no wish to owe Angiolina's affection to the authority of another person. As for her, at the first opportunity, he would show her less gratitude for those signs of affection that had so overjoyed him that day. It was now perfectly clear why she had been so willing to let him fondle her in Balli's presence. She was dominated by the sculptor! For him she had known how to give up all her pretensions of respectability and all the lies that Emilio had not known how to get rid of. With Balli she was completely different. With Balli, who was not her lover, she unmasked herself; with him, no!

Early the next morning he hastened to Angiolina's house, eager to see how he would be treated when Stefano was not there. Splendidly! After ascertaining that it was he, she opened the door herself. In the morning she was even more beautiful. One night's sleep was enough to give her the serene look of a healthy virgin. Her blue-striped white wool robe, somewhat shabby, softly outlined the contours of her body, leaving her white neck bare.

"Am I disturbing you?" he asked darkly, restraining himself from kissing her so as not to weaken the attack he was preparing.

She did not even notice his sulking. She showed him into her room. "I am going to get dressed because at nine I have to be at Signora Deluigi's. In the meantime, you can read this letter." She nervously drew a sheet of paper out of a basket. "Read this carefully and then you can advise me." Sadness clouded her face and her eyes filled with tears. "You will see what is going on. I will tell you everything. Only you can advise me. I also told my mother all about it, but she, poor woman, has eyes only for crying." She left the room but quickly returned. "Take care, in case my mother comes here and talks to you; she knows everything except that I gave myself to Volpini." She threw him a kiss with her hand and walked out.

The letter was from Volpini, a formal letter of farewell. He started out by saying that he had always behaved in good faith, whereas she — now he knew — had betrayed him from the start. Emilio began reading the almost illegible handwriting with growing fear that he would find his name as the reason for the rupture. There was no mention of him in the letter. Volpini had been assured that she had been not Merighi's fiancée but his mistress. He had not wanted to believe it, but a few days earlier, he had heard, again with absolute certainty, that she had been to various masked balls in the company of various young men. This was followed by

ponderous ill-connected sentences, which confirmed the un-
questionable sincerity of the good man, and were comical
only because of a few pompous words that must have been
taken from a dictionary.

In came old lady Zarri. With her hands in their usual
place under her apron, she leaned against the bed and waited
patiently for him to finish reading the letter.

"How does it look to you?" she asked in her nasal voice.
"Angiolina says no. To me this looks like the end of Volpini."

Only one of Volpini's allegations had made an impression
on Emilio. "Is it true that Angiolina has often gone to masked
balls?" As for the rest, that she had an affair with Merighi or
with many others, was no more than fact as far as he was
concerned. If anything, since someone else had been as taken
in as he, and more so, he should feel less hurt by the lies that he
had always found so offensive. But he did learn something
new from the letter. She was even better at dissembling than
he had suspected. The day before she had fooled Balli himself
with her cries of joy over the idea of attending a masked ball
for the first time.

"All lies," the old lady said with the calm assurance of
someone reporting something presumed to be already believed by the hearer. "Angiolina comes home directly from
work every evening and goes to bed at once. I see her go to
bed myself."

Crafty old woman! She was certainly not fooled, but she
would never admit to fooling someone else.

As soon as the daughter reappeared the mother left.

"Did you read it?" Angiolina asked, sitting down beside
him. "What do you make of it?"

Looking very sullen, he told her gruffly that Volpini was
right: it is not fitting for a fiancée to go to masked balls.

Angiolina protested: she, masked balls? Had he not seen

her excitement the day before at the idea of going to a masked ball, her first ever?

Said that way, her argument lost all its power. That excitement, remembered as a proof, must have cost her considerable effort if she made such a point of remembering it. She proffered many other proofs: she had been with him every evening she had not had to go to Signora Deluigi; she did not own a stitch of clothing that could be used for a masquerade; in fact, she counted on his help to procure what she would need for the costume she had in mind. Emilio was unconvinced, by then certain that she had often attended the carnival balls that season. But so many proofs, presented with such seductive intensity, finally softened him. She was not offended to be doubted. She clung to him, tried to convince him, tried to gain his sympathy, and Balli was not present!

Then he understood why she needed him. She was not yet ready to let go of Volpini, and in order to hang on to him, counted on Emilio's advice, in which she placed the great faith that the uneducated have for the educated. That observation did not diminish Emilio's satisfaction with the affection being given him: it was a lot better than owing it to Balli. Moreover, he wanted to be deserving of all that expansiveness, and so he set himself to examining the problem that had been placed before him.

He was immediately forced to recognize that she understood it better than he did. She pointed out with great acuity that in order to know how to respond, it was first of all necessary to know whether Volpini believed the information he had communicated to be reliable, or whether he had written that letter merely to verify a number of vague rumors; and then, had he written with the firm intention of leaving her, or merely as a threat, prepared to give in at Angiolina's first move in his direction? Emilio had to reread the text and had to admit that Volpini had piled on too many arguments to have a really solid one. The only name mentioned was Merighi. "As for that, I know just how to reply," Angiolina said irately. "He has to acknowledge that he was the first to possess me."

Following that line of reasoning, Emilio made an observation that corroborated Angiolina's position. In his grandiloquent closing, Volpini had declared that he was leaving her, first of all because she was unfaithful to him, and then, because he found her extremely cold toward him, thus indicating that she did not love him. Was that the place to complain about a deficiency, perhaps merely a deficiency of temperament, if the other complaints were as damning as the writer would have her believe? She was enormously grateful to him for that point, which provided clear proof of the accuracy of her own interpretation, having forgotten that it was she who had directed him toward that argument. Oh, she wasn't cultivated and didn't care about getting credit. She was engaged in a struggle and would use with equal determination any weapon that might work, unconcerned who had made it.

She did not want to write to Volpini right away because she had to rush off; Signora Deluigi was expecting her. But at noon she would be back home and asked Emilio to come then. She would wait for him, and until then, he as well as she had to think single-mindedly about that subject. In fact, he should take the letter with him to the office to study it at his leisure.

They left together, but she warned him that they had to separate before they reached the city. She no longer had any doubt that there were people in Trieste hired by Volpini to spy on her. "The scoundrel!" she exclaimed emphatically. "He has ruined me!" She loathed her aged fiancé, as though he had really been the one to ruin her. "Naturally, now he would love to be free of his obligation, but he will have to deal with me." She confessed that she despised him. He was as revolting to her as a dirty animal. "It was your fault that I gave myself to him." Seeing him taken aback by the accusation, made for the first time in anger, she corrected herself: "If it wasn't your fault, it was certainly your love."

With these tender words she left him, and he remained convinced that her only motive for incriminating him was to make him assist her with all his power in the campaign she was about to wage against Volpini.

He followed her for a while and seeing how, in the middle of the street, she brazenly offered herself with her glance to every passerby, he relapsed into the sickness that dominated every one of his emotions. Forgetting his fear that she would put her hooks into him, he was overjoyed by what had happened. Volpini's abandonment made her need him, and at noon, for another whole hour he would be able to have her all to himself and feel that she was intimately his.

In the busy center of the city, where no one was strolling for pleasure at that hour, Angiolina's soft rosy appearance, her unhurried stride and her eyes attentive to everything but where she was going, attracted general attention. He was sure that anyone seeing her would immediately think of a bedroom, for which she was ideally made. The excitement aroused by that image did not leave him all morning.

He decided that at noon he would make Angiolina understand how much his help was worth, and would exploit every advantage that his exceptional position offered him.

The old woman received him, very hospitably inviting him to make himself comfortable in her daughter's room. Tired from his rapid climb, he sat down, certain that Angiolina would walk in any moment.

"She isn't here yet," the old woman said looking toward the corridor as though she too were expecting to see her daughter arrive.

"Not here?" Emilio asked, so deeply disappointed that he could hardly believe his ears.

"I don't understand why she is late," the old woman added, still looking out of the doorway. "Signora Deluigi must have kept her."

"How late could she be?"

"I don't know," she replied most innocently. "She could be here any minute, but if she has already had lunch at Signora Deluigi's, she might not come back until late afternoon." She said nothing more for a moment, then, very thoughtfully and with growing certainty, added, "But I don't think that she will stay out for lunch since her lunch is ready in there."

Keen observer that he was, Emilio clearly saw that all those doubts were fabricated, and that the old lady surely knew Angiolina would not be coming back so soon. But as always, his powers of observation were of little use to him. Held there by his longing, he waited for a long time while Angiolina's mother stayed with him, so silent and serious that later, thinking back on it, Emilio discovered that she was ironic. The youngest of her daughters came to stand beside her mother, rubbing against her hip like a kitten against a doorjamb.

Disconsolate, he left amid warm goodbyes from mother and daughter. He stroked the child's hair, which was the same color as Angiolina's. Except for Angiolina's healthy complexion, the little girl looked very much like her sister.

He thought it might be a good idea to take revenge for Angiolina's dirty trick by not going to see her until she came to him. Now that she needed him she would go looking for him quickly enough. However, that evening, right after work, he took the same road back, planning in the process to determine the cause of her inexplicable absence. It was highly possible that some emergency had arisen.

He found Angiolina still dressed as she had been when he left her that morning. She had just come home. She let him kiss her cheek with the kind of docility she showed when she was seeking his forgiveness. Her cheeks were flaming and her breath reeked of wine.

"I did drink a lot," she said grinning at once. "Signor Deluigi, he's an old man of fifty, wanted to see if he could get me drunk, but he sure didn't, so there!"

Still, he must have been more successful than she realized, to judge from her excessive gaiety. She was doubled up with laughter. With her uncommonly red cheeks and her shining eyes she was strikingly beautiful. He kissed her open mouth on her pink gums, and she let him, as though it had nothing to do with her. She continued to giggle, telling him in broken sentences that not only the old man, but the whole family had been involved in trying to make her woozy, but no matter how many there were of them, they did not succeed. He tried to sober her up by talking about Volpini.

"Leave me alone with that stuff!" she shouted, and seeing that he persisted, instead of answering him, she began kissing and embracing him as he had been kissing her until then, on the mouth and neck. She was more aggressive than she had ever been, and before long they were on the bed, she still in her hat and coat. The door had remained open so that it was impossible for the sounds of that battle not to reach the kitchen, where her mother, father, and sister were.

They really had intoxicated her. Strange family, those Deluigis. But he held no grudge against Angiolina because his pleasure that evening was utterly perfect.

The next day at noon they found each other in excellent spirits. Angiolina assured him that her mother had not heard a thing. Then she regretted having let herself be taken in that condition. It was not her fault. "That old bastard Deluigi!"

He reassured her, telling her that if it were up to him, she should get drunk every day. Then they composed a letter to Volpini of a precision that would not have seemed possible given the state they were in.

Angiolina may have been sharper in her interpretation of Volpini's letter, but the reply flowed entirely from Emilio's expert hand.

She would have liked to write an insulting letter, wanting to vent the indignation of a respectable girl, wrongly accused. "As a matter of fact," she remarked with theatrical ire, "if Volpini were here, I would slap him, without any explanation. He would immediately be convinced that he was wrong."

That was not a bad idea, but Emilio wanted to proceed more cautiously. Very ingeniously, and not wanting to offend her, he told her how, in order to analyze the problem more carefully, he had asked himself, "What would a respectable girl do in Angiolina's position?" He did not tell her that Amalia was his notion of a respectable woman, and that he had asked himself how his sister would have responded to Volpini's letter. He communicated the results to her. A respectable woman would first of all have expressed enormous surprise; then, the thought that there must be a misunderstanding; and finally, but only as a last resort, the horrible suspicion that the letter could only be attributed to the fiancé's wish to renege on his commitment. Angiolina was entranced by this reconstruction of an entire psychological process, and he set to work at once.

She sat next to him, quiet as a mouse. Here was someone

working on her behalf. She rested her hand on his knee, held her head close to his to be able to read along with what he was writing, and made her presence felt without in any way preventing him from writing. That proximity diminished the intended rigor of the letter and — had it not been intended for a man like Volpini — even its efficacy, since it lost the dignified moderation that he had planned to give it. Thus something of Angiolina entered those sentences. Pretentious words came to his pen, and he left them, delighted to see her ecstatic admiration and the same expression that had been on her face a few days earlier when she was looking at Balli.

Without rereading it, she set to work copying his prose, vastly pleased to be able to affix her own signature. She had seemed much more intelligent when she discussed what attitude to take than now, with her unconditional approval. While copying she could not pay much attention to the text of the letter because she was much too concerned with her handwriting.

Looking at the sealed envelope, she suddenly asked whether Balli had made any further mention of the ball he had promised to take her to. The slumbering moralist in Emilio did not wake up, but he advised her not to go, out of fear that Volpini might hear about it. However, she had answers for every reservation.

"Now, I will go to the ball. Until now, out of respect for that scoundrel, I did not go, but now . . . so much the better if he does hear!"

Emilio insisted on meeting her that evening. In the afternoon she was to pose for Balli, then she had to dash over to Signora Deluigi's for a moment, so they could not meet until late. She granted the appointment since, as she said, for the time being she could refuse him nothing. But not in the room of that Paracci woman, because she wanted to be home early. As in the happier moments of their love affair, they would walk together on Sant'Andrea, and then he would bring her home. Still exhausted after all the wine she had drunk the day before, she needed sleep. The proposal did not displease him at all. It was one of his most characteristic traits to indulge in the sentimental evocation of the past. That evening he would once again analyze the color of the sea, the sky, Angiolina's hair.

She left him, and in her parting words asked him to mail the letter to Volpini. Thus he found himself in the middle of the street with that letter in his hand, a material proof of the basest thing he had ever done in his entire life, but that occurred to him only when Angiolina was no longer beside him.

twelve

He had come home but remained standing in the dining room, hat in hand, undecided whether to escape the boredom of an hour face to face with his silent sister. Just then, he heard from Amalia's room two or three garbled words, then a whole sentence: "Get away, you ugly beast!" He shuddered! The voice was so altered by fatigue and emotion that it sounded like his sister's only in the way a scream involuntarily forced from the throat can sound like the person's normal speaking voice. Was she now sleeping and dreaming during the day as well?

He opened the door, trying not to make any noise, and saw before his eyes a sight he would never be able to forget. For the rest of his life, his senses had only to come into contact with one detail or another of that scene for the whole of it to come back to him at once, making him relive the terror, the horror of it. A few country folk, passing through a street nearby, were singing, and forever after their monotonous song brought tears to his eyes. All the sounds reaching him were monotonous, without warmth or meaning. In a neighboring apartment an untalented beginner was limping through a popular waltz on the piano. That waltz, played that way — and he often heard it again — sounded to him like a dirge. Even the time of day, normally cheerful, became somber for him. Noon had struck a short while before, and from the windows opposite so much sunlight was reflected into the room that it was blinding. And yet the memory of that moment would always be linked to an impression of darkness and bitter cold.

Amalia's clothes were strewn all over the floor, and a skirt had kept the door from opening completely. A few things were under the bed; a blouse was caught between the two panels of the casement window, and both shoes, with evident meticulousness, had been placed squarely in the middle of the table.

Amalia, seated on the edge of the bed, covered only by her camisole, had not noticed her brother's entrance and continued rubbing her legs, thin as twigs. At the sight of her nudity, Emilio felt the surprise and discomfort of noting her resemblance to a starving child.

He did not understand at first that he was in the presence of delirium. Unaware that she was hallucinating, he attributed her heavy breathing, which required so much effort that it shook her all way to her hips, to her awkward position. His first reaction was anger: no sooner was he free of Angiolina than he had this one to worry about.

"Amalia! What are you doing?" he asked reproachfully.

She did not hear him, although she had apparently caught the strains of the waltz, since she was marking the rhythm during her concentrated occupation with her legs.

"Amalia!" he repeated weakly, stunned by the evidence of her delirium. He placed his hand on her shoulder. At that, she turned around. First she looked at the hand whose contact she had felt, then at his face; in those eyes brightened by fever there was nothing but the effort of seeing; her cheeks were flaming, her lips purple, dry, shapeless, like an old unhealing wound. Then her eyes moved to the window and, bothered perhaps by so much light, immediately returned to her naked legs, on which they fastened with attentive curiosity.

"Oh, Amalia!" he cried, letting his shock express itself in that cry, which might have brought her back to her senses. A weak person fearfully regards delirium and madness as contagious diseases; the terror Emilio felt was such that he had to force himself not to tear out of the room. Conquering his violent revulsion, he touched his sister's shoulder once again: "Amalia! Amalia!" he cried. He was calling for help.

He felt somewhat relieved when he saw that she had heard him. She looked at him a second time, thoughtfully, as though she were trying to understand the reason for those cries and for the repeated pressure on her shoulder. She put her hand to her chest, as though at that moment she had become aware of her congested breathing. Then she forgot about Emilio and her congestion: "Oh, those beasts again!" Her altered voice seemed to herald imminent tears. She rubbed her legs with both hands, suddenly bending over as if she were going to catch an insect about to run away. In her right hand she found one of her own toes; she clutched it in her hand, then raised her fist as though she had caught something. It was empty, but she kept looking at it. She then went back to her foot, ready to bend over once more and return to that strange hunt.

Seeing her shiver again, Emilio was reminded that he should make her get back into bed. He approached her, shuddering at the thought that he might have to use force. Instead, he succeeded with no trouble at all because she obeyed at the first pressure of his hand; without any embarrassment, she slid one leg after the other onto the bed and let herself be covered. But out of an inexplicable hesitation, she leaned on the bed with one arm, seemingly unwilling to lie down completely. Unable to maintain that position, she soon lay back on the pillow and for the first time emitted a lucid expression of pain: "Oh my God! My God!"

"What happened to you?" Emilio asked, believing that after that single sensible outcry he could now speak to her as though she were in full possession of her senses.

She did not reply, once again busily investigating the cause of her discomfort under the blankets as well. She crouched over, put her hands on her legs, and, in order to achieve the ruse she was planning against the things or bugs that were tormenting her, she had even managed to quiet her breathing. She then brought her hands to her face and with incredulous surprise found them empty again. For some time, under the covers, she was seized by a torment that made her forget that other dreadful torment of her breathing.

"Do you feel better?" Emilio asked pleadingly. He sought consolation in the sound of his own voice, which he modulated sweetly, hoping to forget the threat of violence that had been hanging over him. He bent over so that he could be heard better.

She looked at him for some minutes, exhaling in his face the fluttering breath of her respiration. She recognized him. The warmth of the bed must indeed have restored her senses. Although she later became delirious again, he did not forget that he had been recognized. Evidently, she was improving.

"Now let us leave this house," she said, making every syllable clear. She even extended a leg to stand up, but when he prevented her with more force than was necessary, she immediately complied, forgetting what had prompted her action.

She repeated the same attempt soon after, but no longer with the same energy, and seemed to remember that she had been made to lie down and kept from getting out of bed. Then she began to talk. She thought she had moved to another house and had a lot to do, a huge amount of work putting so many things away.

"My God! Everything is filthy here! I already knew that, but you insisted on coming. And now? Aren't we leaving?"

He tried to calm her by agreeing with her. He stroked her, telling her that he did not find it that dirty, and now that they were in the house, it was better to stay there.

Amalia heard what he said but also heard words he had not said. Then she said, "If that is what you want, I must do as you wish. Let's stay, but . . . so much filth . . . " Two tears fell from her eyes, dry until then, and rolled like two pearls on her burning cheeks.

A moment later she had forgotten that distress, but her delirium created other ones. She was at the fish market and found no fish: "I don't understand! Why do they have a fish market if they don't have fish? They make people come all this way, and in such bitter cold." All the fish had been shipped off so there was none left for them. This particular upset and delusion seemed to stem entirely from that mishap. Her feeble words, rendered rhythmic by her gasping breaths, were constantly interrupted by sighs of anguish.

He stopped listening to her. There had to be some way of getting her out of this; he had to find a way to call a doctor. He weighed each idea born of his desperation as though he could use them all. He looked around the room for something with which to tie her to the bed so that he could leave her alone. He moved toward the window to call for help, and finally, forgetting that Amalia could not understand him, started talking to her to secure her promise that she would not move during his absence. Gently covering her shoulders with the blankets to indicate the she had to remain in bed, he told her: "You will stay like that, Amalia? You promise?"

By then she was talking about clothing. They had enough for a year and would therefore have no expenses for all of the next year. "We are not rich, but we have everything we need."

Signora Berlini, however, could look down on them because she had so much more. But Amalia was pleased that the lady had more because she liked her. Her babbling continued in that childish well-meaning way; it was wrenching to hear her proclaim herself so happy in the midst of such suffering.

The need for a decision was urgent. There was nothing violent about Amalia's delirium, neither her gestures nor her words, so that once he shook off the stupor that had taken hold of him from the moment he found her in that state, Emilio left the room and ran to the door of the house. He would call the custodian, then he would rush to a doctor, or perhaps go to Balli for advice. He did not yet know which he would do, but he had to hurry in order to save that poor woman. Oh, the pain of remembering that heart-rending nudity!

On the landing he stopped, hesitating. He would have liked to go back and see whether Amalia had taken advantage of his absence to commit some delirious act. He leaned against the railing to see whether someone was coming up. He bent over to see farther down, and for a moment his mind wandered. He forgot his sister, perhaps agonizing next door, and remembered how, in that very position, he used to wait for Angiolina. In those few seconds, the memory was so vivid that, forcing himself to look far into the distance, he tried to see the bright figure of his mistress instead of the help he needed. He straightened up, nauseated.

A door on the floor above opened and closed again. Someone — help! — was coming down to him. He tore up the stairs and found himself in front of a tall, strong woman. Tall, strong, and swarthy; that was all he saw, but he immediately found the right words: "Oh, Signora!" he pleaded. "Help me! I would do for anyone in my situation what I am asking of you."

"You are Signor Brentani?" she asked kindly, and the dark figure, which in fact had been about to slip away, stopped.

He told her how, on his return home just before, he had found his sister in the throes of such a delirium that he did not dare leave her, as he must, to call a doctor.

The woman said: "Signorina Amalia? Poor dear! I will gladly come with you right now." She was dressed in mourning. Emilio thought she might be devout and after a moment's hesitation said, "God will repay you."

The lady followed him into Amalia's room. Emilio took those few steps with intolerable anxiety. Who could know what new horror awaited him. Not a sound came from the next room, even though he could have sworn that Amalia's breathing was audible throughout the house.

He found her turned to the wall. Now she was talking about a fire. She was seeing flames that could not harm her except for the terrible heat they emitted. He bent down to get her attention and kissed her flaming cheeks. When she turned to him, he wanted to see, before going out, what impression was made on her by the sight of the companion he was leaving with her. Amalia looked at the newcomer for an instant with total indifference.

"I entrust her to you," Emilio said to the lady. He could readily do so. The lady had the tender look of a mother; her small eyes resting on Amalia were filled with pity. "The young lady knows me," she said, seating herself beside the bed. "I am Elena Chierici and I live on the third floor. Do you remember the day you lent me a thermometer to take my son's temperature?"

Amalia looked at her. "Yes, but it is burning and will go on burning forever."

"It will not burn forever," Signora Elena said, leaning toward her with a warm smile of encouragement, her eyes moist with feeling. She asked Emilio to give her a pitcher of water and a glass before he left. For Emilio it was no small matter to find such things in a house where he had lived with the inattention of a hotel guest.

Amalia did not understand at first that she was being offered cool refreshment in that glass; then she drank avidly in little sips. When she let herself fall back on the pillow, she found relief of another kind: Elena's soft arm was stretched out on it, and Amalia's little head was now held up comfortingly. Emilio's heart swelled with gratitude, and before going out, he expressed it by firmly grasping Elena's hand.

He raced to Balli's studio and ran into his friend as he was going out. He was afraid Angiolina might be there and was relieved to find Balli alone. Later on, he felt no remorse over his behavior during the brief period of that day when he still imagined he could get help for Amalia. He thought exclusively about his sister during those hours, and if he had happened on Angiolina, he would have winced with pain, but only because the sight of her would have reminded him of his own guilt.

"Oh, Stefano! What terrible things have happened to me!"

He went into the studio, sat down on the chair closest to the door and, covering his face with his hands, burst into sobs of despair. He would not have been able to explain why he had dissolved in tears just then. Was it that he was beginning to recover from the terrible shock he had experienced and was finding relief in this release of his pain, or was it the proximity of Balli — who had his share in Amalia's condition — that produced such intense emotion? What was certain was that afterward he became aware of his pleasure in having demonstrated his distress so violently, as much to himself as to Balli. His tears made everything easier and more bearable;

they had relieved him and made him a much better person. Even if — as he believed — she had gone mad, he would keep her near him, no longer like a sister, but like a daughter. And he found such pleasure in his tears that he forgot how urgent it was to call a doctor. This was where he belonged, right there, this was where he could act for Amalia's benefit. In his present state of excitement any enterprise seemed easy for him, and merely through this demonstration of his own suffering he would even make Balli forget the past. At last, he would see to it that Balli got to know what a gentle, good, hapless person Amalia was.

He related the scene in every detail: the delirium, Amalia's labored breathing, and the long interval when, since he was alone, he could not leave the room before the providential appearance of Signora Chierici.

Balli looked like someone stricken by some new misfortune — not at all what Emilio had been expecting — but with the dynamism that came easily to him in such a state, he told Emilio to go at once and get Doctor Carini. He described him as a competent doctor, and what was more, since he was an intimate friend, Balli would be able to talk to him about Amalia's condition.

Emilio continued to cry and made no move to get up. It seemed to him that his tears had not yet come to an end; he did not yet feel he was overcome, and hunted for words to move his friend. The few he found made him shudder: "Mad or moribund!" Dead! It was the first time he imagined Amalia dead, gone. Now that he had discovered he no longer loved Angiolina, he saw himself all alone, devastated with regret that he had not known how to enjoy happiness, within reach until that day, or how to dedicate his own life to someone who needed protection and sacrifice. Without Amalia, any hope of tenderness would vanish from his life. In a choked voice he said: "I don't know which is greater, my pain or my remorse."

He looked at Balli to see if he had been understood. Stefano's face registered genuine surprise: "Remorse?" He had always considered Emilio a model brother, and said so. However, remembering that Amalia had been somewhat neglected because of Angiolina, he added: "It is true that it was not worth getting involved with a woman like Angiolina, but misfortunes like that do happen . . . " Balli had understood Emilio so little that he declared he did not see why they were wasting so much time. They had to hurry to Carini and not despair before knowing what he had to say about Amalia's condition. It could well be that the symptoms that were terrifying to a lay person might appear less alarming to a doctor.

It was a hope, and Emilio clung to it with all his heart. Outside, they separated. Balli thought it wiser not to leave Amalia alone with a stranger for too long. Emilio should return home and he would go for the doctor.

Both of them dashed off. Emilio's haste was prompted by the great hope that had appeared to him a moment earlier. It was not at all impossible that once home he would find Amalia back to normal, greeting him with gratitude for the affection she had seen in his face. His rapid pace accompanied and encouraged his impetuous dream. Never had Angiolina inspired in him a dream like that, dictated by a wish so intense.

He did not feel the harsh wind that had just come up, enough to make one forget the mild, almost springlike day that had seemed to him so starkly inapposite to his distress. The streets quickly turned dark and the sky covered over with heavy clouds, pushed by a current of air that was perceptible on the ground only because of the sudden drop in temperature. Far in the distance, Emilio saw against the darkening sky, the top of a hill splashed with the yellow of the fading light.

Amalia was still delirious. Hearing again her tired voice, that same sweet tone, the same childlike modulation broken by her gasps, he understood that while outside he had been filled with insane hopes, inside, the sufferer in that bed had not been granted a moment's respite.

Signora Elena was bound to the bed because Amalia's head was resting on her arm. She related that soon after he left, Amalia had rejected this pillow, which had become bothersome to her, but now had accepted it again.

The services of the good woman were no longer really needed, and he told her so, expressing his infinite gratitude.

She looked at him with her kind little eyes and did not move the arm on which Amalia's small head moved restlessly. She asked: "And who will replace me?" Hearing that he planned to ask the doctor about hiring a nurse, she implored him: "In that case, allow me to stay." And she thanked him when, deeply moved, he explained that he had never thought of sending her away but had not wanted to impose on her by keeping her. "I have no one at home who might be alarmed by my absence. As it happens, the maid just started working for me today."

Soon after, Amalia lay her head on the pillow, freeing the Signora's arm. She was finally able to take off her little mourning hat and put it away. Emilio thanked her again, seeing in her gesture a confirmation of her determination to remain beside that bed. She looked at him in surprise, not understanding him. She could not have acted with greater simplicity.

Amalia began speaking again, without thrashing or calling out, as if she thought that all along she had been relating her whole dream aloud. Some sentences she began at the beginning, others at the end; some words she mumbled incomprehensibly, in others each syllable was clearly pronounced. She exclaimed and questioned. She questioned anxiously, never satisfied with the reply that she may not have fully understood. She asked Signora Elena, who had bent over her in an attempt to understand better a desire that she seemed to be expressing, "But you aren't Vittoria?"

"I? No," the Signora answered, surprised.

This reply was understood and for a while was enough to calm her. Later she began to cough. She struggled to stop and looked like a suffering child; she must have felt sharp pain. Signora Elena pointed out to Emilio that this same look had appeared during his absence.

"You must tell the doctor about it. Judging from that cough, your sister must have something wrong with her lungs."

Amalia had more fits of weak, suffocating coughing. "I can't take any more," she moaned with tears in her eyes.

Her tears no sooner wet her cheeks again than she quickly forgot her pain. Breathlessly, she began talking about her house. There was a new invention for making coffee inexpensively.

"They can do everything nowadays. Soon we will be able to live without money. Give me a little of that coffee to try. I'll return it to you. I believe in justice. I even told Emilio so . . ."

"Yes, I remember," Emilio said to keep her calm. "You have always believed in justice." He leaned over and kissed her forehead. He never forgot a moment of that delirium.

"Yes, both of us," she said, looking at him with that expression which the delirious have, which could be an exclamation or a query. "The two of us, here, peaceful, together, just the two of us." The seriousness of her face went with the seriousness of her words, and her breathlessness seemed to indicate intense pain. Soon after, however, she spoke of the two of them alone in the inexpensive house.

The doorbell rang. It was Balli and Doctor Carini. Emilio had already met him, a man about forty, dark, tall, slender. It was said that his years at medical school had been richer in amusements than in studies, but now, comfortably settled, he did not look for more patients. He was satisfied with an inferior position in the hospital that allowed him to pursue the studies he had neglected earlier. He loved medicine with the fervor of a dilettante, but he alternated his studies with pastimes of every kind, so that there were more artists among his friends than doctors.

He stopped in the dining room and, remarking that Balli had been able to tell him no more about Amalia's illness than that she must be suffering from high fever, asked Emilio for additional information.

Emilio began telling him about the condition in which he had found his sister a few hours before, alone in the house, where she had apparently been doing strange things that morning. He described with precision the details of the delirium, first apparent in the restlessness that made her look for insects on her legs, then in her interminable chatter. Moved by the memory and his analysis of all the horrors of that day, he spoke tearfully about the gasping, then about the cough, about the thin unnatural sound that seemed to come from a cracked vessel, and the terrible pain that each fit of coughing produced in the patient.

The doctor tried to hearten him with a friendly word or two, then, returning to the subject, asked a question that upset Emilio considerably: "And before this morning?"

"My sister has always been weak, but always healthy." He had tossed the sentence out, but after speaking it, began to have doubts. Were those talking dreams he had overheard not an indication of illness? Should he tell the doctor about them? But how to do so in front of Balli?

"Before today the Signorina was always well?" Carini asked incredulously. "Even yesterday?"

Emilio was embarrassed and did not know how to answer him. He could not even remember having seen his sister during the preceding days. When, in fact, had he seen her last? Perhaps months ago, the day he discovered her in the street so bizarrely dressed.

"I don't think she was sick before. She would have told me."

The doctor and Emilio went into the patient's room while Balli, after hesitating for a moment, remained in the dining room.

Signora Chierici, who was sitting at the head of the bed, got up and went to the foot. The patient seemed to be dozing but, as before, was speaking as though she were still engaged in a conversation and had to reply to questions or add to previous remarks.

"In half an hour. Yes. But not sooner." She opened her eyes and, recognizing Carini, said something by way of a greeting.

"Good day, Signorina," the doctor replied loudly, obviously intending to play along with her delirium. "I have been meaning to come and see you, but it was impossible for me to do so until now."

Since Carini had been in the house only once, Emilio was pleased that she had recognized him. She must have improved greatly during those few hours, because at noon she had not even recognized him. Speaking quietly, he mentioned this to the doctor.

The doctor was concentrating on the patient's pulse. Then he bared her chest and pressed his ear to various spots.

Amalia remained silent, her eyes on the ceiling. Then, with Signora Elena's help, he sat her up to make a similar examination of her back. Amalia resisted for an instant, but when she understood what was wanted of her, even tried to stay upright by herself.

Now she was looking at the window, which had rapidly grown dark. The door was open, and Balli, who had stopped at the threshold, was seen by her. "Signor Stefano," she said without surprise and without moving, since she had understood that the doctor wanted her to stay still. Emilio, fearing a scene, made an imperative sign to Balli to go away, which alone underscored the importance of the encounter.

But it was too late for Balli to back away. He stepped forward as she, with repeated movements of her head, encouraged him and addressed him.

"So long," she mumbled, evidently wanting to say that they had not seen each other in so long.

When she was allowed to lie back, her eyes remained on Balli, whom she continued to regard, even in her delirium, as the most important person in that room. Her breathing had become more labored because of the effort of having had to move. A brief coughing fit made her face contract with pain, but she did not stop looking at Balli. Even when avidly drinking the water the doctor offered her, she kept her eyes fixed on Balli. Then she closed her eyes and seemed to want to sleep. "Now everything is all right," she said out loud, and for a while was peaceful.

The three men left Amalia's room and went into the adjacent one. Impatient, Emilio asked, "Well, doctor?"

Carini, who had little experience with patients' families, candidly voiced his opinion: pneumonia. He thought her condition was very serious.

"Hopeless?" Emilio asked, anxiously awaiting the answer.

Carini gave him a compassionate glance. He said there was always hope and that he had already seen similar cases suddenly improve, to the point of complete recovery — a phenomenon that surprised even the most experienced physician.

Emilio became emotional. Oh, why could such an amazing phenomenon not take place in this case? That would be enough to make him happy for the rest of his life. Was that not the unexpected joy, the generous gift of providence that he had wished for? For a moment his hope was boundless. It could not have been greater had he seen Amalia walk or heard her talk lucidly.

But Carini had not said everything he had to say. He did not believe the illness had suddenly declared itself that day. In view of its virulence, it had to have manifested itself one or perhaps two days earlier.

Once again, Emilio felt the need to excuse himself for that past which seemed so remote to him. "That could be," he acknowledged, "but I think it is unlikely. If it did start yesterday, it must have been so mild that I was unable to notice it." Then, offended by Balli's disapproving look, he added, "Not possible."

In that abrupt manner tolerated by everyone who knew him, Balli said to the doctor: "Look, we don't understand much about medical matters. Will this fever last until the illness ends? Won't it subside now and then?"

Carini replied that he could say nothing about the course of the illness. "I find myself faced with someone I do not know, and with an illness about which I know only the present moment. Will there be a crisis? And when? Tomorrow, tonight, in two or three days? How can I know?"

Emilio thought all this warranted the most reckless hopes and left Balli to continue questioning the doctor. He saw himself with Amalia, restored to health, to her senses, once again capable of feeling his affection.

The most alarming symptom Carini observed in Amalia was neither the fever nor the cough; it was the nature of the delirium, the continuous agitated babbling. Lowering his voice he added: "Hers does not strike me as an organism capable of enduring high fever."

He asked for writing materials, but before writing the prescription, he said: "To relieve her thirst, I would give her wine mixed with seltzer water. Every two or three hours I would let her have a generous glass of wine. It would seem," he remarked cautiously, "that the Signorina is accustomed to wine." With two decisive strokes of the pen he wrote out the prescription.

"Amalia is not accustomed to wine," Emilio protested. "On the contrary, she can't stand it. I could never get her to drink any."

An expression of surprise crossed the doctor's face, and he looked at Emilio as though he could not believe that he was telling him the truth. Even Balli looked questioningly at Emilio. He had already gathered that the doctor, on the evidence of Amalia's symptoms, had concluded he was dealing with an alcoholic, and he remembered having noticed before that Emilio was capable of the worst kind of false propriety. He wanted to prod him into telling the doctor the truth he ought to know.

Emilio guessed the meaning of that look. "How can you believe such a thing? Amalia, drink? She can't even drink water in any quantity. It takes her an hour to swallow a glass of water."

"If you can assure me of that," the doctor said, "so much the better, because an organism, however delicate, can withstand high fever if it is not weakened by alcohol." He looked at the prescription with some hesitation and then let it stand. Emilio understood that he was not believed. "The pharmacist will give you a liquid, a spoonful of which should be given the patient every hour. As a matter of fact, I want to speak with the lady who is looking after her."

Emilio and Balli followed the doctor and introduced him to Signora Elena. Carini explained that he wanted her to see whether the patient would tolerate cold compresses on her chest, which would be extremely beneficial for her.

"Oh, she will!" Elena said with a fervor that surprised the three men.

"Easy now," the doctor smiled, happy to see the patient in such caring hands. "I do not want her to be forced, and if she has too strong an aversion to cold, then we will have to give this up."

Carini turned to leave, promising he would come back early the next day.

"Well, doctor?" Emilio asked again, in a pleading voice. Instead of replying, the doctor said a few comforting words and added that he wanted to defer his prognosis until tomorrow. Balli walked out with Carini, saying he would be right back. He wanted to take the doctor aside and hear whether he had been completely sincere with Emilio.

Emilio clutched at his hopes with all his strength. The doctor was mistaken when he suspected Amalia of tippling; his entire prognosis could therefore be erroneous. Knowing no limits to his dreams, Emilio went so far as to think that Amalia's health might still depend on him. She had fallen sick primarily because he had been negligent in his duty to watch over her. Now, instead, he was there to provide her with every gratification, every comfort, and of this the doctor was ignorant. He went to Amalia's bed as though wanting to bring her pleasure and comfort, but once there, he felt suddenly disarmed. He kissed her forehead and remained beside her for a long while, watching her struggle to get a little air into her pitiful lungs.

When Balli returned, he sat himself in the corner farthest away from Amalia's bed. The doctor had only repeated to him what he had already told Emilio. Signora Elena asked if she could go to her apartment for moment to make some arrangements; she would send her maid to the pharmacy. She went out, followed by a look of admiration from Balli. There was no need to give her money, since the Brentanis had a long-standing account at the pharmacy.

Balli murmured: "Such unassuming kindness impresses me more than the greatest charm."

Emilio took the place left by Elena. For quite some time the patient had not said a single comprehensible word. She mumbled vaguely as though she were practicing the pronunciation of difficult words. Emilio put his head in his hand and stayed there listening to her steady, breathless struggle. Ever since that morning he had heard it, and it now seemed like something in his own ear, a sound he could never be rid of. He remembered how one evening, in spite of the cold, he had gotten out of bed in his nightshirt out of solicitude for his sister, whom he had heard sobbing in the next room. He had proposed taking her to the theater the following evening. He had felt enormous solace on hearing the gratitude in his sister's voice. Later, he forgot the incident and never again tried to repeat it. Oh, if only he had known his life had a mission as important as that of watching over someone entrusted solely to him, he would not have felt the need for a relationship with Angiolina. Now, perhaps too late, he was cured of that passion. He wept silently, bitterly, in the gathering shadows.

"Stefano," the patient called softly. Emilio was startled

and looked at Balli, who was in the part of the room still slightly illumined by the light coming from the window. Stefano must not have heard, for he had not moved.

"If that's what you want, then so do I," Amalia said. Her old dreams were coming back with the identical words, dreams that had been snuffed out by Balli's abrupt abandonment. "I am willing," she said, "go ahead, but quickly." An attack of coughing twisted her face in pain, but immediately after she said, "Oh the great day! So long awaited!" And she closed her eyes again.

Emilio felt he should get Balli out of the room, but could not find the courage. He had already done so much harm by interfering with Amalia and Balli.

The patient's mumbling became unintelligible again for a while, but just as Emilio was starting to relax, she called out clearly, after another fit of coughing, "Oh Stefano, I am so sick."

"Is she calling me?" Balli asked, rising and approaching the bed.

"I did not hear," Emilio said, embarrassed.

"I don't understand, doctor," she said, turning to Balli. "I stay in bed, I take my medicine, and I don't get better."

Amazed not to be recognized after having been called by name, Balli talked to her as though he were the doctor. He advised her to continue following his orders and she would soon be well.

She went on: "Why do I have to have all this . . . this . . . " and she touched her chest and her hip, "this . . . " Her labored breathing could be heard with every pause, caused by hesitation, not a lack of breath.

"This illness," Balli interjected, offering her the words she vainly sought.

"This illness," she repeated gratefully. But shortly after,

she once again feared that she had expressed herself badly and added with great difficulty, "Why do I have to have this . . . just now! How will we manage with this . . . this . . . on a day like today?"

Only Emilio understood. She was dreaming of a wedding.

Amalia, however, did not say this openly. She repeated that she did not need this illness, that she thought no one had wanted it, and yet just now . . . just now. But the adverb was never clarified in any way, so Balli could not comprehend. When she lay back on the pillow and looked straight ahead or closed her eyes, she was addressing the object of her dreams in total familiarity; when she reopened them, she did not recognize that the very object was standing beside her in flesh and blood. The only one who could understand her dream was Emilio, who knew all the facts and all the dreams that had preceded this delirium. Beside that bed, he felt more useless than ever. Amalia did not belong to him in her delirium; she was even less his than when she had been in full possession of her senses.

Signora Elena returned, bringing with her the cold compresses already prepared, and everything needed to insulate them and keep them from making the bed wet. She bared Amalia's chest, shielding her from the eyes of the two men by placing herself in front of them.

Amalia emitted a weak cry of shock on feeling the sudden sensation of cold.

"It will do you good," Signora Elena said, bending over her.

Amalia understood but, doubtful and breathless, asked, "Do good?" She nonetheless wanted to be rid of that unpleasant sensation: "Not today, however, not today."

"I beg you, dear sister," Emilio pleaded with emotion,

having finally discovered something to do, "try to keep these compresses on your chest. They will make you well."

Amalia's condition seemed to get worse; once more her eyes filled with tears. "It is dark," she said, "very dark." It was indeed dark, but when Signora Elena hastened to light a candle, the patient took no notice of it and continued to complain about the darkness. She was trying thereby to express an entirely different sensation of oppression.

In the light of the candle Signora Elena saw that Amalia's face was bathed in sweat; even her nightgown was soaked all the way to her shoulders. "Could this be a good sign?" she exclaimed cheerfully.

In the meanwhile, however, Amalia, who in her delirium was humility personified, in order to free herself from the weight on her chest without disobeying the order that still rang in her ears, pushed the compresses toward her back. But even there the sensation they provoked was disagreeable, and so, with remarkable agility, she shoved them under the pillow, pleased to have found a place where she would keep them without having to endure the discomfort. Then she examined the faces of her caretakers, whose help she knew she needed. When Signora Elena removed the compresses from the bed, Amalia looked and sounded vaguely surprised. For the rest of the night, it was her most lucid moment, and at that, it was the intelligence of a docile animal.

Balli had told his servant Michele to bring an assortment of red and white wines. It so happened that the first bottle he picked up was a sparkling wine; the cork popped out with a loud explosion, hit the ceiling and fell on Amalia's bed. She was completely unaware of it, whereas the others, stared in fright at the path of the projectile.

Then the patient drank the wine offered her by Signora

Elena, making a face of disgust. Emilio watched her grimace with satisfaction.

Balli offered a glass to Signora Elena, who accepted on condition that he and Emilio drink with her. Balli drank, first making a toast to Amalia's health in a husky voice.

But health was far away from the poor woman. "Oh, oh, what do I see!" she cried out with clarity, looking straight ahead. "Vittoria with him! It can't be, or he would have told me."

This was the second time that she mentioned Vittoria, but now Emilio understood to whom that pointed *him* referred. She was having a dream of jealousy. She went on talking but less intelligibly. From her babbling, Emilio was able to follow this dream, which lasted longer than any of the preceding ones. The two people created by her delirium had moved closer to one another, and Amalia said that she was pleased to see them and see them together. "Who says this displeases me? It gives me pleasure." Then, there was a long interval during which she uttered only garbled words. Perhaps the dream had ended earlier, but Emilio was still searching in those labored sounds for the pain of jealousy.

Signora Elena was once again at her post at the head of the bed. Emilio went to join Balli, who was leaning on the window sill looking out at the street. The storm that had been threatening for the past few hours continued to gather. As yet, not a drop had fallen on the street. Yellowed by the turbulent air, the last rays of the setting sun that fell on the cobblestones and on the houses seemed to be reflections of a fire. With eyes half-closed, Balli enjoyed watching that strange color.

Again, Emilio tried to devote himself to Amalia, to protect and defend her, although even in her delirium she kept him away from her. He asked Balli: "Did you notice that look of disgust when she drank the wine? Is that the expression of someone accustomed to drinking?"

Balli agreed with him but, eager to defend Carini, said in his usual ingenious way of turning a phrase, "It could be, however, that her illness has affected her palate."

Emilio, his throat tight with anger, exclaimed, "You still believe what that imbecile said?"

Seeing how upset he was, Balli apologized: "I don't understand anything about all this, but Carini's certainty left me wondering."

Emilio started to cry again. He said it was not Amalia's illness or her death that brought him to the point of desperation, but the thought that she had lived her life misunderstood and scorned. Now, implacable destiny was amusing itself by deforming Amalia's sweet, gentle, virtuous face with the agony reserved for the dissolute. Balli tried to calm him: on second thought, even he found it unthinkable that Amalia had a vice. Furthermore, he had not meant to insult the poor woman. Looking toward the bed with deep commiseration, he said, "Even if Carini's supposition had been accurate, I would have felt no contempt for your sister."

They stood together in silence at the window for a long time. The yellow rays on the street were doused by the quickly creeping darkness of night. Only the sky, where the clouds continued to swell, remained luminous and yellow.

Emilio thought that perhaps Angiolina herself would fail to keep their appointment. But all of a sudden, forgetting from one moment to the next what he had decided that morning, he said, "Now I will go to my last meeting with Angiolina." And why not? Living or dead, Amalia would always have kept him from his loved one, so why not meet Angiolina and tell her that he wanted to break off permanently with her? His heart burst with the joy of that final encounter. His presence in that room was of no use to anyone, whereas by going to Angiolina, he was making an immediate sacrifice to Amalia. To Balli, who, astounded by his words, tried to dissuade him from his plan, he explained that he wanted to take advantage of his present state of mind to free himself forever from Angiolina.

Stefano did not believe him. He was hearing the same old weak Emilio and thought he might galvanize him by telling him how that very day, he had been forced to send Angiolina away from the studio. He said this in words that could leave no doubt about the reason.

Emilio paled. His adventure was still not over! It was reborn right there, at his sister's bedside. Angiolina was deceiving him yet again in the most outrageous way. He felt he was suffering the same oppression as Amalia. Just when he had become aware that for Angiolina he had neglected all his obligations, she was betraying him with Balli. The only difference between the rages he had experienced at other times and this one, which was impeding his breathing, was that the only revenge he could think of taking on that woman was to leave her. His troubled mind no longer comprehended the nature of vengeance. Events would unfold exactly as though Balli had told him nothing. He was unable to hide his pained surprise. "I beg of you," he said with an intensity he made no attempt to control, "tell me what happened."

Balli demurred: "Aside from the embarrassment of having had, for the first time in my life, to play the chaste Joseph, I certainly don't want the additional embarrassment of consigning to history all the details of my adventure. For you, however, there is absolutely no hope if on a day like this you can still think about that woman."

Emilio defended himself. He said that he had already

decided to leave Angiolina that morning, and that the only reason Balli's words had pained him was because he regretted having devoted so much of his time to a woman of that kind. Stefano must not believe that he was going to that appointment with Angiolina for the purpose of making a scene. He smiled wanly. He was so far removed from that! On the contrary, Balli's words affected him so little that he did not think his determination to end that relationship was any greater than before.

"All this moves me because it reawakens the past."

He was lying. It was the present that had become so remarkably fervent. Where was the anguish that had overcome him during his long, fruitless watch over Amalia? The excitement he now felt was not at all unpleasant. He would have liked to race away in order to arrive all the sooner at the moment when he would tell Angiolina that he never wanted to see her again. But he felt the need for Balli's consent before doing so. It was not hard to obtain, for that day Stefano felt so sorry for him he could not bring himself to deny him something he wanted.

Hesitating briefly, Emilio asked Balli if he would keep Signora Elena company. He expected to return shortly. Angiolina was thus once again responsible for bringing Stefano and Amalia together.

Balli urged Emilio not to demean himself by reproaching Angiolina. Emilio smiled with the assurance of a superior person. Even if Balli had not asked, he could assure him that he would not even mention this final betrayal of which he had just been apprised. And that really was his intention. He was imagining his final conversation with Angiolina. It would be gentle, perhaps even affectionate. That was how it had to be. He would tell her that Amalia was dying and that he was leaving her without resentment. He did not love her any more, nor did he love anything else in this world.

With his hat in his hand, he went over to Amalia's bed. She examined him carefully and asked, "Are you coming for lunch?" Then, trying to look behind him, she asked again, "Have you both come for lunch?" She was still looking for Balli.

He said goodbye to Signora Elena, but had one last hesitation. Fate had always seemed to enjoy incongruously juxtaposing Amalia's misfortune with his love for Angiolina. Could it therefore be that his sister would die just when he was with his mistress for the last time? He went back to the bed and saw in the poor woman's face the very image of suffering. She had collapsed on her side with her head off the pillow, off the bed. That head, with its thin hair all damp and tangled, vainly sought a place to rest. It was obvious that this state could immediately be followed by the final agony. All the same, Emilio left her and went out.

He had replied to Balli's renewed urgings with another smile. The frigid evening air stunned him, chilling him to the bone. He, violent with Angiolina! Because she was the cause of Amalia's death? But she could not be held guilty of that. Misfortune happened, it was not committed. An intelligent person could not be violent where there was no place for hatred. From his old habit of turning inward and analyzing himself came the suspicion that perhaps his attitude was the result of his need to be forgiven and absolved. He smiled at this as though it were terribly funny. How mistaken he and Amalia had been to have taken life so seriously!

At the shore, after checking the time, he stopped. Here the weather seemed worse than in town. Accompanying the whistling wind was the mighty din of the sea, a great roar composed of many smaller sounds joined in unison. The night was impenetrable. All that could been seen of the sea was the white foam of a wave that broke in the tumult before reaching land. People were watching out for the boats on the beach, and a few seamen could be seen high up on those masts, bobbing around in all directions, working in darkness and in danger.

It seemed to Emilio that this turmoil reflected his own. This gave him an even greater sense of calm. His literary bent made him think of the parallel between that spectacle and his own life. In that turmoil, as in his own, he saw the impassivity of fate — in the way each wave passed to the other the motion that had brought the previous one out of inertia, an attempt to rise up that ended in a horizontal displacement. There was no culprit in this, however great the ensuing damage.

Close to him a portly seaman, firmly planted on feet shod in boots, shouted a name out to sea. A moment later he was answered by another shout, upon which he hurried to a nearby pile, untied the cable wound around it, gave it some slack, and then tied it up again. Slowly, almost imperceptibly, one of the larger fishing boats moved farther out, and Emilio understood that it had been moored to a nearby buoy to keep it from being hurled against the shore. Then the heavy seaman took on a very different posture; leaning against the pile, he lit his pipe and in the midst of that devilish whirlwind enjoyed a moment of repose.

Emilio reflected that the inertia of his destiny was the cause of his misfortune. If, just once in his life, it had been his duty to untie or retie a rope; if the fate of a fishing boat, however small, had been entrusted to him, to his care, his energy; if he had been obliged to prevail over the howling of the wind and the sea with his own voice, he would be less weak, less unhappy.

He went to the rendezvous. His pain would return immediately after, but for the moment, he was filled with love in spite of Amalia. There was no pain in the hour during which he could do what his nature demanded. He savored voluptuously that calm feeling of resignation and pardon. He did not prepare a single sentence to communicate his state of mind to Angiolina. Quite the contrary, their final tryst had to be absolutely inexplicable to her; he would behave as though some higher intelligence were there judging them both.

The weather settled into a cold harsh wind but a steady, even one; there was no more turbulence in the air.

Angiolina came toward him from viale Sant'Andrea. Seeing him, she exclaimed with considerable irritation — striking a very sour note, given Emilio's emotional state at that moment — "I have been here for half an hour. I was about to leave."

Very gently, he pulled her to a street lamp and showed her the clock that marked the exact time set for their appointment.

"Then I was mistaken," she said with little more grace. While he considered how he would tell her that this was their last encounter, she stopped and said "You will have to let me go this evening. We can see each other tomorrow. It's cold, and . . . "

He was shaken out of his chronic musings about himself and looked at her, observing her. He understood immediately that it was not the cold that made her want to leave. In addition, he was surprised to see her dressed with greater care than usual. She was wearing a brown dress that he had never seen before, very elegant, that seemed to have been chosen for some special occasion. Even the hat looked new to him, and he even noticed her shoes, hardly suited for walking on Sant'Andrea in that weather.

"And . . . ?" he repeated, stopping beside her and looking squarely at her.

"All right, I'll tell you the whole story," she said with an air of resolute confidentiality that was totally inappropriate, and proceeded unperturbed, not noticing that Emilio's expression was growing grimmer by the minute. "I received a telegram from Volpini announcing his arrival. I don't know what he wants of me, but by this time he is certainly at my house."

She was lying; there was no doubt about that. Volpini, to whom that very morning he had written that letter, was now here, before he had received it, contrite, apologetic? Appalled, he gave a sick laugh: "Is that so? The same person who yesterday wrote you that letter is coming today to retract it and even notifies you of his arrival by telegram! Important business! Affairs of state! So important as to require a telegram? And what if you are wrong and instead of Volpini it is someone else?"

She smiled, sure of herself: "Ah-ha, Sorniani told you that the day before yesterday he saw me late in the evening accompanied by a gentleman? I had just left the Deluigi's house, and since I'm afraid to walk alone at night, that escort was very convenient."

He was not listening to her, but her last sentence, which she considered an exculpation, he heard and retained because of its strangeness: "That was just an ordinary *Deo gratias*." Then she went on: "Pity I left the telegram at home. But if you don't want to believe me, too bad. Don't I always come to our appointments on time? Why would I have to invent an excuse for missing this one?"

"That's easy to figure out!" Emilio laughed furiously.

"Today you are meeting someone else. Go, now! Someone is waiting for you."

"If that's what you think of me, it's better that I leave!" She spoke with conviction, but did not move a step.

Her words affected him as they would have had they been immediately followed by the act itself. She wanted to leave him! "Wait a minute. We need to talk." Even in the rage that was taking complete hold of him, he thought it might still be possible to retrieve the state of calm resignation which he had enjoyed only a few minutes earlier. But wouldn't he be justified if he threw her to the ground and trampled her? He grabbed her arm to keep her from leaving and, leaning against the streetlamp behind him, brought his distraught face close to her rosy tranquil one.

"This is the last time we see each other!" he shouted.

"All right, all right," she said, only concerned to free herself from that grasp which was hurting her.

"And do you know why? Because you are a . . . " He paused for a second, then roared the word that seemed excessive even in his fury; he roared it in victory, victory over his own doubt.

"Let go of me," she shouted, tense with anger and fear, "let go of me or I'll scream for help."

"You are a . . . " he replied. At last, seeing her shaken, he no longer felt like hurting her. "Do you really think that I haven't known for a long time what kind of person I was dealing with? When I caught you dressed like a servant on the stairs in your house," he said, evoking that evening in every detail, "with that vulgar flowered shawl on your head, your arms still warm from some bed, I thought at once of the word I just called you. I did not want to say it then and I used you the way all the others did, Leardi, Giustini, Sorniani and . . . and . . . Balli."

"Balli!" she laughed, shouting to be heard over the wind and Emilio's voice. "Balli is bragging; there's not a word of truth in it."

"Because he didn't want to, that fool, out of respect for me, as though it mattered to me whether you were had by one man less, you . . . " and for the third time he pronounced the word. She was working harder to free herself, but the effort of holding on to her was the best outlet for Emilio; he dug his fingers into her soft arms with intense pleasure.

He knew that the moment he let go of her she would take off and it would all be over, all of it, and very differently from the way he had imagined. "I loved you so," he said, trying perhaps to gain control, immediately adding, "but I always knew what you are. Do you know what you are?" He had finally found a means of reparation; he would force her to admit to what she was. "Go on, say it! What are you?"

By then, evidently at the end of her strength, she became frightened. Her face paled and she stared at him with an expression that begged compassion. She let herself be shaken without resisting and looked as though she were about to fall down. He loosened his grasp and supported her. Suddenly she tore herself loose and started to run desperately. So she had lied again! He would have been unable to catch up with her. He bent down, looked for a rock, and not finding one picked up a handful of gravel and threw it at her. The wind carried it off and a few stones must have hit her because she let out a cry of fear; the others were stopped by the bare branches of the trees and made a noise utterly inappropriate to the anger that had hurled them.

What to do now? The final reparation he had yearned for had been denied him. In spite of all his resignation, everything around him remained harsh and unyielding. He himself was brutal! His arteries were pounding with agitation. In the midst of that biting cold, as he burned feverishly with rage and stood immobilized on paralyzed legs, the calm observer in him was already working again and was reprimanding him.

"I will never see her again!" he said as though replying to a reprimand. "Never! Never!" And when he was able to start walking, this word resounded in the noise of his own steps and in the whistling of the wind across a desolate landscape. He smiled to himself as he passed the streets by which he had come, remembering the thoughts that had accompanied him to that appointment. Reality was full of surprises!

He did not go home right away. In his present state, it would have been impossible for him to resume his role of caregiver. He was so totally possessed by his reverie that he would not have been able to say which streets he had taken to get back! Oh, if only his meeting with Angiolina had gone the way he had wanted, he could have gone straight to Amalia's bedside without even altering the expression on his face.

He discovered another analogy in his relationships with Angiolina and Amalia. In both cases, he was detaching himself without being able to say that last word which might have sweetened his memory of the two women. Amalia could not hear it, and to Angiolina he could not say it.

thirteen

He spent that entire night at Amalia's bedside in an unbroken dream. Not that he was thinking ceaselessly about Angiolina, but between him and his surroundings a veil kept him from seeing clearly. A heavy fatigue denied him both the reckless hopes he had still nourished during much of the afternoon, and the utter despair that had produced the relief of tears.

In the house everything seemed to him to be as it had been. Except that Balli had left his corner and was sitting at the foot of the bed, beside Signora Elena. Emilio kept looking at Amalia in the hope of reviving his tears. He analyzed her, scrutinized her, so as to feel all of her suffering and to suffer with her. Then he turned his glance away in shame. He realized that in his search for emotion he had been hunting for images and metaphors. A fresh impulse to do something came over him. Thanking Balli for his help, Emilio told him that he was free to leave.

But Balli, who had not thought for a moment to ask him about his farewell meeting with Angiolina, took him aside to tell him that he did not want to leave. He looked sad and embarrassed. There was something else he wanted to say, something so delicate he did not dare launch into it without some introduction. They had been friends for many years, and he had experienced as his own every misfortune that befell Emilio. Finally resolved, he said, "That poor woman keeps saying my name. I'm staying." Emilio clasped his hand without any particular feeling of gratitude. Already then —

and he was so convinced that it brought him great serenity — there was no hope whatever for Amalia.

They told him that during the past few minutes Amalia had not stopped talking about her illness. Could this not be a sign that the fever was going down? He sat listening, certain that they were mistaken. She did indeed say in her delirium: "Is it my fault that I am sick? Come back tomorrow, doctor, and I will be well." She did not seem to be suffering. Her face was small and pathetic, just about the right face for that body. Still looking at her he thought, "She will die!" He imagined her dead, at peace, relieved of congestion and delirium. He was pained to have had so unfeeling a thought. He moved away from the bed and sat at the table where Balli had also sat himself.

Elena remained at the bed. In the feeble light of the candle, Emilio noticed that she was crying.

"This takes me back to my son's sickbed," she said, aware that her tears had been seen.

Suddenly, Amalia announced that she felt very much better and asked for food. Time did not evolve in its normal rhythm for those who were watching and living her delirium. From one moment to another her mood changed, or else she had new delusions, taking her caregivers with her through phases that in ordinary life would have taken days and months.

Signora Elena — remembering an order left by the doctor — prepared and offered Amalia coffee, which she drank gluttonously. All of a sudden, her delirium brought her back to Balli. Only to a casual observer did this hallucination lack cohesion. The ideas intermingled, one was submerged by another, but when it reappeared it turned out to be the same one that had disappeared earlier. It was that rival she had invented, Vittoria. Amalia had received her warmly, then — as

Balli related — a quarrel broke out between the two women, revealing to Balli that he was the patient's dominant concern. Now Vittoria was coming back. Amalia saw her approach and was horrified.

"I won't say a word to her! I will stay here quietly, as though she didn't exist. I don't want anything, so leave me alone."

Then she called loudly for Emilio. "You who are his friend, tell him yourself that she has invented the whole story. I never did anything to her."

Balli thought he could quiet her. "Listen, Amalia! I am here and I would not believe anything bad that was said about you."

She heard him and examined him at length. "You, Stefano?" She did not recognize him. "Then you tell him!" Exhausted, she let her head fall back onto the pillow. From previous experience, they all knew that, for the moment, that episode was over.

During the lull, Signora Elena moved her chair to the table where the two men were sitting and begged Emilio, who looked worn out, to go to bed. He refused, but these few words gave rise to a conversation among the three of them that managed to distract them for a little while.

Signora Chierici, whom Stefano, with his indiscreet curiosity, had plied with questions, related that when Emilio ran into her, she had been on her way to mass. Now, she said, it seemed to her that she had been in church ever since that morning and felt the same lightness of mind that came with ardent prayer. She said this without any embarrassment, in the tone of a believer invulnerable to the skepticism of others.

Then she told a strange story, her own. Until the age of forty, she had lived without affection, having lost her parents when she was very young. Unloved, she watched the lonely uneventful years go by. Then, at forty, she met a widower who married her so that the son and daughter of his first marriage would have a mother. Both children spurned her from the start, but she nonetheless felt such fondness for them that she was sure they would come to love her. She was wrong. They never ceased regarding her and loathing her as a stepmother. Relatives of the first wife came between the children and their new mother, trying to making her hate them with lies, and trying to make them believe that their first mother's soul would suffer jealousy over a new attachment.

"Instead, I became all the more attached to them, to the point where I even loved the rival who had given them to me." Examining this idea like an dispassionate observer, she added, "Perhaps it was the hostility on their pretty pink faces that made me love them still more." The little girl was taken from her soon after her father's death by a relative who persisted in believing that the child was mistreated.

The boy was now entirely hers, but even without any other relatives to fan his hatred, he clung to his contemptuous malevolence, with an obstinacy amazing in a child, which he demonstrated by spitefulness and disrespect. He fell sick with pernicious scarlet fever, yet even in high fever he continued to resist her until a few hours before he died, when, utterly exhausted, he threw his arms around her neck, called her mama, and begged her to save him. Signora Elena then warmly described the boy who had made her suffer so much. Daring, vivacious, intelligent, he could understood everything, except the affection that was being offered him. Now her life was spent between her empty house, the church where she prayed for the person who had loved her for a brief moment, and the grave where there was always so much to do. Yes! Tomorrow, without fail, she had to go there to see whether the attempt to support a sapling that refused to grow straight had been successful.

"If Vittoria is here, I am leaving," Amalia cried out, raising herself to sit up. Emilio, frightened, lifted the candle to see better. Amalia was livid. Her face was the same color as the pillow behind it. Balli looked at her with obvious admiration. Amalia's damp face reflected the yellow glow of the candle so brightly that the light seemed to be emanating from it: a shining, suffering bareness that was shrieking. It looked like the sculpted image of a furious shriek of pain. That little face, for a moment marked with firm resolution, looked imperiously threatening. The expression was gone in a flash. She suddenly fell back, soothed by words she had not understood. She began to mumble weakly again, following her racing dreams with an occasional word.

Balli remarked, "She looked like a kind sweet Fury. I have never seen anything like it." He sat down and raised his eyes to the ceiling with that dreamy expression he had when he was groping for ideas. What was clear, and Emilio was pleased to see it, was that Amalia was dying enveloped by the noblest love Balli could offer.

Signora Elena took up the conversation where she had left off. Not for a moment while attending Amalia had she been distracted from her cherished memories. Even her resentment of her in-laws played a role in her life. She related how they had scorned her because her father sold farm implements. "In any case," she added, "the name Deluigi is an honorable name."

Emilio marveled at the way fate brought into his house a member of that family so often mentioned by Angiolina. He immediately asked whether Elena had other relatives. She said she did not and even denied the possibility of there being another family of the same name in the city. She was so positive about it that he had to believe her.

Thus, even that night, his thoughts turned to Angiolina. As in that now distant period when a healthy Amalia had been no more for him than a troublesome presence, to be avoided, now too he was overcome with a burning desire to run to Angiolina and rebuke her for this most outrageous of her deceptions. These Deluigis had been pulled out of a hat at the very start of their relationship, each member of the family produced as needed. First, it was old Signora Deluigi who loved Angiolina like a mother, then the daughter who was her friend, and finally the old man who had wanted to get her drunk — lies repeated at each one of their meetings, so that every trace of fondness was erased from his memories of Angiolina. Even those rare expressions of love which she had managed to simulate were now obvious to him for what they were — lies. And yet, before long, this fresh betrayal soon felt to him like another new bond. Amalia was moving pointlessly, laboriously in her bed of pain, but for a long time Emilio saw nothing. Once he regained some composure, he was distressed to recognize that no sooner would Amalia's illness disappear, or Amalia herself, than he would be off to Angiolina's again. To exert control over himself, he sat stiffly in his chair for some time and swore never again to fall into that trap: "Never again, never."

Even that interminable night, the worst sleepless night he had ever spent but which could yet become a nostalgic memory, that too passed. A clock struck two.

Signora Elena asked Emilio to find her a cloth to wipe Amalia's face. In order not to leave the room, he unlocked his sister's wardrobe when he finally found the keys. He was instantly struck by a strange medicinal smell. The few undergarments were distributed among the large drawers, most of which were taken up by vials of various sizes. Unable to understand at first, he went for a candle. Some of the drawers were filled to the top with cheerful shining vials giving off mysterious yellow reflections of some treasure inside; in other drawers there was still space and from the way the vials had been arranged, one could surmise that the orderly completion of this strange collection had been planned. Only one vial was out of place and that one still held some transparent liquid. The odor of the liquid left no room for doubt: it had to be ether. Doctor Carini had been right. Amalia had been seeking oblivion in intoxication. Not for a moment did he blame his sister, because his mind rushed instantly to one conclusion: Amalia was beyond hope. That discovery, however, was what finally brought him back to her.

Very carefully he closed the wardrobe. He had not known how to watch over his sister's life, but now he would try to protect her reputation.

Dawn approached, darkly, haltingly, sadly. It brought a pale light to the window but left the night intact inside the room. A single ray seemed to have penetrated the darkness, for the glasses standing on the table refracted the daylight into delicate shades of blue and green. In the street, the wind was still blowing the same even, triumphant gusts as when Emilio left Angiolina.

Within the room, however, there was deep quiet. For quite some time the only sign of Amalia's delirium had been a few truncated words. She was lying quietly on her right side, her face close to the wall, her eyes wide open.

Balli went to lie down in Emilio's room. He had asked not to be allowed to sleep more than an hour.

Emilio returned to the table and sat down. He started, terrified: Amalia had stopped breathing. Even Signora Elena had noticed and had sat up straight. Amalia was still staring at the wall, and a few seconds later began to breathe again. Her first four or five breaths sounded normal, and Emilio and Elena smiled at each other hopefully. But the smile soon died on their lips because Amalia's breathing came faster and faster, only to become labored and then stop again. The halt this time lasted so long that Emilio cried out in fright. She began breathing as before, easily for a short while, then she suddenly started to pant heavily. For Emilio this was an ex-cruciating phase. Even though after an hour of intense atten-tion he was convinced that the temporary cessation of her breathing did not signify death, any more than the even breathing that followed it heralded recovery, he too, out of fear, held his breath when Amalia's stopped, gave himself up to unbridled hopefulness when he heard her breathing re-turn to its even rhythm, and wept with disappointment on seeing her fall back into her agony.

By then the dawn was casting light as far into the room as the bed. The gray neck of Signora Elena — who was mak-ing do with the light sleep of a good nurse — supported her drooping head and seemed made of silver. For Amalia that night would no longer end. Her head was now sharply silhouetted against the pillow. Her black hair had never been so impressive as during her illness. It was the profile of a dynamic individual with prominent cheekbones and a pointed chin.

Emilio placed his elbows on the table and cradled his forehead in his hands. The time when he had been rough with Angiolina seemed far away; once again, he saw himself incapable of such behavior; he could not find in himself the energy or the force needed to accomplish it. His eyes closed and he fell asleep. It later seemed to him that even in his sleep he had continued to hear Amalia's breathing and to feel as before the same sequence of fear, hope, and disappointment.

When he awakened it was broad daylight. Amalia's eyes were wide open and staring at the window. Hearing him move as he stood up, she looked at him. And what a look! Not that of a feverish person, but of someone exhausted to the point of death, no longer in control of her eyes and exerting great effort to direct them.

"What's wrong with me, Emilio? I'm dying!"

Her senses had returned, and he, forgetting his observation of that expression, was once again flooded with hope. He told her that she had been very sick, but that now, clearly, she was getting better. The affection in his heart overflowed and he began weeping with relief. Kissing her, he cried out that from then on they would live together united, one for the other. It seemed to him that the whole agonizing night had been nothing but a preparation for this unexpected joyful solution. Later, he remembered the scene with shame. He recognized that he had taken advantage of Amalia's single flash of lucidity to soothe his own conscience.

Signora Elena rushed to calm him and to warn him against upsetting the sick woman. Alas, Amalia understood none of it. She seemed so focused on one thought that all her senses were involved in it.

"Tell me," she pleaded, "what happened? I'm so frightened! I saw you and Vittoria and . . . " The dream was entwined with reality, but her enfeebled mind could not disentangle the twisted threads of the confusion.

"Try to understand!" Emilio implored her. "You have been dreaming steadily since yesterday. Rest now, you can think later."

This last phrase was said in response to another signal from Signora Elena which only attracted Amalia's attention.

"It's not Vittoria," said the poor woman, evidently reassured.

No, it was not the kind of lucidity that could be considered a sign of recovery; it appeared only in flashes which could do little more than revive her suffering and aggravate it. Emilio was as terrified of this as he had been of the delirium.

Balli walked in. He had heard Amalia's voice, and he too was surprised by the unexpected improvement.

"How do you feel, Amalia?" he asked affectionately.

She looked at him incredulously.

"So it wasn't a dream?" She held her gaze on Stefano, then looked at her brother, and back at Stefano as though she wanted to compare the two bodies to see if one of them might be unreal.

"Emilio," she exclaimed, "I don't understand!"

"Knowing that you were sick," Emilio explained, "he wanted to keep me company during the night. He is the good friend of the family that he has always been."

She had not heard him. "And Vittoria?" she asked.

"That woman has never been here," Emilio replied.

"He has every right to do this. And you can even stay with them," she mumbled with a flash of rancor in her eyes. Then she forgot everything and everyone as she watched the light in the window.

Stefano said to her, "Listen to me, Amalia. I have never known the Vittoria you are talking about. I am your devoted friend and I stayed here to help you."

She was not listening. She watched the light in the window with obvious difficulty, trying to focus her veiled vision.

She watched ecstatically, in admiration. She made an ugly grimace which nonetheless resembled a smile.

"Oh," she exclaimed, "all those lovely children!" She watched admiringly for some time. The delirium had come back, but there was a break between the dreams of the night and the luminous visions bathed in the colors of the morning. She saw rosy children dancing in the sun. A hallucination of few words. She described what she was seeing but nothing else. Her own life had been forgotten. She made no mention of Balli or Vittoria or Emilio.

"So much light," she said, fascinated. She too lit up. Beneath her transparent skin, one could see the blood rise tinting her cheeks and forehead. She was changing but did not feel it. She was looking at things that were moving farther and farther away.

Balli suggested calling the doctor.

"Useless," Signora Elena said, understanding from that blush what was happening.

"Useless?" Emilio asked, frightened to hear his own thoughts spoken by others.

In fact, soon after, Amalia's mouth contracted in that strange spasm which, at the very end, apparently forces even ineffective muscles to promote respiration. Her eyes were still staring out. She did not utter another word. Before long her breathing was joined by the death rattle, sounding more like a lament, the lament of that gentle soul who was dying. It seemed to come out of meek despondency; it seemed intentional, a humble protest. What it was, in fact, was the lament of matter, already left behind and breaking up, that emits sounds learned during the long travail of conscious suffering.

fourteen

The image of death is enough to occupy the mind completely. Any effort made to hold onto it or erase it is titanic, because every terrorized fiber of our being re-members it after having experienced its presence, every one of our molecules rejects it in the very act of preserving and producing life. The thought of death is like a trait, a flaw of the organism. It cannot be summoned by an act of will, nor can it be resisted.

Emilio lived with this idea for months. Spring had passed and his only awareness of it had been its flowering on his sister's grave. It was an idea that entailed no remorse. Death was death; it was no more horrible than the circumstances that had surrounded it. Death, that heinous crime, had de-parted, and he felt that his own mistakes and misdeeds had been all forgotten.

During that period he lived, insofar as possible, a solitary existence. He even avoided Balli, who, after having behaved so admirably at Amalia's deathbed, had already lost all mem-ory of the brief interest she had awakened in him. Emilio could not forgive him for not being more like himself in this regard. By then, it was the only thing he held against him.

When his agitation subsided, he felt unbalanced. He ran to the cemetery. The dust of the road made him suffer, and even more so, the heat. At the grave, he assumed the pose of someone meditating, but he did not know how to meditate. The most powerful sensation he had was the smarting of his skin from sun, dust, and sweat. Back home, he washed, and once his face was freshened, he forgot all about his excursion. He felt terribly lonely. He went out with the vague intention of looking for someone, but on the landing where one day he had found the help he sought, he remembered that close by he could find someone who would teach him to remember — Signora Elena. He — so he told himself as he climbed the stairs — had not forgotten Amalia, he remembered her only too well, but he had forgotten the emotions of her death. Instead of seeing her in the death rattle of her final struggle, he remembered her sad, weary; her gray eyes reproachful for his neglect; or disconsolate, when she replaced the cup prepared for Balli; or what he remembered of the end, her gestures, her words, her cry of anger and despair. Those were all memories of his own guilt. All that had to be buried under Amalia's death, which Signora Elena would re-evoke for him. Amalia herself had not been significant in his life. Nor, as he remembered, had she had shown any desire for renewed closeness when he had tried to make their relationship more affectionate in order to free himself from Angiolina. Only her death was meaningful for him; at least it had liberated him from his disgraceful passion.

"Is Signora Elena at home?" he asked the maid who came to the door. That house doubtless received few visitors. The maid, a pleasant blonde, prevented him from entering and loudly called Signora Elena. She came into the dark hallway through a side door and stood in the light coming from the room.

"What a great idea to have come here!" Emilio thought gleefully, moved by the sight of Elena's gray head in that pale aureole, just like the light that had made such an impression on him the morning Amalia died.

Signora Elena greeted him very warmly.

"I have been hoping to see you for such a long time. This really gives me pleasure."

"I thought so," Emilio said with tears in his voice. The friendship that woman had extended to him at Amalia's deathbed still moved him. "We have known each other only a short time, but the kind of day we lived through together is more binding than years of intimacy."

Signora Elena led him into the room she had left; it was the shape of the Brentanis' dining room, which stood below it. Although simply furnished, even sparsely, everything was in such meticulous order that the room needed no more furniture. As for the walls, left completely bare, the simplicity went a bit too far.

The maid brought in an oil lamp, already lit, said good evening, and exited.

The signora watched her go with a benevolent smile. "I cannot break her of that country habit of saying good evening whenever she brings in a lamp. To be truthful, it is not an unpleasant custom. Giovanna is so good. Too naive. It is rare to find a naive person today. One feels like curing her of a malady that in fact is charming. Whenever I tell her anything about modern customs, she looks shocked." She laughed heartily. She imitated the individual she was talking about, opening wide her sweet little eyes. She seemed to have observed Giovanna closely in order to appreciate her all the more.

The story about the maid had interrupted Emilio's agitation. To settle a question in his mind, he told her he had gone to the cemetery that day. His question was immediately answered, because Signora Elena unhesitatingly told him, "I never go to the cemetery. I have not been there since the day of your sister's funeral." She then remarked that she now knew there was no way of fighting death. "Whoever dies is dead; comfort can come only from the living." Without any bitterness she added, "It is sad, but that's how it is." Then she told him that her brief care of Amalia had lifted the spell of her memories. Her stepson's grave no longer produced in her the kind of emotion that overpowers and renews. She was expressing Emilio's very own thoughts, although not when she concluded with a moral axiom: "It is the living who need us."

She returned to the subject of Giovanna. The girl had fallen sick and, to her good fortune, Elena had nursed her and saved her. During that illness they found each other. When the girl recovered, Elena felt that her son had been resuscitated in her. "Gentler, kinder, more grateful, oh, so grateful!" But her new attachment was also a cause for worry and distress. Giovanna was in love . . .

Emilio had stopped listening. He was wholly engrossed in the solution of a serious problem. Upon leaving, he respectfully said goodbye to the servant, a human being who had succeeded in saving another from despair. "How curious," he thought, "it would seem that one half of humanity exists to live and the other half to be lived through." His thoughts immediately turned to his own case: "Perhaps Angiolina exists only so that I can live."

At peace, feeling reborn, he walked in the cool night air that followed a sultry day. The example of Signora Elena had proved to him that he too might find in life his daily bread, his reason to exist. This hope stayed with him for some time. He had forgotten the elements that constituted his drab life and thought that the day he chose to do so, he would be able to turn his life around.

His first attempts fell flat. He tried to go back to art but reaped no emotion from it. He tried women but found they were not important enough. "I love Angiolina!" he thought.

One day, Sorniani told him that Angiolina had run off with the disloyal cashier of a bank. The story had unleashed a scandal in the city.

For Emilio, this was an unpleasant surprise. "Life has abandoned me," he told himself. Instead, Angiolina's elopement brought him back to life for a while, in the most exquisite pain and acrimony. He dreamed of love and vengeance, as he had the first time she left him.

He went to see Angiolina's mother once his emotions had subsided, just as he had gone to Elena when the memory of Amalia threatened to fade away. He was similarly compelled to make this visit by a particular state of mind that required at that very moment a fresh stimulus, and so urgently that he made it during working hours, unable to postpone it by even a few minutes.

The old woman greeted him hospitably as in the past. Angiolina's room looked somewhat different, stripped of all the knickknacks that Angiolina had collected during her long career. The photographs were also gone, probably adorning the walls of some other room somewhere else.

"So she ran off?" Emilio asked with bitterness and irony. He relished the moment as though he were speaking directly to Angiolina.

The Zarri woman denied that Angiolina had run off. She had gone to stay with relatives who lived in Vienna. Emilio did not contradict her but, quickly yielding to an urgent impulse, resumed the accusatory tone that she had tried to discourage. He said that he had foreseen it all. He had tried to correct Angiolina and show her the righteous path. He had not succeeded and was left heartsick. So much the worse for Angiolina. He would never have left her if she had treated him differently.

He would have been unable to repeat the words he used during that momentous scene, but they must have been very powerful because the old woman started to sob in a strange dry way, then turned away from him and left the room. He watched her, taken aback by the effect of his words. Her sobs were surely genuine; they shook her entire body to the point of hampering her steps.

"Good day, Signor Brentani," Angiolina's sister said, entering the room with a little curtsy and extending her hand. "Mama went in the back because she does not feel too well. Perhaps you can come another day."

"No!" Emilio declared gravely, as though he were in the process of leaving Angiolina. "I will never come here again." He stroked the little girl's hair, not as thick as Angiolina's but the identical shade. "Never!" he repeated, and with deep feeling kissed the child's head.

"Why?" she asked, throwing her arms around his neck. Stupefied, he let his face be covered with kisses that were anything but childish.

When he managed to get out of that embrace, a wave of nausea submerged every other emotion. He felt no need to continue the homily he had begun and left the house, after placing a paternal, indulgent hand on the child, whom he did not want to leave disheartened.

A terrible sadness overcame him when he was alone in the street. He felt that the caress he had given out of compassion marked the absolute end of his adventure.

He himself did not know which important period of his life had ended with that caress.

For a long time his adventure left him disoriented, dissatisfied. Love and pain had crossed his life and now, deprived

of those elements, he felt like someone who had been ampu-
tated of an important part of his body. The void nonetheless
ended up being filled. He regained his taste for peace and
security, and the care he devoted to himself freed him from
all other desires.

Years later, he was entranced by that period of his life, the
most meaningful, the most luminous. He relived it the way
an old man remembers his youth. In the mind of this idle
writer, Angiolina underwent a strange metamorphosis. All of
her beauty remained intact, but in addition she had acquired
all the characteristics of Amalia, who died, a second time, in
her. She became downcast, inconsolably inert, but with a
candid and intelligent look. He saw her before him as though
on an altar, this personification of thought and pain, and he
loved her forever, if love is admiration and desire. She represented everything noble that he had thought and observed
during that period.

That figure finally became a symbol. Her eyes were always turned in the same direction, the horizon, the future,
from which emanated the red rays reflected on her pink,
yellow, and white face. She was waiting for him! The image
embodied the dream he had once had with Angiolina beside
him, which that lower-class girl had not understood.

On occasion that lofty, magnificent symbol was reani-
mated, turning once again into a loving woman, but always a
sad and thoughtful woman. Yes! Angiolina thinks and weeps!
She thinks as though the secret of the universe and of her
own existence had been revealed to her; and she weeps as
though in all of that vast world she never again found another *Deo gratias*.